INDIGOBIRD

MICHAEL STUART

This book is a work of fiction and names, businesses, organizations, houses, places, events, and incidents are used in a fictitious manner. Any resemblance to actual persons (living or deceased), situations, events, etc. are coincidental.

Self-published by: Michael Stuart
ISBN: 9798856131191

First edition.

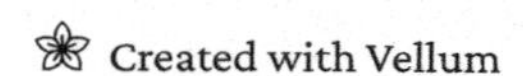

For Ireland, Aidan, and Alana

PROLOGUE

My body is borderline catatonic in this moment. Under normal circumstances, I'd be screaming in pain, sadness, and confusion. But these are far from normal circumstances.

The acrid stench of my bloodied feet, cut from the jagged rocks below, saturates my fluid-filled nostrils. The saltiness of the ocean thickly coats my throat, but no water is visible on this moonless night. I am in complete darkness. A wave violently crashes into the rock that I'm standing on, splashing sheets of frigid water against my bare feet. Finally, I feel something.

The powerful screaming from the northeast wind is deafening, as whirls of approaching sirens hum in my ears. My face is numb. My teeth are chattering. The sirens intensify as the lights continue to brighten. Maybe nothing matters. Maybe everything does.

The siren quickly cuts out but the accompanying flashing light, projecting through the dense fog, creates a surreal blue aura. Suddenly, a large spotlight is illuminating the beach and moving in the direction of the jetty. Over the howls of the wind, someone is yelling. I hear my name.

The sound echoes over the frenetic waves, now crashing toward me from all directions. The voice is friendly and recognizable, but it doesn't matter. Brightness sweeps across the jetty, inching closer to where I stand. Next to me, a pulsing red light, affixed to the top of the channel marker, blinds me with darkness. My thoughts transition to the water temperature and how cold it will be if I jump.

The voice is getting closer and echoes over the choppy water, reverberating with each wave that splashes on the rocks. I hesitate and have second thoughts. Maybe it is time to give up and deal with everything that I have been running from for what seems like a lifetime. The lies and the secrets. The horror of learning the things shielded from my life.

The spotlight is directly on me. I can't see and there is nowhere to run. A loud explosion crashes through the dense air, and I no longer see the light. Seconds later, another blast rips through the darkness. I raise my arms slowly toward the sky.

Then, I jump.

PART ONE
EMERALD

CHAPTER 1
THE PARTY

Happiness generally eludes me, and each morning I wake up with the hope that this will be the day that it finds me. I knew, upon opening my eyes, that today was going to be different. Mid-spring sun transcended warmth into my room, casting beams of radiant light across my oversized bed. Within minutes, the sweet aroma of strong coffee permeated the bedroom, which was usually my cue to get out of bed and head downstairs to the kitchen. Today, I decided to wait under the covers. After all, it was my birthday. While pondering how long I'd wait for breakfast in bed, footsteps echoed outside the door.

"Happy Birthday Emerald Woodley. Fresh from your favorite bakery."

I was never sure when he addressed me that way if he was being polite or if it was out of discontent that I kept my family name. He did not seem to understand that I was the last of the Woodley's and, in addition to keeping the name, we needed to have a son who would have the last name Woodley and not Crossman. We have not had that conversation yet, but it should be a good one.

There he stood. My exceptionally handsome husband, dutifully standing at the foot of our bed with a tray of green roses, steaming coffee with my usual splash of almond milk, and a brown paper bag. He was wearing a dark jogging suit and the glazed perspiration on his forehead was evidence that he had run to the local bakery to get my favorite pastry. A plain croissant for a simple, unhappy girl.

"Samuel Crossman. You are too much. Thank you."

He placed the tray on the bed and took a step back. To me, Samuel was a gentle giant. He was just over six feet tall, rugged, and full of sinewy muscle from a lifetime of physical activity. Blessed with a head of thick, black hair and a closely trimmed beard, he was the vision of the man all girls dreamed of calling their husband. Although he was not much taller than me, his power and presence made him seem larger than life. He recently entered my life of chaos and, most of the time, I was thankful that I found him.

"I'd join you in bed, but I need a shower, and then I'll be back. Wait here for me." He shot up his index finger. Before I could respond, he retreated toward the bathroom.

Defiance is a longstanding family tradition, so I disregarded his order, gingerly arose from the bed, and carried the tray to the bedroom window seat which sat high above the ocean and provided sweeping views of the sound. This comfortable perch was my favorite spot in the house and hundreds of hours of my life have been spent sitting on this ledge gazing mindlessly at the ocean below.

Mesmerized by the rhythmic ebb and flow of waves reaching and retreating from the beach, the inevitable sadness won my constant battle of conflicting emotions. My mind had the magical ability to transition to a negative emotion whenever I was feeling good. Even though it was my birthday, it was also the day my mother died. I never actually knew her because she died giving birth to me. This irrational guilt will not go away.

A bird was staring at me. The chipped, ceramic mug that held my coffee was inscribed with the word *Indigobird* and had a faded silhouette of the bird. *Indigobird* was the name of the beautiful house where I lived. As a kid, I never understood the concept of houses, or boats for that matter, having names and I never reconciled the meaning behind the home that had belonged to Harold and Mary, my grandparents, who had raised me since birth and had tragically died together less than a year ago.

Indigobird. I thought about riding my bike around town as a little girl and stopping at the other houses to check and see if they also had names. Sometimes, I'd stop if someone were in their yard and ask them if their house had a name. Most were confused by my question, and when they said their house did not have a name, I'd proudly tell them the name of my house. If they did have a name, it was usually nautically themed. *Captain's Quarters, Seaview, Seaside Serenity, Sand Dollar*. I often asked Harold about the name and never got a straight answer. Why name a house after a bird indigenous to Africa and not after a downy woodpecker or piping plover? Something related to Cape Cod. Other than the tattered, weather-beaten wooden plaque, meekly affixed over the front entrance to the house, and the faded coffee cups, the only other homages to *Indigobird* were two pieces of art. One was a small painting of an indigobird nestled in a tree that had been in this room until Samuel decided that it did not match our new bedroom set and moved it to a guest bathroom. Defiant Emerald let him win that battle.

The primary tribute was another painting, a much larger five-foot by five-foot piece that proudly hung over the never used fireplace in the living room. The massive oil on canvas had a hand painted nautical map of our little corner of the world and the surrounding marine area with an out-of-place bird looming on the left side of the painting. The bird was dark and creepy. The oversized, gold-colored eyes of the bird were directed at the center of the room. It always made me anxious, especially as a child. The portrait was out of place and, as Mary used to say, aesthetically offensive.

Samuel steadfastly wanted to remove this piece, but out of respect for Harold, I stood my ground, and it was still hanging. I thought about the hours that Harold would stand in front of the painting and use it to tell wild stories of the old family. He would excitedly point out places on the map where his great, great, great grandfather had a farm and raised sheep for the merino wool. And the place where another ancestor kept his fleet of boats. He would point at the red dots on the nautical map while telling stories of his family, the local pirates, and of buried treasure to entertain me when I was younger. No princess stories for me. Maybe this is why I am a hot mess.

Maybe it's time to move on from the name *Indigobird*. That might make me happy. I wondered if it was possible to change the name. But then I'd have to buy new coffee mugs and find another oversized painting to hang over the fireplace. That seemed like too much work.

Indigobird sat in the secluded, oceanside part of Woods Hole, a small town at the southwest end of Cape Cod. It was technically a village of the town of Falmouth in Massachusetts. For as long as I could remember, this was the only place I called home. I lived in this house through elementary school, but once completing fifth grade, they shipped me off to a boarding school outside of Boston. The school years were long, and I counted down the days to get back here for the summer.

The Woodley's had once been important people in the area, arriving here even before the *Mayflower* hit the shores of Provincetown and Plymouth. The first Woodley arrived on this spot in 1602 on a ship captained by Bartholomew Gosnold. The Woodley family has been a fixture in Woods Hole since that time and prospered through the years. They were farmers and fished in the 1600s, and then active in maritime trade and shipping by the 1700s. In the next century, they owned a fleet of ships and were notorious whalers, fueling the settlement and increasing their legend. As the stories went, recent years were not kind to the family. Untimely deaths, economic downfalls, and other tragedies reduced the Woodley family and fortune to only Harold and Mary. And their daughter Justine.

Samuel's voice interrupted my thoughts. "I hope you're ready to party tonight." He placed his hand on my shoulder. "It's going to be a great evening."

The unexpected noise caused me to startle. The mug tumbled from my hand, spilling coffee on the window seat.

"You scared me. Don't do that again."

"Sorry. I thought you heard me coming." He looked at me with a weird expression. "Lost in your thoughts?"

"Do I really have to host a party tonight?"

Samuel offered a quizzical look. "First of all, you are not the host. You are the guest of honor. I've taken care of everything."

"But it's my house, and I feel like we're hosting."

"I was under the impression that this was *our* house, since we are married." The attitude in his voice was obvious as he rolled his eyes while shaking his head.

"You know what I mean. *Our* house. With twenty of your closest acquaintances coming, including your father who does not seem to like me."

"Guest list is twelve as some of the people we invited are not down for the season yet. You only turn twenty-eight once. Listen, this is important to *us*." He said, ignoring the comment about his father.

"*We* invited? And remind me again why this is important to us?"

"It is important. It might bring you out of your darkness."

"Samuel, we've been married for four months. And I'm not depressed. It's just that, well, a year ago, I was finishing school and about to start preparing for my dissertation. Since then, I have lost my entire family and got married, and now we are here," I waved a hand in front of me. "I'm supposed to host a party for people that I barely know, and this is going to somehow make me feel better?"

"We will have fun. It will be a night to remember."

"I just don't know if I'm ready. It feels sudden and..."

"Do you trust me?"

I looked at him and before I could respond, he started to walk away. This new habit of his was becoming annoying. Was he always like this and I never noticed?

He turned and looked back. "Trust me. Tonight, everything changes."

After finishing the remaining coffee and munching on the flaky croissant, I went to my dresser and pulled on a white shirt, black leggings, and socks. It was just after seven on this sun-splashed morning, and I wanted to get outside for air. Walking downstairs, I forced myself to smile and think positively. That worked for about ten seconds until I remembered the appointment. Samuel had convinced me to start therapy and had booked a session for me for eleven this morning. A little birthday gift. Not thrilled about the idea in general, and my anger was amplified by the fact that it fell on my birthday. Was it a coincidence or purposeful? I wanted to give him the benefit of the doubt, but it made me wonder.

Downstairs in the foyer closet, I grabbed a light sweatshirt, slipped on running shoes, and checked myself out in the hallway mirror. My long, brown hair was a mess and reminded me to think about making an appointment. My blue eyes were as clear as the sky on this day, and I decided I looked not a day over twenty-eight. With purpose in my steps, I walked outside to the patio overlooking the water and onto the short path that took me to the rocky beach. When I was a kid, I thought there was no way this could be a beach because there was no sand, just soft, small stones that crunched under your feet. Harold loved it though and always tried to convince me that this was better than a sandy beach. As I got older, it dawned on me that he had a valid point.

The early morning ocean was calm. There was barely a ripple, and the sounds of the powerful sea were muted. The water in this part of town made me think of the Caribbean, and once you traversed the rocky beach area, your feet enjoyed the soft, silky sand underneath the clear surface of the ocean. I looked over at the rack holding two yellow kayaks that we recently purchased and briefly considered that the conditions would be perfect for a morning glide. I thought otherwise when I leaned over and allowed my fingertips to graze the frigid water.

Across the sound, the island of Martha's Vineyard sat in front of me, and I slowly trained my head to the right and could see the outer point of the cove where Harold and Mary took their last breaths. Less than a year ago, they had died in each other's arms on their sailboat. I had just finished my eighth year at Harvard University and was living in a tiny Cambridge apartment. I was in the shower when I heard my cellphone ring. Before I leapt out of the shower and still managed to miss the call, I knew there was an urgency to the ringtone. The cellphone display told me it was from a restricted number. I went and finished the shower, dried off, and brushed my teeth. After getting dressed, I checked the phone, saw a voicemail message, and pressed play. I replayed the message three times. The detective's cold voice telling me that there was an accident, and that I needed to get to Woods Hole, continues to haunt me. I left the apartment that day, and never returned.

My thoughts transitioned to the last time we were together. It was my second graduation ceremony after eight long years. My grandparents arrived in town the night before and we dined outside at my favorite Italian restaurant. A night filled with stories, laughter, and a few tears. I had broken the news of my plan to remain in Cambridge for the summer to prepare my dissertation. Harold did not like this. He was especially unhappy about my decision not to come home the following weekend for the annual sail. Almost caving into his pleas, it turns out that my decision to stay in Cambridge likely saved my life.

Harold called me the night before they embarked on their final trip on the *Woodley*, Harold's second child. The *Woodley* was a 1963 Classic Schooner sailboat that was accompanied by the legendary story that Harold won her in a poker game. I always questioned the veracity of the tale because whenever he told the story, which was usually late at night, and after too much whiskey, Mary would look at me and give the slightest headshake. Our final conversation replays often in my head. They had me on speaker and Harold intimated, in his own way, that I was needed on the boat and should be with them for their annual, first of the season voyage. It was a rite of passage to summer, and there were only a few times in my life that I was not present on the sailboat for that trip.

The sail was a family tradition, as its roots went back over a hundred years when members of the Woodley family would race their respective boats around Martha's Vineyard. In recent years, it was known as the Woodley Figawi, named after the infamous race from Hyannis to Nantucket. The trek started in Woods Hole, with the sailors headed toward Edgartown, looping around Cape Poge and the backside of the Vineyard. The goal was to round the rainbow-colored, clay cliffs of Aquinnah at sunset and race across the sound to a cove further down the Elizabethan Islands. There they would drop anchor, break out the champagne and whiskey, and make the proclamation that summer had arrived. They would party all night in the cove before heading back to the harbor the following afternoon. These days it was just the *Woodley* that continued the tradition.

Harold assured me that he and Mary, both nearing eighty, were experienced mariners and could do this journey in their sleep. He insisted that, although the boat was more than fifty years old, she was thoroughly serviced at the marina just weeks before and deemed as seaworthy as the day it was christened. According to the GPS, which the Coast Guard was happy to show me, there must have been favorable winds on both sides of the island, and they completed the loop in record time. It would have made for a remarkable story if not for a mechanical problem that caused a leak in the generator's exhaust system and a carbon monoxide alarm that failed to make a sound. Silent death.

The gravelly crunch of seashells and stones made me turn, and I watched Samuel navigating his way down the path.

"You want me to drive you to your appointment this morning?" He asked in a gentle tone.

I pondered his offer. "You know what, I'm going to take the bike into town. It's a beautiful day, and I'd like to get some exercise."

"Sounds like a great idea. I'll pull it out of the garage and check the tires to make sure everything is good. When you get to the doctor's office, there is a side door on the left by the driveway. The waiting room is right there when you enter that door. He practices out of a small cottage in town."

"You sure seem motivated to get me to the shrink." Samuel seemed to know a lot about the layout of the house. I found that curious.

"A husband is supposed to look after his wife. You've been through a lot in the past year. The guy is good and maybe he can help."

"Help what? I'm just going through a normal process. You know – the stages of grief."

"That is a great discussion to have at your appointment." He said, dismissively. Thoughts of telling him to cancel the appointment and the party were on the tip of my tongue but I forced them to stay there.

"I'm planning to leave around ten to get extra riding in and plan to hang out in town after my appointment. Maybe have lunch there. Unless you need me to be around to help get ready for the party."

"Not necessary. I have everything under control. The guests will arrive around five, dinner will be at six, and everyone will be gone by eight or nine. Then it's just you and me for the night."

I forced a smile. "Sounds good. What's for dinner?"

"So, there's this guy in town famous for grilling chicken at the summer parties. They call him Spatch. It has something to do with the way he cooks the chicken. I ordered a bunch of salads and vegetable plates from your favorite caterer. I also hired a sommelier to pick out wines that pair well with the food. And for music..."

"Sounds a little excessive?"

"It's going to be perfect."

THE BIKE RIDE to town was glorious. Veering off the bike trail and up a steep incline, my route took me around the lighthouse, through the end of town and down the main street to bump up the miles. My legs were pumping hard, and the welcomed drips of salty perspiration beaded on my forehead and began trickling down my face. The traffic was light since the summer crowds were still weeks away. It was a perfect day for biking, and the temptation to keep on riding and blow off the appointment was strong.

Riding through town, I thought about my journey in life and tried to come to terms with the idea that maybe talking to someone could help me. A year ago, I was finishing my doctorate and desperately trying to figure out life. Harvard was a weird experience for me and there was no clarity in my mind about what came next. The first four years there felt like an extension of the boarding schools. Classes with notable professors, the mix of first-generation, hard-working students with the spoiled and privileged kids from here and abroad, my ongoing struggle to fit in and make friends. The second four years in the doctoral program were different. I had given up on trying to fit in and slowly became a recluse, living in isolation from the world. Classes were attended, and I was physically present at all the meetings and internship rotations. It just felt like I was sleep-walking through this experience and pretending that I had it all figured out. The thought of what I was going to do after completing my dissertation made me anxious, depressed, and put me into a dark place. But I never had to deal with it because of the accident.

After their deaths, I inherited *Indigobird*, which had an assessed value at around two million dollars. When I met with the attorney to review the will, I was surprised to learn that Harold and Mary were living off declining investment money and their estate essentially consisted of the house and the boat. The attorney let me know that they each had small life insurance policies that totaled around one hundred thousand dollars and neither had any debt. Even amidst the shock I had from their accident, I remember thinking that they had more assets. They certainly did not live an extravagant lifestyle but Harold, especially after dark-colored drinks, would proclaim that there would be money for me, that I was set for life, and he would someday tell me the secret. Mary would simply shake her head and extract the glass of liquor from his hand.

Downshifting the bike, I swerved onto Gardiner Road. The psychiatrist's office was in a typical Cape Cod gray house on the edge of the downtown area beyond the marine laboratory buildings. Walking into the appointment wearing sweaty biking clothes caused a slight smile to tug on my lips. I was not going to dress up for this appointment. True Woodley defiance.

During the ride, I felt my anger toward Samuel start to boil. He pushed the idea for the party without any discussion with me, and he should have known that I would've preferred a more somber celebration or nothing at all. And why do I have to sit in a stuffy office for the next fifty minutes on such a beautiful day?

Following his specific instructions, I entered through the side door and took a seat on a lumpy leather couch across from a door that adorned a plaque reading *Nathan Ferguson, MD*. The doctor was prompt, and precisely at eleven, he opened the white door and ushered me into the office. Seated in an even more uncomfortable chair that he directed me toward, I noted that his chair was different and looked newer. Fresh leather tickled my nose. The office had a second door that appeared to lead to the street. I surmised that it was his way of preventing patients from running into each other.

He was clearly in his late sixties, and it seemed that he put earnest effort into looking doctorly. The fully gray beard that shadowed his face was masked with thick, clear-framed glasses. The doctor had wild hair and needed a haircut. He wore a wide, paisley tie over a light-green shirt, and a tweed sports jacket. There was an awkward minute of silence where we both just looked at each other, and then he spoke.

"Hi, I'm Doctor Ferguson. I'm excited to begin working together and getting to know you. So, what brings you here today Mrs. Crossman?"

Crimson colored my face. Breathe Em, breathe.

"First, my name is Emerald Woodley." Accentuating my last name. "Please call me Em."

"Fair enough." He replied with an attitude. I immediately disliked this man, and seriously contemplated walking out of the room.

"Before we get into why I'm here, I have a few ground rules. First, under no circumstance will I ever consider taking any medications. Second, I want to pay out of pocket for this and don't want my insurance company billed or to even know that I'm seeing a shrink. Agreed?"

He paused. "As for the billing, your husband already paid me for eight sessions. We will not have to discuss payment until those sessions are completed. But I get what you are saying. Related to the medications, I hear your position, but you need to understand mine. If, during our work together, I think that adding a component of psychotropic medications may be a benefit to your well-being, I'll be ethically obliged to inform you of such. It is understood that the decision to accept any treatment recommendations is entirely up to you, in most circumstances."

My head was spinning, and anger continued to build. "Wait, what do you mean *by most circumstances*?"

"A court could order a person to take psychiatric medications on an involuntary basis. It is called a Rogers guardianship, but that is rare."

"I know about the Rogers case. But wait, Samuel paid for eight sessions, is that standard for your practice?"

"It was his idea. He indicated that you would be, um, looking for at least eight sessions."

I was seething and it showed. It took every ounce of composure to not walk out of the office. Ferguson quickly changed the flow of conversation and outlined the logistics around his duties and responsibilities. After general housekeeping items, such as session length, appointment cancellation, and calling his answering service if there was a crisis, he talked about the Tarasoff case. He explained his obligation to notify the police if I discussed causing physical harm to myself or another person. I rolled my eyes a little and he sensed it.

"Something I said?" He bristled with condescension.

"I was just thinking I'd like to punch Samuel in the face when I get home."

He paused. "Do you feel violent?"

"Dr. Ferguson, I feel violated. I have been through significant life stressors in the past year. I'm going through things but managing them. Apparently, my husband thinks I need intensive psychoanalysis. You may not know this, but I just completed a doctorate program. I should be sitting in your comfortable chair and not on this one."

"I'm aware of that. Quite an accomplishment."

I glared and it was a moment before he spoke.

"That brings us to the next key point we must discuss, which I know you understand but need to review anyway. Confidentiality. I'll give you a document that outlines your privacy rights and HIPAA. Basically, what we discuss here is protected in most cases, save for the duty to warn, medical emergency, court order, or if you provide written consent or authorization. Is there anyone that you would like to consent for me to discuss your treatment with, maybe your husband?"

"Hard no." I said with aggression in my voice.

"Okay then. Can we start at the beginning? Take the next ten minutes to walk me through your life to this point."

So, I did. I told him about my mother dying while giving birth to me. I recounted my early childhood growing up with my grandparents. I talked about my experiences in boarding schools, summers in Woods Hole, eight years at Harvard. I gave him a succinct synopsis of the early life and times of Emerald Woodley. When I finished the story about the phone call informing me of the accident involving Harold and Mary, he interjected.

"What do you think of your life up to the point of that phone call?"

"I don't think much about it. Things were normal." Leaving out my constant sadness, the isolation, and the dark thoughts that never seemed to go away.

"Normal. That is an interesting word." He paused for dramatic effect. "Em, your life was not what most would consider normal."

"Maybe not, but it was all I knew. It was just my life."

"What about relationships with other people? You didn't mention any close friends or boyfriends or important people in your life. I ask because I sense that, with everything you went through, you feel some sort of abandonment which may complicate current relationships. It may be something that we talk more about."

There was a period of awkward silence. I didn't know if he was waiting for me to respond or if I was waiting on him.

He broke the void. "Continue with after leaving Cambridge. And keep in mind that we have twenty minutes before the end of the session, and as I mentioned in the beginning, I want to use the last five minutes to recap this session and schedule the next."

I recounted coming back to Woods Hole after learning what happened to Harold and Mary. At the time it was all a blur, but as I spoke today it seemed more vivid and real. When I arrived at the Falmouth Police Department, I was driven by a sympathetic police officer to the harbor. We boarded the harbormaster's boat accompanied by several uniformed people, including police and Coast Guard personnel. During the quick trip to the cove, the officers explained that, based on GPS data, the sailboat had been anchored at that spot since seven the previous evening. They stated that shortly before ten the following morning, a fishing boat radioed in that the sailboat was slightly smoking and there was a smell of diesel fumes in the area. The Coast Guard responded and found the bodies. I'm composed as I talked about this life-altering event, but also told him that I always felt some level of ease that they died together on the boat that they loved and that they lived a full and happy life.

"So, how did you meet Samuel?"

"We met at the reception after the funeral. He introduced himself to me and two days later he brought me flowers and croissants from my favorite place in Woods Hole. I was alone and scared, and he was kind to me. We started taking walks each morning and he just helped me when I was helpless. I was planning to stay here for the rest of the summer to deal with the estate and house, and then head back to Cambridge, find a place, and continue my life."

"What changed?"

"I'm not exactly sure. Sometime in August, I realized that I didn't want to leave. I was with Samuel all the time. In the beginning, he was there for me, and suddenly he was always around. We clicked and I was afraid to be alone. On Columbus Day, or whatever it is called now, he took me out on my grandparents' sailboat. I had accepted an offer to sell her and wanted to take one last sail. I wanted the last memory of that boat to be a good one. It was weird, but cathartic in a sense. We anchored in the sound and swam in the chilly water like kids, doing cannonballs off the side, drinking champagne out of the bottle. Then, he proposed to me. It was like a fairy tale. We got married on New Year's Eve."

"That was a fast courtship. Why did things move so fast?"

I did not have a satisfactory answer for that. "I don't know. It kind of just happened and I went with it. It was impulsive."

"Impulsive, I see. Any regrets?" His arrogance and tone offended me.

"Honestly, he made me feel safe at a time that I was scared and alone. But I'm not sure I want to be married, it was never part of my plan, and after today, I'm clearly having second thoughts. I could kill him for making me spend my birthday in this office. I feel controlled.

And he is making us host a party at the house tonight. I'm less than thrilled."

He looked at me with intensity. "I'm going to trust that your comments of violence are in jest. Quickly tell me about him."

"Samuel is an interesting man. He is in his mid-thirties, so a few years older than me. He is the only child of a prominent New York City doctor, he attended private schools and lived in privilege. He graduated at the top of his high school class and was accepted early at Johns Hopkins for pre-med. His father has a house down here. From what he has told me, before he was set to head off to Baltimore, he enjoyed a wild summer here and never left. His parents were mortified at his poor choice and slowly shut him off. Then his mother suddenly passed away. It didn't seem to faze him, and even when his father threw him out of his houses, he found a small apartment here. He basically had been doing odd jobs... landscaping, bartending, working as a mechanic, kind of drifting."

"So, there are two things we need to discuss related to some, um, ethical murkiness. First, I know Doctor Crossman, and have for many years. It is a small community down here and we have socialized on occasion. I have known Samuel since he was a child, but only in passing. I have determined that this will not interfere with our work here in any unethical way." He paused. "Thoughts?"

I wanted to scream. "Only that it seems messed up that you would wait until this point to mention that. Way to bury the lede doc, what with seven minutes left in this session. What is the other thing?"

"We will get to that in a minute. It is a little more complicated. I have one more question."

"Shoot." I said in a hostile way, but if I had a gun and knew how to use it, I'd be in prison tomorrow.

"What about your father?"

"I didn't have one."

"I understand that you did not have a father in a parental sense, other than Harold, but you did biologically."

"As a child, I thought Harold and Mary were my parents. Nobody said anything to the contrary and they, you know, functioned as my parents. At the end of fifth grade, I was friendly with an Asian boy in my class. I went to his birthday party and saw that his parents were... not Asian. I was confused and asked him about it, and he told me that he was adopted because his parents were killed in a car accident in China. I went home and asked Mary if I was adopted. It was an innocent question from a ten-year-old girl. I mean, I was not really focused on how much older they were than the parents of other kids my age."

"How did Mary react?"

"She had no reaction."

"She did not say anything?"

"Mary said something to the effect of 'wait until Harold gets home.' Later that night, they came into my room and told me that they were my parents and explained that my mother had gone to the angels when I was born. Harold cried and Mary just watched. He said that my mother had some problems and had moved far away but had come back to them when she was pregnant with me. They were clear that this was the end of the discussion, and, for all intents and purposes, they were my mother and father. Years later, I must have been fifteen, Mary and I were sitting on the beach. I begged her to tell me about my mother. She told me that my mother got involved in drugs and other reckless behavior when she was in high school and eventually ran away and ended up somewhere in Florida. They lost contact and didn't see her for a long time until she showed up at their door eight months pregnant. I asked her if she knew who my father was, the biological one."

"Her response?"

"I don't recall her specific words, but she said that I would never know and not to go down that road."

"Emerald...Em, you never tried to find out?"

"What's the point? I mean, I went to town hall when I turned sixteen and got a copy of my birth certificate and saw the name listed. Not sure where to begin looking for Mr. John Doe."

"You said in the beginning that you've had a normal life. Does our session today change that perspective or give you any insight?"

"I feel like we are dredging up things that I have already come to terms with for the sake of creating some sort of treatment plan. It's like the tail wagging the dog."

"The goal of this is to help you." He said with condescension. "And this is the beginning of the process."

"I don't think this has helped, to be honest. I understand this is what you and people in your profession do for a living, but I'm beginning to think that there are some things in life that you just don't want to know. Some things are better left unknown. I have not thought about my biological father for years, and now I'm forced to think about that. The more I know the less I understand."

He smiled. "People in your profession? Is this not the career you are pursuing?"

"I'm having second thoughts." In periods of darkness and self-reflection over the past months, it had dawned on me that the only reason I went to Harvard was the prestige of being an Ivy-leaguer and entering the doctoral program in psychology was more of a quest to understand my perpetual unhappiness. I hated the school and helping other people was clearly not my calling.

He looked over my shoulder which I knew was an effort to glance at the clock behind my head. "Please commit to at least one more session. You may feel differently, but we have something to work with here."

"I'll consider it. But no promises."

He pushed the issue. "How about next Monday. I have a late opening, how about six?"

"As I said, I'll consider it." There was less than a one percent chance.

"I'll put you down for next Monday then. The other quasi-ethical issue that I debated internally before agreeing to have this session is something that we should discuss when we meet next time."

This guy will not quit. "Yeah, and what might that be?"

He paused and took off his glasses, methodically cleaning the lenses with his ugly tie. His soulless eyes looked up at me. "Your mother. She was a patient of mine."

IT TOOK two shots of house whiskey to calm down. I was sitting on the outside deck at Captain Kidd's, a pub for the locals in the off-season which transformed into a tourist trap from Memorial Day through the end of summer. Legend had it that this was an actual tavern for pirates hundreds of years ago. I chose to sit outside to be away from people and so I could wear my sunglasses to hide my tears and anger. This day was supposed to be beautiful. The golden sun stood directly overhead and brought warmth and light that conflicted with my darkness and anger. The alcohol warmed my body and things were moving in slow motion. Day drinking was not my thing, and this was not going to turn out well. I was sure of that.

The server approached and spoke with annoying vocal fry. "Ready to order?"

The menu had not been touched, and I pointed at the empty shot glass. She gave me a sympathetic look.

"Okay. But maybe you should order some food, you know, we have several great specials today. I just sampled the dayboat scallops and they were super good."

"Bay or sea?"

Her fake smile quickly transformed into confusion. "Um, what do you mean?"

"Bay or sea scallops? You know, bigger ones like half-dollar sized or smaller ones like a dime?" *Stop being a bitch Em.*

She thought about it before speaking with more exaggerated fry. "These were more like a quarter."

Glaring at her nametag, I almost snapped at her but instead took a deep breath.

"Jessie. I'll have the house burger, medium with cheddar and extra bacon with well-done fries and coleslaw."

"Sounds good. I'll be back with your drink."

After Jessie walked back into the inside restaurant, I felt a vibration in the side pocket of my pants. Samuel. No chance of taking that call.

When Jessie returned with the whiskey, I asked her to bring a pint of beer, a local IPA, with the burger. Time to slow down. From the deck, I gazed at the harbor which was only about half-full this time of year. A small fishing boat pulled up to the dock below me, and the air became thick with evidence that their trip was a success. The two guys on the boat gave a wave in my general direction, but I pretended not to notice, I had on sunglasses after all. The small glass of whiskey was slammed like an amateur, and some dribbled down my chin. *Don't judge me, I'm having a tough day.*

The burger dripped with white cheese and was accented nicely by crunchy bacon. Harold used to say to never trust a person that eats a burger without bacon. The icy beer was surprisingly hoppy, and my mouth enjoyed the subtle notes of citrus and pine. The messy appointment came back into my head, and I thought about how to handle Samuel when returning home. Part of me wanted to race the bike back to the house and have him cancel the party and have it out with him. My anger was palpable, and the whiskey and beer were not doing me any favors.

The fishing boat beneath me unmoored from the dock and was replaced by a family of ducks circling in the brackish water. I started breaking apart the soggy, not well-done French fries, and tossed them over the railing causing a feeding frenzy below. This led to dirty looks from the other patrons on the deck. Suddenly, an idea came to mind. One of Harold's favorite sayings, which I was sure was not an original, was 'don't trust a brilliant idea until it survives the hangover.' In my defense, this idea was far from brilliant.

Motioning Jessie to bring me the check, I paid the bill and slowly walked through the restaurant, gazing at the pirate murals on the wall. The bright afternoon sun blinded me after walking through the dimly lit bar, and the quickly consumed alcohol caused a swaying motion in my step. Walking the bike down the street to the nearby office seemed like the right thing to do. Of course, I did not have an appointment, but was hoping that he would see me for a quick consultation.

Haphazardly leaving the bike on the sidewalk and tossing my helmet into the bushes, I entered the building and took the stairs to the second floor. In the office, I was greeted by the familiar receptionist, and asked if Len was available for a few minutes. She said she would check and asked me to take a seat. I stumbled a little bit before landing on the black leather couch. With the phone pressed against her ear, she spoke to me over the desk.

"Mrs. Woodley, he asked what this is in regard to."

"Tell him I want an annulment or a divorce or some way to get unmarried." It probably sounded more dramatic than intended. I wondered what my blood alcohol level was, and I knew my words came out smashed together in a slur. I had not noticed that there was another person sitting in the waiting area until she emitted a slight chuckle at my comment.

The receptionist nodded and hung up the phone. "You can go into his office." She did not have to tell him the reason for my visit, which indicated that he must have heard me through the earpiece. Or maybe my voice echoed down the hall, and he heard it in stereo.

Leonard Fiore was the Woodley family attorney. He was the one who prepared the last wills and testaments for Harold and Mary. I knew him a little when I was younger and met with him a few times after their deaths. He seemed like a nice guy. Seated at his desk behind a large computer monitor, he was reclined in a chair gazing at a flat screen television mounted to the wall. He was a short, stocky man and was wearing a dark, pinstriped suit, crisp white shirt, and maroon tie. Big city lawyer in a sleepy little village.

"Mrs. Woodley. Nice to see you. Please have a seat." He motioned to the chair in front of the desk. "What's going on?"

"You can call me Em. I may need to retain your services. I'm not sure if I want to be married anymore."

He pondered my statement. "I see. You understand that I'm not a divorce attorney, but I could certainly recommend someone that could handle that...or maybe a marriage counselor?"

More counseling. "I don't want marriage counseling. I just want to know what would happen, I mean, financially if I divorced him."

"You just got married, right? Two, three months ago?"

"A little over four months ago...about." My mouth was heavy with alcohol, and I struggled to sound coherent.

"I see." He gazed at me for an awkward moment. "Listen, are you okay? Not really my business but you look like you've been crying and, well, you seem impaired."

"I'm fine. I had a few drinks at lunch and don't drink often, and it sort of hit me funny. I know we signed a prenup and I just want to make sure that it protects the state...I mean estate. I got married too quickly and he... kind of orchestrated the whole thing. I'm having second thoughts and getting a weird vibe from him."

"Again, I'm not a divorce attorney and want to be careful here. But we did execute a prenuptial agreement, upon my insistence I might add, and the estate is protected in the event of divorce. As far as any type of settlement or financial remuneration is concerned as part of the divorce, you would have to speak with someone that is better versed in that world. I'll reach out to some colleagues in the area this afternoon and call you tomorrow with a referral."

"I appreciate that. Thank you."

His sympathetic eyes looked at me. "No problem. Do you need a ride home? I hope you're not driving. I don't do DUI cases either."

I stood. "All set. On foot today. But thanks for the consideration. Appreciate you taking a few minutes to talk with me."

The walk of shame out of his office was quick and I kept my head down while passing the receptionist desk. After retrieving my bike and helmet from the bushes in front of the building, I thought about going back to Captain Kidd's for more beer. Sobering up was not part of the plan. It struck me that this was a bad idea, and I'm better than that. I went to Harvard, right?

Instead, I went to the market and purchased a half pint of sour mash whiskey and a large bottle of spring water. I walked the bike down to the park next to the beach, drank half of the water, and then added the whiskey to the plastic bottle. Creating a loud clang when tossing the empty glass bottle into a metal trash barrel, two Coast Guard dudes sitting on a bench looked at me. One gave me a thumbs up.

There was an empty wooden bench in the park next to a bronze sculpture of Rachel Carson, and I decided to keep her company. For the next hour, the sour mash water coated my palate while I chatted with Ms. Carlson. I did most of the talking, and half expected the local police to roll up and take me into custody.

As low clouds moved over the glowing sun, I noticed a man who had pushed his bike into the park and was sitting on the rock wall overlooking the water. He had a black hybrid bike and was wearing all black, from his helmet to his shoes, with large, reflective sunglasses that seemed too big for his chiseled face. I found it strange that he never took off his helmet and was tempted to yell for him to take off his helmet and stay a while. Alcohol rushed through my body, and I was ready to ride. Normally, the bike ride back to the house was seven minutes. That used to be my target as a teenager, and I remembered the proud moment the first time I broke that mark. It was time to go home. Saddling up on the bike, I exited the park and pedaled to the main street and around the corner past the steamships. The route continued through the long-term parking area and onto the bike path. As my front tire hit the beginning of the paved bike trail, I casually turned my head and saw him in the distance. The man in black was following me. *Why?*

Emerald. Get ahold of yourself. It is the middle of the day and a public bike path. My pace accelerated and I focused on the pavement in front of me. Drunk biking is not something I have ever done, and it was not as easy as it seemed. The path was strangely deserted this afternoon. *Weird.* I turned to look, and the man on the bike was closing the gap and about a hundred feet behind me. To get to the house, which was on my right, I needed to veer off the paved path and take a sharp right to get down a narrow dirt trail that took me to the bottom of an embankment. The driveway for the house was two hundred feet from there. I sensed the man gaining on me as I readied myself for the turn. Fifty feet. *Why is he chasing me?*

I made the sharp right turn like an Olympian, leaning in perfectly and timing the downshift with precision, decelerating like a champion. I quickly looked back and realized no one was behind me. I was about to scream in triumph, and then I saw the tree.

EVERYTHING HURT. I rolled over and violently retched. The vomit bounced off the dusty trail and splattered on my face. Whiskey, beer, bacon.

My legs were shaking, and I took that as a good sign. Raising my right arm to my head, I felt the warm blood dripping into my right eye. Using the sleeves of my sweatshirt, I wiped the blood from my eyes and face. I had never had a serious accident before, no stitches, no surgeries. The only visits to the doctor had been routine appointments. Thoughts of an ambulance ride sent shivers through my body. Using the slope to my advantage, I was able to sit up. With limited visibility, I saw the bike at the base of the tree, about five feet behind me. It took all my strength and effort to rise to my feet. I managed to stand for a moment before I vomited again and fell to the ground. This bout eased the throbbing pain in my head, and I rose again to my feet, taking baby steps toward the bike.

The walk back to the house was slow and painful. By the time I reached the driveway, a second wind propelled me forward. Using the code to open the garage door, I started to roll the bike toward the back and the sound of the metallic screeching along the cement floor echoed loudly. The front tire was flat, and the forks were bent. I placed the bike on the wall next to a storage shelf. Entering the house through the garage, I crept up the stairs to my bedroom moving stealthily to avoid being noticed by Samuel and his father, Bill, who were sitting on the back patio.

In the bathroom, I shut and locked the door, quickly stripping out of my bloody clothes. I was about to throw them in the laundry basket, but it was lined in cloth, and I didn't want it to get stained from the blood and dirt. I found a trash bag under the vanity and stuffed the clothes in and dropped the bag in the basket. Naked, my image in the mirror was horrifying. The cut over my right eye oozed blood down my face, however; I decided it wasn't deep enough to warrant stitches. I was sure of that. I turned on the shower and peered out the window to the patio below. *Ugh.* While I was out getting drunk and crashing my bike, Samuel had set up the patio in an extraordinary way. Beneath a large tent, there were round, ten-top tables with crisp white linens. On each table, the same green roses he gave me this morning, sprouted from vases, contrasting nicely with the backdrop of white. I watched Samuel, his father, and another man setting up a cocktail bar. Sliding open the window, I heard the sizzle of the grill and smelled olive oil, garlic, and herbs sweetening the late afternoon air.

Everything outside was pristine, elegant, and white. Inside the house, I was a battered and bloodied mess.

Water cascaded down my aching body for an hour, or so it seemed. The shower was set at the highest temperature possible and pulsing with pressure. It was painful but I deserved it. The visibility in the glass encased shower was lacking due to the accumulated steam. My good eye noted a shadowy figure beyond the steam, and I sensed someone was watching me. Using my hand to wipe off the condensation on the glass, I saw him, and he did not look happy. I turned off the shower, opening the door as a funnel of steam shot out through the bathroom.

"Emerald, what the... what happened to your face?"

"I had an accident on the bike. But I'm okay." I shrugged. "Hand me a towel."

He leaned to the rack and his entire body jerked as he roughly pushed the towel toward me. "You don't look okay. You are bleeding."

"It is just a small cut. I'll survive."

He put his hand on my head and waves of pain radiated through my body.

"It is not just a small cut. You have a big welt, and your eye is black. Where did this happen?"

"I thought someone was chasing me on the bike path. A man was following me." I said, and then a memory hit the surface of my mind. "On the trail from the bike path to the driveway. I misjudged a turn and hit an oak tree or something. That therapy session set me off, Samuel. I'm angry. I had a few drinks. I'm not happy that you made me go there. Today, of all days. But we can talk about this later, let me get ready for the party."

Confusion filled his face. "Chasing you? What are you talking about? Are you sure you're up for the party? Maybe—"

"I'll be fine. Just... I have a headache and I'm not in the mood to argue." I said as I wrapped the towel around my body. "Can you bring me a glass of whiskey? I need something for the pain. I'll be ready in ten minutes, and we can walk down together."

"Can I have my father come up and check you out just to make sure you don't have a concussion or some type of head trauma. This doesn't look good."

"No. Absolutely not."

"Well, at least let me put Neosporin on it, and a bandage."

With the skill of a Boy Scout working on a first aid merit badge, Samuel struggled to get the ointment out of the small cylinder and fumbled with the bandage wrapper. He seemed nervous and I sensed something was off. *Why was he distracted?*

I asked Samuel to get me the drink and give me fifteen minutes to get ready. I walked into my closet to pick an outfit and saw two feather hem sheath dresses with the tags still on them, one white and one off-white. I chose the off-white one. I rushed my hair and makeup, but it was nearing the fifteen-minute mark and I didn't care anymore. I was going to look like a mess regardless. Exiting the bathroom, I found Samuel sitting on the window seat gazing at the festivities below. On the ledge, I could see a healthy pour of amber liquid in a highball glass and two small, white pills.

He stood, giving me a sympathetic look. "I told my father about the accident, and he had some nonnarcotic pain medications in his medicine bag," he said as he handed me two oval white pills.

Sweet. I grabbed the glass and drank half the whiskey. I was sore and achy, and needed to rally. I wanted tonight to go well and wanted the pain to go away. We would talk tomorrow, but tonight I was committed to forgetting about everything. Maybe I would actually enjoy the night. I took the pills and sipped more whiskey. For the next few minutes, Samuel and I stood looking out the window. We watched his father below, greeting guests as they arrived on the back patio and acting like a maître de. Through the open window, sounds of laughter and happiness carried up to my bedroom, echoing over the ocean. His voice broke the silence.

"Are you sure you are up for this?" He asked with his arms folded across his chest and speaking to me like I was a child.

Peering deeply into his dark eyes, I saw deceit. I panicked. I can't go down there. "I need ten minutes. You go down first, and I'll be down soon, and I'll you know...make a grand entrance."

He looked at me with disappointment. Like he had planned this whole event out and I was ruining everything. But he smiled.

"Of course. I'll see you when you're ready."

He kissed my cheek and left the bedroom. I sat at the window and watched the party below. Soft classical music filled the air, and the intensity and volume of the laughter seemed to have risen in the last few minutes. I watched Samuel greeting people, shaking hands, embracing guests as they arrived. It felt voyeuristic.

I saw him talking with his father and sensed negativity. Bill had just turned sixty and looked exactly like an older version of Samuel, only grayer and more wrinkled. There was headshaking, and at one point, they both looked up to the window. Looking at me. Could they see me watching them?

I quickly retreated from the window, stumbling backwards toward the bed. I caught my balance and used my left hand to steady myself against the mattress so I wouldn't fall. My shoes were on the bed, and I had selected flats that matched the dress. No chance I could do heels tonight. I laid on my back to slip them on. Lightheadedness and confusion took control of my body. Slowly, I was wheezing and gasping for oxygen. *Was I having a panic attack?* My eyes closed and the music started to fade. I recognized it and tried to hum along with the symphony. The room started spinning, and visions of darkness took over my still body. Suddenly, my body jolted forward, and sensations of sudden alertness radiated throughout. I inhaled oxygen into my lungs, tasting a mixture of unnatural chemicals with each breath. My eyes fluttered again and closed. *What was happening to me?*

For as much as I dreaded this party and as angry as I was about the many things that transpired during the day, somehow against all odds, I had an amazing night. Everything was perfect. The wine selection was amazing, and I was careful not to drink too much considering my day drinking and injuries. The food was incredible. Samuel was right, it was the best chicken I had ever eaten. There was a champagne toast right before dinner with Samuel, showcasing his charisma, professing his love and adoration for his beautiful wife. It brought me to tears, but they were classy tears.

After dinner, we all headed down to the beach. Some of the guests that knew Harold and Mary told funny stories. The minister from the church said a kind and powerful prayer on the rocky shore just mere miles from where they died. It was touching. The night was perfect. When we got back from the beach, the tables had been removed and rows of chairs lined the bricks. Majestic flames were shooting out from the firepit at the corner of the patio. One of the guests broke out an acoustic guitar and sang all my favorite songs.

The encore was our wedding song, and before he started strumming, the guitar guy invited Samuel and I to the front of the patio. Under the stars, we slowly danced pressing our bodies together. After the song and applause from the guests, Samuel spoke and asked everyone to mark their calendars for next year, for this was going to be an annual tradition. He thanked everyone for coming and, in a polite way, told everyone the party was over and he needed alone time with his beautiful wife. Everyone laughed, including me.

Each guest left with a smile. I had an enjoyable conversation with Samuel's father who was the last one to leave the house. In my mind, he was always cold to me for reasons I did not understand, but tonight our interactions were warm and friendly. He professed his adoration of me and told Samuel that he better take care of me. I gushed with happiness at the idea that maybe he was finally coming around and maybe we would actually have a decent relationship.

We sat underneath a warm blanket in an oversized chair by the dwindling fire, drinking glasses of port while people removed and loaded up the tent, tables, and chairs. Beneath the starry sky, we listened to the rolling sounds of the ocean water and the crackling of the dying flames. I begged Samuel to add more wood to the fire. He shook his head and nodded toward the house. We went inside and made our way upstairs to the bedroom. I went to the bed and laid on top of the blankets. I watched him as he stood by the window looking at the waning moon over the sound. He took off his jacket and neatly laid it on the chair as he started to unbutton his dress shirt.

I had to hand it to him. He was right.

Tonight, everything changed.

CHAPTER 2

AFTER PARTY

Without question, this morning was different. There were no illusions that happiness would enter into my lexicon of emotions. When my eyes opened, it felt like I was being stabbed by needles and all I could see was darkness. Instead of soft Egyptian cotton sheets grazing my skin, I felt as if I was wrapped in a steel wool sponge. I tossed the rough blanket off me and that's when pain radiated over my entire body. I reached for Samuel, but instead of touching his warm skin, my hand ricocheted off a firm surface with an odd sounding thump. *Where was I?* I panicked and pulled in breaths that didn't reach my lungs. A surge of heat passed through me as my heart threatened to jump out of my chest.

My eyes fluttered but all I could see was blackness. When I moved my mouth, the edges of my lips felt as if they were bruised, along with my arms and limbs. In place of the strong coffee that normally awoke me each morning, I inhaled the unpleasantness of chemicals. My body shifted, again thumping against a solid surface that in no way resembled a bed. *Where was I?* Surrounded in darkness, my hands discovered soft plastic. Using them for sensory guidance and as my good eye adjusted to the darkness, I realized that I was curled up in the rear cargo area of my Jeep Cherokee.

I pushed the liftgate from the inside, but it wouldn't budge so I slammed my palm on the hatch until I could calm myself down enough to open it with the inside handle. Painful tears burned my eyes. The second the latch unclicked, bright light from above illuminated the cargo area. Swiveling my cramped legs to the concrete, I placed my bare feet on the cold floor and braced myself for more pain. I released a grateful exhale when I realized that the Jeep was parked in our garage. It took me more than a minute to walk the fifteen steps into the house, each step carefully thought out to limit the pain.

My first stop was the bathroom across from the garage entryway. Straddling my arms on the sink to keep my aching body upright, I used my elbow to flick on the light and looked in the mirror with abject horror. My right eye was completely shut. There was a crimson foam caked around the sides of my mouth. My hair had flecks of what looked like crusted vomit. I was wearing running shorts and a sweatshirt. When did I put this on? *Why did I sleep in the Jeep?*

Staggering through the house like I was ninety, I yelled his name over my tears. My weak voice was met with silence. The house was spotless, but the strong scent of chemicals caused my gag reflex to kick into high gear. In the kitchen, there were no signs of a party that ended less than twelve hours ago. No empty bottles, no remnants of food. Slowly making my way to the back sliding door, I stepped out onto the patio. The smell of smoldering embers triggered a thought from last night when I sat beside the fire with Samuel.

Hobbling slowly down the sandy path to the water, the sun flickered in the cloudless sky. Samuel was nowhere to be found. In the distance, I could make out eight or more boats in the rip current about a mile from the shore. They were circling the area, and I heard yelling. There were dozens of birds diving in the water adding to the chaos that was inside my aching head. *Where was he?*

My cell phone. I retreated, as fast as my legs would allow, back up the path and into the house, making my way back upstairs hoping it was in its usual spot on the nightstand. Halfway up the stairs, I heard a faint ringtone and was able to get to the phone just before it went to voicemail.

"Hello." I said between sips of air.

"Em, Len Fiore. Good morning."

"Oh... hey...um, hi Len," I forced myself to string coherent words together. "Good morning."

"So, I have the name of an attorney that has agreed to meet you for a consultation. He is a good guy, and I think you will work well together. Do you want me to text you his name and number?"

Awkward.

"Len. Um, I made a mistake yesterday." I thought back to the boiling rage I felt after my appointment with the therapist, when I stormed into the innocent attorney's office. "I appreciate your call, but I won't be needing an attorney."

"Okay." He paused for a moment. "Are you sure?"

"Listen, I'm sorry for wasting your time. I really am. Yesterday was a bit messy. But everything is good. I'm kind of in the middle of something but thank you for following up." I ended the call abruptly. With my facial features distorted, normal access to my iPhone would not work, and I struggled to remember the code to open the phone. It took me four attempts. I checked my call history and there were no missed calls and no texts. *What happened last night?*

I scrolled down to earlier yesterday and saw the missed call from Samuel in the afternoon. Right. When I was doing shots of whiskey before lunch. I pressed the screen to call him, and it went right to voicemail. It was then that I ran to the bathroom and kneeled before the white porcelain gripping it harder with every surge of pain that ripped through me as I vomited.

Gently removing my clothes, I entered the shower and chilly water cascaded over my body for the next ten minutes. Without drying off, I moved back into the bedroom, and crawled below the soft, fluffy blankets. Weakness and fatigue washed through my body. I closed my functioning eye and tried to remember what happened. *Something is not right.*

Shaken by a boom that echoed throughout the room, I opened my good eye, and saw waves of lightening flash through the dark sky outside of the window. The sun that provided a bright light was gone, replaced with dark clouds. The bedside clock told me that it was after three in the afternoon.

After the lengthy, unplanned nap, some of my agility had returned, and I was able to exit the bed with less of a struggle. Dressing in my seemingly endless supply of matching sweatsuits and throwing my hair in a ponytail, I once again went through the house calling Samuel's name and only heard the echoes of my weakened voice. I tried calling him again. Straight to voicemail. Dreading the next call, I scrolled through my contacts and pressed the screen. The father who did not like me. We had made some progress last night, but I was still filled with anxiety over interacting with him. The phone stopped ringing and there was silence on the other end until I spoke.

"Hello? Bill?"

"Yes... who is this?" More unpleasant than usual. And he sounded confused.

"Hi, Bill. It's Em. Good afternoon, I hope I'm not catching you at an inconvenient time."

"Who...? Oh... Now is fine. What... what can I do for you?" His stuttering was disconcerting.

"I haven't seen Samuel since last night. He wasn't here this morning when I woke up. His car is in the garage, and he is not answering his phone. I was wondering if he is with you. Or if you have seen or heard from him today."

"No. I called him a few times earlier today and it went right to voicemail."

"Strange. This is not like him." A boom of thunder exploded outside, shaking the windows.

"What was that?"

"Thunder, the storm outside?" His house was less than five miles away.

"I'm back in New York." He lived in Manhattan for most of the year, but it surprised me that he had already returned so soon after coming up for the party.

"Okay, well if you hear from Samuel, please tell him to come home or call me. I'm worried."

"Right."

"I also just want to say that it was such a beautiful party last night. I really enjoyed it, especially our conversations. Thank you for being a part of it."

Click. The call ended. I checked my phone to see if I lost service, but five bars were visible on my screen. I debated calling him back but decided that I was in no shape to deal with his attitude.

I paced aimlessly through the kitchen, and waves of weakness pulsed through my body. I took out almond butter and pita bread, and haphazardly made a sandwich, eating while standing over the kitchen sink. My vision was obstructed by the welt over my eye, and I noticed something in the deep, metallic basin. There were rust colored spots around the edges of the stainless steel. I picked up the sponge to wipe them off and saw that the cellulose fibers had turned from yellow to brown. I put the sponge in the sink and poured bleach on top of it while steaming hot water from the faucet drizzled down. Within seconds, the once yellow sponge that had turned crimson was a much lesser shade of yellow. I splashed more bleach in the sink and washed it again.

Still ravenous, I ate another almond butter pita and painfully slurped down a bottle of water before I returned upstairs to the bedroom. My mind was all over the place. I had a flashback of last night and I can hear Samuel's yelling voice as if it's happening in this moment. *Why was he yelling at me?* I looked up and around the bedroom, but I was alone. *Did we have a fight last night? Is that why he is not here?*

For the next twenty minutes, I sat on the window ledge and looked outside. The violent rain and thunderstorm had given way to clearing skies, and it looked like the sun was about to reappear. I dialed his phone again. Nothing. I thought about calling the police. What would I say?

My mind was racing, and I thought about yesterday. Waking up with happiness. The horrible appointment. The doctor that knew my mother. Excessive day drinking. The man that chased me on the bike trail. The accident.

Remembering that I left my bloodied clothes from yesterday in a trash bag in the laundry basket, I went into the bathroom and grabbed it, making my way down the stairs. About halfway down, the bag hit the metal stair railing and a clanging sound echoed through the house. When I reached the bottom of the stairs, I opened the bag to see what made the noise. On top of my balled-up biking clothes was a knife, glistening with reddish, brown fluid. *What the fuck?* Underneath the knife was my dress from last night, also covered in blood. The bag escaped from my hand and thudded to the floor. I screamed.

Then, the doorbell rang.

FROZEN AND UNABLE TO MOVE, I heard the chimes of the bell again, only they were amplified this time. Through the full-length panes on the sidelights, I could see someone standing on the steps. A man in a blue sport coat. He was well-dressed, looked muscular for his smaller frame, and his shiny head of gray hair glistened in the sunlight. I watched him reach over toward the doorbell. When he moved to press the button, I could see the steel metal of a gun holstered on his belt. I started to open the bag to grab the knife but realized that would be pointless. The man then pounded on the door. *Bang, bang, bang.*

"Detective Chase, Falmouth PD. Please open the door."

His hand moved over the gun, and he slowly drew the weapon from his holster and spoke louder.

"I know someone is in there. I heard someone yelling. I need to enter the house."

"Everything is okay. I'll be there in a second." My voice came out, barely audible.

Looking over at the adjacent foyer closet, I had an idea. The side-lights were reflective, and I knew that he would not be able to see me. Slithering away from the front door, I slowly opened the closet and slid the bag inside, gently closing the door.

"Can you please show me your identification?" I stalled to compose myself wondering why feelings of guilt pulsed through my body.

The man complied and pressed his open wallet against the side-light. Badge and identification. Lincoln Chase, Falmouth Police, Detective Division. I could see that his gun was back in the holster, covered by his large hand. I unlocked the deadbolt and opened the door halfway. He gave me a sympathetic look and trained his eyes behind me.

"Are you alone in the house?" His hand was still on the gun.

"Yes. I'm alone."

"I need to enter the house." He said directly. "Are you sure you are alone?" He spoke with a clear tone of skepticism.

Swinging the door fully open, I took a step back. "Yes. It's just me."

He walked past me, and I followed.

"I heard someone scream."

"That would be me. I banged my knee on the railing coming downstairs. Clumsy."

He looked around the downstairs area of the house, moving his oval head from side to side. It was evident that he didn't believe me. He turned back and set his gaze on me, scanning me from head to toe.

"Are you sure that you're okay? You look injured?"

"I had a bike accident yesterday afternoon. Went off the path and into a tree." I pointed to my bruised face and shrugged my shoulders. "Can we go out on the back patio to talk? I need fresh air." We should move away from the knife and bloody dress.

He nodded and I led him out the back slider to the patio. The chairs outside were wet from the rain and I excused myself to go into the house to grab a towel. I offered to bring him a water and he politely declined. Returning with a towel, I sopped up the standing puddles on two of the chairs. He slowly took a seat and I lowered myself into the other dry chair.

He took out a notepad. "You are Emerald Woodley? This is your house?"

I nodded in the affirmative even though I could tell that he already knew.

"Ms. Woodley, we got a call a short while ago from Bill Crossman. He reported that his son, your husband, is missing. He requested that we conduct a wellness check at this residence."

"Yes. I spoke with Bill about an hour ago to see if he had heard from my husband."

"When did you last see your husband?" Checking his notepad.

"Last night, after the party. It was my birthday. We went to bed around eleven. When I woke up this morning, he was not here." I skipped the part about sleeping in the Jeep.

He looked at me. "Is that out of the ordinary?"

"Very much so. He communicates well with me. We've been married for only four months, and he has never been off the grid like this. He always calls or texts. I have tried calling him, but it goes straight to voicemail."

"Did he have plans for today? Did he mention not being home, maybe he was going somewhere?"

I paused. "I don't recall him discussing anything about today. If anything, we would have been doing yard work and cleaning up from the party last night. I was shocked that he was not home when I awoke this morning, and I don't understand why he hasn't called."

"What time did you wake up?"

I had no idea, and by the way, I woke up in the back of my car. "Around eight."

"Did anyone stay here last night? Any of your guests?"

"No. Everyone left before ten. His father was the last guest to leave, and then the people that my husband hired to help were still around to clean up."

He consulted his notes. "How was the party by the way?"

"It was great." A smile crossed my nervous face. "Samuel did an amazing job putting it together. I enjoyed myself very much."

He looked at me with dead eyes. "This might seem like an odd question but bear with me. Were you intoxicated last night? I mean, it was your birthday party."

"Full disclosure. I had a rough day yesterday. I don't want to get into it, but I had some drinks, too many drinks, in the afternoon. Before the bike accident. But I rallied after getting home and did not drink much at the party. It was more like a wine tasting thing."

He continued to gaze at me with increasing levels of incredulity. "Did you use any drugs last night?"

"What? Drugs? Absolutely not! I mean... no, I never use drugs. Why would you even ask that?"

He changed the subject. "Do you mind if we walk around the property, just so I can check that off in my report?"

I thought about the bag in the closet. The one with the knife and my bloodied dress. "Go ahead. Anything you need. Where do you want to start?"

He shrugged. "How about the beach?"

We made our way down the path to the beach area. I was buzzing with intense trepidation and anxiety. I felt guilty, like I had done something terribly wrong, and the tension was compounded by the fact that I had no idea what happened last night. I need to show him the bag with the knife and my bloody dress. It would be the right thing to do. *There must be a logical explanation for that, right?*

After the earlier downpour, the sun was out in full force and the air was thick. Warm wetness moistened the back of my shirt. I watched the detective walk the beach in a grid-like manner. At times, he curiously bent down to investigate things in the sand.

"Do you mind if I go back up to the patio and sit down? I'm feeling a little sore from the accident."

"The accident?" He raised his eyebrows.

"On my bike."

"Oh, right. Sure, I'll only be another few minutes."

As I started walking back to the patio, out of the corner of my eye, I saw something. One of the kayaks was missing. I know it had been there yesterday when I was out here. But was it here this morning? I could not remember. Is Samuel out on the kayak?

He started following me and stopped at the rack. "You been doing any kayaking this spring?"

"Not yet. Water is still a little too cold for me."

"The water temperature is warmer than you think. Did you see the commotion out there this morning?" He pointed toward Vineyard Haven.

"I did see boats circling out there. Figured they were on some early season bass."

"Not stripers. There was a white shark siting. About a mile out. Two guys in a fishing boat saw it drag a seal or another shark under the water. I heard it was quite a scene."

"Great white? A little early in the season, isn't it?"

"That's what I thought too. But the harbormaster said it can happen." He began to hum the Jaws theme song.

He finished combing the beach and told me that he wanted to look around the house. We started in the basement, a place where I had not been since we moved my grandparents' belongings down here sometime in the late fall. There was also a stack of boxes from Samuel's apartment. I was shocked when I saw how everything was in disarray. We had carefully moved their books, pictures, and other items to a corner of the basement and stacked everything neatly. Samuel had thought that moving their things to the basement might be beneficial for me in my grieving process. Papers were strewn across the cold, concrete floor. It looked like someone had rifled through the boxes, but he didn't seem to notice. *Why would he?*

On the main floor, the detective casually looked through each room. I half expected him to peek under all the beds, in each closet, and behind the curtains, but his process seemed to be more cursory. We went into the garage, and he spent time looking through Samuel's BMW and then the Jeep. He even popped open the back of the Jeep and picked up the grey wool blanket that served as my bed the night before. On the way back into the house, he looked over at the mangled bike leaning against the work bench.

"Quite an accident." He offered after surveying the damage.

"You should see the tree."

We entered the house and walked right by the foyer closet before ascending the grand staircase to the second floor. He went through each room, this time more methodically. In my bedroom, he checked the bed, looked under it, and asked permission to look through Samuel's dresser. He pulled out a wallet and cell phone from the top drawer.

"Your husband's?"

I walked over and looked at the phone and wallet. "Yes. These are his."

"Well, the phone is powered off." He showed me. "I'm going to turn it on. Do you know his password?" He asked as the phone screen came to life. I shook my head. He left the wallet and the phone on top of the dresser, and walked to the large window that overlooked the patio and the sound. He looked over the ocean in silence before finally speaking.

"I need a little more of your time. Can we go downstairs?"

I nodded and we walked down to the main floor in silence. I ushered him into the living room, and we sat across from each other on opposite couches. I looked over at the indigobird on the oversized painting, his eyes taunting me. Detective Chase once again pulled out his notepad.

"If I may recap what you have told me." He then proceeded to walk through the information that I provided earlier. Then he probed a little more about the party and what happened after the guests left. I recounted what I told him before, and then he interrupted me.

"Emerald, I'm really counting on your cooperation here. I'm not sure if you are being honest with me." His tone was accusatory.

"What do you mean?" I weakly stammered. "I have answered all your questions."

"You told me about the party and provided details about conversations with guests and the great night."

"Okay. And?"

"Do you believe Dr. Crossman to be an honest person?"

I shrugged. "I've only known him for six months, but I have no reason to think that he is dishonest."

"According to him, when the party started, you were in the bedroom window in a light dress, looking down at everyone. Then you were gone. And you never came downstairs. You were not at your party."

THAT STATEMENT TOOK the wind out of me, and I struggled to catch my breath. Was this some kind of joke? How was I not at the party? I had vivid recollections of the conversation with Samuel's father and remember eating the perfectly seared chicken drizzled with a sweet vinaigrette paired with a fragrant pinot grigio. The hippie with the guitar around the fire. This doesn't make sense.

"Care to explain this discrepancy?" He asked, provoking me.

"I don't have an explanation and I told you everything that I remember. I drank a lot of alcohol yesterday and hit my head hard against a tree. Maybe I have a head injury. I remember details from the party, so how could I have not been there?" I slowly rose to my feet and paced the room as waves of nerves stimulated a layer of sweat under my clothing.

"What's the last thing you remember before going to the party?"

"I showered after the accident. Samuel came into the bathroom and saw my injuries. He wanted me to go to the hospital." *The pills.*

"Then what happened?"

"Samuel went downstairs while I got ready. Then, he brought me a drink and Dr. Crossman gave me pills for the pain."

"So, you saw Dr. Crossman?"

"Let me rephrase. Samuel gave me two pills that were from his father. He said they were nonnarcotic and would help with the pain. He said his father recommended that I take them."

"Okay. Then what happened?"

"I finished getting ready... and yes, I did stand in the window and look down at the people on the patio. I remember making eye contact with Bill...Dr. Crossman."

"How long were you at the window?"

"I don't know, two minutes. Maybe more. Then I went over to the bed to put on my shoes and then..." I struggled to complete the sentence.

"Then?"

"I thought I went down to the party. But you're telling me that's not what happened."

"I'm not telling you that. I want to be clear. I'm telling you what Dr. Crossman reported to us."

"What else did he say?"

Detective Chase consulted his notebook. "Nothing else relevant at this point."

"Listen. I'm tired and not doing great. I want to call my doctor. This is enough for now."

"I understand and appreciate your cooperation with looking around the house. Two things, if I may. One, can I take your husband's phone? Maybe one of our tech guys can get into it and that might help us in understanding what happened. Is that okay?"

I debated for a moment. "Yes. That's fine."

"Also, the white dress and shoes from last night. Can I see them, you know, get a visual on them?"

Behind him I could see the foyer closet. *Sure, let me give you my bloody dress and a kitchen knife that inexplicably seems to have blood on it. It's in a bag in the closet. I don't know why there is blood, but please take it to your lab and find out what happened.*

"Why?" I stammered.

"Seeing those items would be helpful." He persisted.

"Okay, I'll go upstairs and grab everything," I paused and looked around the room. "You can wait here, and I'll be back in two minutes."

"I'd prefer to go up there with you."

"No. Please wait here." This time I'm assertive and it works because he nods.

My head was spinning with guilt. In the bedroom, I grabbed the phone from Samuel's dresser. *What am I going to do about the dress?*

Walking toward my closet, I remembered the other dress. I pulled it off the hanger and looked at it closely. It was the same exact dress as the one in the bag, just a shade lighter. I grabbed a random pair of light-colored flats from the shoe rack and started making my way back downstairs. On the way down I purposely wrinkled the dress to make it look worn, and then saw that the tags were still on it. In my haste to pull them off, I dropped the shoes and the cell phone, and they softly tumbled down the carpeted stairs and met the cold marble tiles at the base of the steps with a thud. Detective Chase came running into the foyer just as I slipped the tags and plastic piece in my pocket. He met me at the bottom of the stairs, picking up the shoes and the cell phone, facing the newly shattered screen toward me.

"These stairs, they've been giving me a lot of problems today."

He had put on a pair of latex gloves and that made me anxious. He slipped the phone into a translucent plastic bag, sealed it, and dropped it into his sport coat pocket. He then lifted the shoes, carefully inspecting the soles which hadn't been walked on since last summer. I handed him the partially wrinkled dress. He looked it over and seemed satisfied with his review.

"This is the dress you wore last night?" He asked, narrowing his eyes.

"That is the dress and those are the shoes," I lied with confidence, ashamed of how easy it came to me.

"Do you mind if I take the dress and the shoes?"

"Why do you need to take them?"

"It might help us figure out what happened here," he didn't hide the sarcasm in his voice and his response came with raised brows. "You do realize I could come back with a warrant and obtain these items?"

"I'm not sure how that would possibly help you find my husband, who apparently left the house and has not returned." I took the dress from him. "I'll leave the dress and these shoes on the table here, and if you get a warrant, they will be waiting right here for you." I placed the dress and shoes on the table in the foyer.

"Fair enough."

We were standing less than five feet from the closet. *Could he smell the blood?* I walked toward the front door and opened it. Giving him a little headshake toward the front, he noticed my body language. Out in front of the house, we had a quick conversation about the next steps. He was going to see if they could get anything from the cell phone. We exchanged phone numbers and he said he would be following up. I wanted to ask him how soon he would be back with the warrant, but that would make me seem guilty and at this point I couldn't really prove that I wasn't guilty. *What did I do?*

I WATCHED the detective walk back to the car with his obnoxious, arrogant stride. Standing weakly in the foyer, I locked the door and saw his car exit the driveway, holding my breath until the taillights disappeared. It was after seven, and darkness had taken over the skies and was taking over my life. I wondered if he was going to stop down the road, and then watch to see if I did anything suspicious. It felt that *Indigobird* had suddenly transitioned into a haunted house with no way out. The thoughts that I have done something bad will not go away, but I don't know what it is, and I'm sure that I don't want to know. If only Samuel would walk through that door. That would solve everything. *Try to focus Emerald.* First things first, I had to push through my frozen state and deal with the bag holding the knife and bloody dress. I remembered that in addition to the dress and the knife, my biking clothes were at the bottom of the bag and could be contaminated with the unknown blood.

In the kitchen, I sat on a barstool in front of the island. My mind cycled through the thousands of hours of police and forensic shows that I have watched in my lifetime. I thought about all the things that criminals tried to do to cover up their crimes only to get caught in the end by some nerdy forensic scientist. I couldn't seem to let go of the fact that maybe, just maybe, I am the one who actually committed a crime.

I thought about my options. I could wait until later tonight and walk through the woods to the trash containers in the steamship parking lot. That seemed too obvious, and I was sure that the police would be waiting there for me, their bright lights blinding me right when I opened the bin. Visions of burning the clothes in the fire pit entered my mind until I recalled an episode where they were able to extract DNA from the ashes of a fire. The cell phone in my pocket vibrated. *Ugh, Samuel's father.*

"Hello." I said meekly.

"Emerald, what's the status? Have you heard from Samuel?"

"No. He's still not home. He left without—"

"I know, I just spoke with Lincoln. His wallet and cell were at the house. Something happened, and I'm coming to the house. My GPS has me there in an hour and ten."

Lincoln? As in Detective Lincoln Chase. "The house?"

"Yes. The house. I'm coming to my son's house to find out what the hell is going on."

Could I say no? I mean, I did not want him here. At the same time, I needed to play it cool. I just had this feeling that everything I have done today and everything I do in the next few days will be scrutinized by someone at some point.

"Okay. Please call me when you pull into the driveway. With everything going on, I'm a little on edge."

"Right." He hung up on me, again.

Leaping out of the chair, I went to the pantry and grabbed two heavy duty trash bags. I placed one inside the other, and then went and opened the foyer closet, grabbing the bag with my clothes and the knife. I brought it into the kitchen and placed it inside the two bags. Grabbing the sponge from the sink, I threw that in the bag just in case. On my hands and knees, I rolled up the bags letting as much air out as I could, while trying to make it as compact as possible. I found a roll of duct tape in a drawer and wrapped it around the outer bag. Now, I just need a hiding spot, at least on a temporary basis. Then, it hit me. My old bedroom.

When I was around five, Harold had renovated the guest suite on the second floor and turned it into my bedroom. It was on the opposite end of the house with sweeping views of the garden and the ocean. Part of the renovation included replacing the carpet with planks of oak flooring. On the first night in my new room, Harold came in and told me that he had a secret. He got on his hands and knees and asked me to watch. Carefully, he pushed the small nightstand a few feet away from the bed. There was a piece of white trim baseboard that he pushed in, and a section of the oak plank popped up near the wall. He showed me how to remove the short plank and revealed the secret compartment below. I asked him why he did this, and I remember him responding that it was always good to have secret spots to hide things. He pointed inside and there was a bright yellow book with a white bow. It's funny how I remember this like it happened yesterday, but I have no idea what happened last night.

I grabbed the bag and headed back to my old room. Fueled by adrenaline and panic, my body responded with energy. I knew it was not a perfect plan, but it was all I had, given the circumstances. In my old bedroom, which now served as a guest suite, I picked up the nightstand and slid it away from the bed. Using my foot, I pushed the baseboard trim like Harold had shown me and as I did many times in my earlier years after writing things in the yellow book. Nothing happened. I pushed harder against the trim. Still nothing. I tried to remember the last time I accessed the secret hiding spot. I did remember writing in the book and journaling some of my summers in Woods Hole, but I lost interest by the time I was eleven or twelve. More than fifteen years ago. All these years of the house settling paired with the salty air moisture seemed to have sealed the trim to the floor and wall.

Losing patience, I kicked the baseboard as hard as my weak body would allow and heard a cracking sound. The splintered oak was pushed in, and pieces of paint chips had cascaded over the floor. Bracing myself, I knelt and pushed the damaged trim back. I was able to pull up the flooring plank without much of a struggle. Using my iPhone's flashlight, I illuminated the secret compartment. There it was. The yellow book was in the center of the secret hiding spot. I did a double take noticing that the book still had the white bow on top, still adhered after all these years. As I reached to grab the book, bright lights shot through the side windows, accompanied by the sound of crunching seashells in the driveway. Dropping the bag inside, I replaced the floorboard. Still on my hands and knees, I slid the nightstand over to cover the splintered piece of trim. Loud, angry banging on the door echoed through the house. The banging intensified as I descended the stairs and reached the door. As I peered through the sidelight, I saw Samuel's father and another man standing on the front steps. My first thought was that the other person was Samuel, and this nightmare was over. But why would Samuel be knocking? I unlocked the door and opened it a crack.

"Hi Bill. Who's with you?"

The other person stepped forward and got in my face.

"My name is Guy Simon. I'm a friend of Dr. Crossman. I asked to join him and see if I can help." He obnoxiously spelled his first name but made the point that it was pronounced like the clarified butter used in Indian cuisine. Ghee.

There was something off about this whole situation. The Indian butter guy looked familiar, but I could not place him. "Okay, come in."

I ushered the two men into the living room and made a vague offer of coffee or tea which both thankfully declined. My offer was less than sincere, and they seemed to notice.

Bill spoke first. "Emerald, I'm losing my patience here and I want to know what the hell happened last night. My son is missing, and you have been less than cooperative which is aggravating me."

His aggressive, accusatory tone threw me off. Admittedly, I didn't know the man very well and most of our interactions had been in social settings. He always seemed proper and composed. I don't think I ever heard him swear.

"I don't know what happened!" I leaned back. "What I do know is that Samuel was not here when I woke up. His car, wallet, phone, keys...everything is here but I don't know where he is."

Simon glared at me. "Walk us through yesterday. We are concerned for Samuel's safety and need your help. And talk to me about your black eye and other cuts and bruises. You look like you had a fight or something."

"My bruises have nothing to do with Samuel's...not being here." I pointed at my face. "I had a bike accident yesterday afternoon."

"Okay, tell us about yesterday." Simon said with an interrogatory tone.

"I had a rough day. I was angry at... unhappy about things and had a lot to drink during the day. I crashed my bike coming home from town before the party. I showered and was getting ready to join the guests when Samuel came up and saw my injuries. I took two pills and then I... I must have passed out." At this point, it did not seem useful to explain my memories of being at the party.

Simon spoke again. "What kind of pills?"

"I don't know. Samuel gave them to me and said they would help with the pain." I exclaimed. "Wait, he got them from you Bill..."

"I did not give—" Bill started before being interrupted by Simon, who shot him a sideways look and raised his arm before speaking.

"Wait, you took pills that you knew nothing about? Why would you do that Mrs. Woodley?"

"Samuel told me that they were from his father, and they would help me. I wanted to ease the pain I was in and make it to my birthday party. I was drunk and hurting, and I trusted that my husband was trying to help me."

Simon spoke again. "So, you have no recollection of anything that happened after taking the pills until this morning? Is that your story? Please give me a straight answer to that question."

I paused for a moment and looked past the two men sitting on my loveseat, to the ugly portrait over the fireplace. I need to take it down.

I inhaled and spoke softly. "I remember taking the pills and laying down in bed and then waking up in the morning to an empty house. I don't know where Samuel is, and I don't remember my dreams while sleeping last night. Does that answer your question?"

Bill started to speak but was interrupted by Simon once again.

"Well Mrs. Woodley, we don't seem to be getting anywhere. Bill and I just want to do a quick look around the house and then we'll leave. We might find something that will help us discover what happened to your husband."

Before I could respond, Bill interjected.

He turned to Simon. "Fuck that. After we search this place, you take the car and stay at my house. I'm staying here until we find Samuel. I'll sleep in the guest suite."

"Not a search Bill, we just want to look around. Your cooperation is appreciated Ms. Woodley." Simon said softly as both men stood.

I stood up with purpose and spoke loudly. "It's a hard no to both of your requests. You can't look around my house and, Bill, you are not staying here. In fact, I ask that you leave right now."

Bill got defiant and demanded to stay at the house, making claims that he had every right to stay in his son's home. I stood my ground and threatened to call the police if they would not leave. After the verbal tennis match, Simon stepped in and convinced Bill to leave. As they walked toward the front door, Bill delivered a parting shot.

"The police will be back tomorrow with a search warrant. Maybe even later tonight. I have connections and you will not get away with what you did."

LESS THAN TWO DAYS AGO, I was ready for new chapters in my life. Today, I just wanted to die. After the two men left last night, I had crawled into bed and cried myself to sleep. Fully expecting to hear loud knocks on my door in the middle of the night, my sleep was restless, and my dreams were angry. Visions of blue monsters tearing apart the house and finding my little secret led to a terrible night of sleep. In my mind, Samuel was gone and not coming home, and I was confused as to why my hope was already lost. Worse than the relentless guilt, was the realization that I didn't care anymore. I just want to know what happened. The questions continue to spiral in my head. *Did I kill Samuel? If I did, how did it happen and where is his body? Where is the second kayak? Why is the basement all torn apart like someone was looking for something? How do I know that he is not coming home?*

It was a quiet, peaceful morning with warm air sweeping in from the ocean. I felt lost and had no idea what to do. For some reason, I never got close to people and even my friends from school were more acquaintances that I had avoided over the past year. No family, no friends, and my husband was missing. Analyzing the situation, it came down to two choices. One, turn myself in for *maybe* killing my husband. Two, try and get away with *maybe* killing him which would start with getting rid of the bag. Grabbing my phone from the table, I scrolled through my contacts and pressed send on a name. I want this to be over and need to tell someone what happened. After being on hold for ten long minutes, Len got on the phone and spoke rapidly.

"I was sort of expecting a call from you this morning."

"Why would you be expecting a call from me?" I asked, stunned by his words.

"Well, Falmouth PD was down here to speak with me early today. Lots of activity in town this morning related to you and, um, your husband, who is thought to be missing. It's the talk of the town."

"Len, I need your help." I was ready to tell him everything.

"Listen Em. I've known you and your family for a long time, and you know that I'd help you, but this is not my area of expertise and there are conflicts here. I need to stay out of this. Don't say anything else."

"Can you at least give me some names?" I pleaded.

"I can't. I don't want any involvement in this although I'm tangentially dragged in a little."

"What do you mean?"

"They followed your tracks from Tuesday. From the shrink to the restaurant, and then to my office."

"And?" I asked as I started to realize where this might be going.

"You understand what you say to me is generally protected by privilege, but you said things in the waiting room in front of the receptionist and another client. Privilege does not apply here. What you said is not protected and if your husband is missing and they suspect that you had something to do with it, well, what you said is not going to do you any favors."

"What did I say?" I ask, trying to remember.

"Something to the effect of ways to get unmarried to your husband."

"Well, I said that in a law office...not an Italian social club." It was the wrong thing to say to an attorney named Fiore, and I immediately regretted it.

"That's offensive Mrs. Woodley." *No more Em.*

"I apologize. Sincerely."

"The challenging part of this is that the next morning when I called you with a recommendation, you told me that it was no longer necessary. You understand how that looks, correct?" *I'm screwed.*

"Did you tell that to the detective?"

He paused. "I did not. If they pressed or if I were called as a witness in any type of legal proceeding, I could be compelled to disclose the context of that conversation. And that is all I can say about that and need to take another call. Good luck Ms. Woodley."

It took every ounce of self-control to not smash my iPhone on the brick patio. Why was this happening? Everything I have done in the last few days is coming back to haunt me. I went back into the house to take a long, hot shower.

Later that afternoon, as the sun gave way to building cumulous clouds and winds whipping from the southeast, I walked through the yard toward the beach. The trees to the right of the house danced rhythmically in the strong ocean breeze. My left knee throbbed, and walking was painful, but I endured the discomfort to get down to the water. I had mentally conceded that the police would be showing up in the next few hours with a search warrant and would find all the evidence they needed for me to be wearing an orange jumpsuit for the next decade or longer.

I thought about what life would be like in prison, how I'd handle it, and where I'd end up being incarcerated. I was tempted to search the internet for answers to these questions but thought better of it.

Images danced through my head of my search history on a large screen in a packed courtroom as twelve of my peers looked at me with contempt. My life was never too hard, never easy, but I always felt like I knew what was happening and that I was in control. I wondered what was taking them so long to search the house and find the bloody dress and knife that I'm starting to think will be Exhibit A in my murder trial.

Sitting on the beach, I was desperately trying to remember what happened two nights ago. I thought about the man on the bike chasing me and wondered if that was real. I remember everything up to right after taking the mystery pills. I know that my dress was splattered in blood and had a knife wrapped inside of it. I needed to get rid of that bag but had no great plan to make that happen.

Lost in these visions of despair, I failed to notice the picturesque sunset that was happening to my right. Shades of pink and red rippled over the blue waters, sparkling like diamonds. It almost looked like ominous flashing red and blue lights. Looking toward the neighbor's house, I suddenly had an idea. It was not a great one, but it was all that I had. Back in the house, I put on a pair of latex gloves and went up to the guest suite to retrieve the plastic bag. It was tightly wrapped in duct tape, and I used the rest of the roll to completely secure the bag to the point that you could only see the metal-colored tape and none of the bag itself. It ended up looking like a large diameter metal pipe and I was impressed by the symmetry of the finished product. The yellow journal remained in hiding and I replaced the floor plank, sliding over the nightstand and cleaning the remnants of paint from the damaged trim.

Earlier on the beach, as I looked at the jetty, I noticed that the neighbor to the east had an old, wooden shed that abutted *Indigobird.* It always struck me as unfair that their ugly shed was likely not visible from their oceanfront home but, for most of the year, the eyesore was partially visible from my house. They were very private and reclusive, and I can't recall their name, but I did know that they lived in Florida for most of the year and would not be back until

June. In my mind, the search warrant would only be for my property and temporarily storing the bag there was the best plan in this moment.

Indigobird was set further back from the road than the neighbor's house and the shed was easiest to access from my front door. I left the bag in the foyer and walked out the front door up the driveway to the street, pretending to get my mail in case there was a caravan of police cars ready to swarm. My heart raced during the walk, and I tried to take slow, shallow breaths to remain calm. The walk was uneventful, and there were no cars or anyone watching. I opened the mailbox and retrieved its contents, slowly retreating to the house. The silence was eerie.

Back in the house, I put on another pair of latex gloves and used a dish towel moistened with bleach to wipe down the wrapped bag. I shut off the front lights that illuminated the driveway and fervently walked through the darkness, veering left through a small wooden area until I reached the back of the shed. Creeping around to the front, my heart sank when I saw the rusty padlock. I shook it in a futile attempt to pop it open.

Improvising, I walked around to the rear of the shed, which was closest to my property, and went down on my knees and saw that the structure was raised off the ground with the help of concrete footings. I cleared away crunchy leaves and pushed the bag under the shed as far as my arms would allow. I shuffled the leaves to cover my tracks in an attempt to make it look undisturbed. In the darkness, it was impossible to be sure. My retreat to the house was uneventful as I half expected to hear a click followed by bright lights shining in my face as I got back to the driveway. *Stop Em, if you are going to get away with this, you need to be positive.* Bypassing the front door, I went around to the backyard where I had purposely left the lights on as part of the plan. I went straight to the fire pit, and dropped in the latex gloves, duct tape roll, the dish towel, and some kindling wood and started a fire fueled by excessive amounts of lighter fluid. I could not decide if this was a genius plan or would someday be showcased in an episode on a forensic television show. I could only hope that the actress that portrayed me was pretty, and that I'd be able to watch the episode while in prison. I pictured me and the other women in orange overalls watching the show, eating stale popcorn from the commissary, and laughing at my stupidity.

LATER THAT NIGHT, I was lounging under a blanket next to the roaring fire with a bottle of whiskey by my feet. I was on my third healthy pour of Maker's Mark when I saw a parade of bright lights streaming through the trees headed toward my house until they stilled in my driveway. And then, the sound of knocking and loud voices. Glass in hand, I walked toward the house.

"Relax. I'm coming from the back." I yelled.

Entering the house through the rear sliding door, I walked through and opened the front door. Detective Chase greeted me.

"Emerald Woodley, we have a warrant to search these premises." He presented me with a folded blue form.

"What are you looking for?"

"Information that will help us find your missing husband."

I took a sip from my glass and looked deep into his exasperated eyes. "Search away."

Six men and one woman entered the house and dispersed in different directions.

"Detective Chase, I'm going out back to my fire pit. I'll be there if you need me."

I went back through the house, and he followed me. I kept walking and plopped down in the Adirondack chair and poured more whiskey into my glass. Using his radio, Detective Chase called someone.

"This is Chase, send Keith out back with a fire extinguisher. There is a firepit at the back of the property."

He looked at me. "What's in the fire?"

"Wood, probably oak and pine if you want to be specific. I'm cold. Do you really have to put out my fire?"

"You know, for a recently married woman whose husband is missing, you seem pretty cavalier about the whole thing."

"I don't know how you expect me to act. Two days ago, on my birthday, my husband made a psychiatry appointment for me because he thinks I'm crazy. I go to the session, it does not go well, I have a few drinks and get into an accident on my bike because someone was following me. I suffered a head injury. My husband plans a party at my house that I don't want to have, then gives me some unknown pills to help with the pain. I remember going to the party, and to my surprise, I had a fun time. One of the best nights in recent memory. I wake up the next day and he is gone, I don't know what happened to him, I learn that I was never at the party, people think that I did something wrong, and you are tearing apart this house. Tell me, how should I feel?"

"Just doing my job Ms. Woodley and trying to find out what happened to your husband."

"And I appreciate that, as I'd also like to know where he is."

A female officer, who had a male name, came out with the fire extinguisher, and methodically put out the fire. Without saying a word, I grabbed my glass and the bottle and went back into the house. I sauntered over to the living room and was aware that Detective Chase had followed me into the house and was watching me. I sat in the oversized chair in the living room, Harold's favorite chair, which had a direct line of sight to the oil on canvas above the fireplace. The bird mocked me.

"Unusual piece of art." Detective Chase commented.

"My grandfather's favorite. He commissioned a local artist to paint this and paid a lot of money for it. I think you could go down to the marina and buy a nautical map that would look the same, except for the ugly bird. I'm thinking of taking it down."

"Harold liked to support the locals."

"You knew my grandfather?" His comment caught me off guard.

"I knew him a little. My father and he were friendly. They used to fish together right back there." He pointed toward the rocky beach. "After I was here yesterday, I went through one of my dad's scrapbooks, and he had a picture of Harold holding a big striped bass caught from the beach. I knew your beachfront looked familiar. Also, I went to high school with your mother."

For the second time this week, someone referenced my mother. I stayed silent but my insides were screaming.

"I didn't know. Listen, how long is this going to take? I'm getting tired."

"We should be done in a few hours. It's a big house, but we brought extra people."

I closed my eyes for a minute which must have turned into hours because when I opened them, I saw that it was after two in the morning according to my fuzzy iPhone screen. As I rubbed my eyes and sat up from the chair, I realized that there were still officers and techs walking through the house. I rose from the chair and approached Detective Chase, who was talking with an officer in the kitchen.

"I'm going to make coffee. You want a cup?" I yawned. I looked up at Detective Chase and froze. In his hand was the yellow journal book with the white bow. *Compose yourself, Em.*

"That would be great." He responded.

I walked past him to the Keurig. As I was brewing a cup, the other officer walked out of the room, and Detective Chase sidled up to me, pushing the yellow book in my direction with his gloved hand. "Found this during our search of the bedrooms upstairs. Look familiar?"

I handed him the coffee. "Oh my god. It does. It looks like my diary from when I was a kid. I remember it being a lot bigger and a brighter shade of yellow though. You found this in my bedroom, under the floorboard, right?"

"Not your bedroom but a different one down the hall. The yellow likely faded over time. When was the last time that you saw this?"

"That bedroom down the hall was mine when I was growing up. It has been a long time since I journaled in there. I do remember that secret hiding place. Harold showed it to me when I moved into that room."

He handed it to me. "Here you go. Last entry was more than sixteen years ago."

"Tell me you did not read my childhood diary."

"I skimmed it. The tech believes that spot has recently been accessed. Have you been in there recently?" It seemed more like a statement than a question.

"I forgot about that hiding place many years ago. How do they know it has been accessed?"

"The trim that held the floorboard in place looks to have recent damage. More recently than your last journal entry. He thinks the damage is within the last few weeks or less."

I struggled to come up with my next words and stood before him in a frozen state.

"Was it you?" He asked pointedly.

"Nope. It wasn't me. I forgot about that spot a long time ago. Maybe Samuel? Some nights I don't sleep well and thrash around in bed and he leaves and sleeps in that room. He is in there much more than me. About a month ago, he moved the bed, so it no longer faced the ocean. I didn't like it that way and had him move it back. Maybe he found my hiding spot then? Or the damage you reference was from moving the furniture." *Quick thinking, Em.*

"If he found your childhood diary, do you think he would give it to you?"

"I would think so." I changed the subject. "Did you find anything that will help in locating him?" I slid the diary on top of the stainless-steel refrigerator. In my nervous state, I used too much force and heard it slide across the top and tumble behind the appliance. I turned back to Detective Chase, who wasn't paying attention and handed him a mug of coffee.

"Not much. We're just finishing a search of the perimeter, the beach, and the Morgan's yard."

"The Morgan's?" I turned my back to him as I dropped another pod into the Keurig.

"Your neighbors. Do you know them? They live here in the summer, right over there." He pointed to the east.

"They're very private, and I haven't met them. They're not around much and are new to the area." My legs are increasingly weakening, and my heart feels like it paused mid-beat.

"They bought the house two years ago and you're right, they aren't in town often. They're mostly in Palm Beach. We called them and they gave us permission to search through their yard and—"

A chirp on his radio made me jump. My hands shook as I lifted my mug full of steaming liquid. He raised the radio toward his mouth.

"Chase. Go ahead." He said, then slurped his coffee.

"Detective, please respond to the Morgan's. There is a shed here on the edge of the property. We found something."

CHAPTER 3
COLD WATER

The arctic water burned my skin. I plunged in and out of the light with angry limbs as strange voices echoed. I heard my name being called but all I could see was darkness. Lights and prisms danced through my head like I was inside a kaleidoscope. Time was lost and my breath was gone. This was the end. This life was over, and I was moving on to whatever came next. Then, I was drowning in icy water and my body was stiff.

"Emerald!"

I opened one eye and saw Detective Chase and other figures above me. Beyond their silhouettes, I saw something familiar spinning above. A whirling fan. *Thap, thap, thap.* I was sprawled out on my kitchen floor.

"What...what happened?" I asked.

"You had a syncope episode." An unfamiliar voice bellowed from behind Detective Chase.

He translated for the voice. "You fainted and probably burned your chest from the coffee you were holding."

It was all coming back to me. The shed. They found the knife and dress. I knew it was a stupid idea. Putting both hands in the air toward the officers, I was ready for them to slap on the handcuffs and end this nightmare. Detective Chase leaned forward, took my arms, and carefully helped me up and into a chair at the kitchen table. The handcuffs were still attached to his belt. For now, anyway.

"What happened? Why is my face all wet?"

"I splashed some water on you to try and help." Detective Chase replied. "We called an ambulance, and the paramedics are on the way. Are you okay?"

"No. It's just...this whole thing is stressful, and I haven't been sleeping. And I think my blood sugar is low. Can you get me some water and a piece of pita bread from the fridge?" I asked, as I realized the irony of the request. This will likely be my meal plan for the next decade. Might as well start assimilating.

I looked over and saw two officers enter the house and motion for Detective Chase to come over. They spoke by the door and then he called to the officers attending to me. "Keep an eye on her. I'll be back in a minute."

He went out the front door with the two officers. My thoughts raced as I sat there drinking chilly water and munching on hardening pita bread. Time was frozen, and when Detective Chase returned there were a half-dozen people behind him making a loud entrance. *This is when the handcuffs come out.* Then, I saw that the people behind him were paramedics wheeling a stretcher into the house.

"Despite your resistance, we're taking you to Falmouth Hospital for a medical evaluation. I'm not negotiating here," Detective Chase asserted.

That option seemed better than a jail cell. Over the next ten minutes, paramedics assessed me, checked my vital signs, asked stupid questions. I was lightheaded and distracted during the assessment. I wanted so badly to know what happened at the shed. Why isn't anyone mentioning the shed? A scrawny paramedic with 'Evans' sewed into a shirt pocket, strapped me into the stretcher. Panic and fear took over. As they were wheeling me through the foyer, Detective Chase turned to me and handed me my iPhone.

"What about locking the house?" I asked.

"The back doors are locked and secured, I just checked them. We'll make sure the rest of the house is locked." He casually responded.

"I need my house keys and the alarm needs to be set."

He walked back to the kitchen and brought me the keys. "How does the alarm get set? I'll do it."

"Once we are at the front door, go to the panel on the wall to the left and hold the ARM button until it beeps. Then you have thirty seconds to get out the door."

The paramedics wheeled me out of the house and waited on the driveway for Detective Chase to emerge.

"All set." He announced as he walked through the door, closing it behind him. I watched him whisper to the other paramedic as Evans loaded me into the ambulance. He placed the house keys on my lap next to my phone. I closed my eyes during the quick ride to the hospital and cried softly.

THE INCESSANT BEEPING of medical machines forced me to open my eyes. I gazed around at my surroundings and tried to recall what happened. The gray, sterile hospital room provided me no comfort and the hospital gown tore into my skin like sandpaper. This was hell. The next few hours consisted of visits from doctors and nurses, all types of scans, and endless blood draws and intravenous punctures that made me want to scream. By ten in the morning, I was crawling out of my skin and wanted to rip out the IVs and run out of the hospital. A soft knocking at the door took me away from this macabre fantasy.

Detective Chase appeared in the doorway. He quietly entered the room with a head nod toward me and peered at the computer monitor across from my bed. His suit was crisp, and he looked freshly shaven. A delicate scent of musky cologne was welcomed over the antiseptic smell of the hospital. It was my first opportunity to check the detective out. He was becoming my nemesis. On the shorter side with a full head of thick hair, which stress and time had turned to a grayish white. He wore old school sideburns but had a gentle face.

"How are you feeling?" He asked in a soft voice.

"Worse every minute. Thanks for asking." I replied, matching his softness.

"Seen the doctor recently?"

"I think so. But not sure. It's a little blurry."

"I bet." He took a seat next to the bed.

"The last thing I remember is that you found something next door. In a shed or something." I hated myself for asking the question and was deathly afraid of his response.

"Right... false alarm. We don't think it's related to Samuel. The padlock to the shed was smashed... might have been a theft. Not sure who did it or when it happened. Working to see if anything was stolen but a tractor and some other quality tools were in there untouched. Honestly, it doesn't seem like a theft to me." He shrugged his shoulders. "Not sure what to make of it."

Words escaped me. How was that possible? The padlock was intact and in place when I was there just hours before. Was this some sort of psychological torture? A new investigative technique? I had no response. He interrupted my frantic thoughts.

"There are a few things that came up while we were searching your property that we need to discuss. You up for it now?"

"Okay." Did I have a choice? I thought about lawyering up, but I didn't have the energy. *Emerald and her penchant for self-pity.*

"We found this on the beach behind your house." He held up an evidence bag that contained a silver ring.

"A ring?" I scrutinized the bag.

"It is. Looks to me to be a white gold wedding ring, a man's probably size 11 or 12. Someone with large hands."

I reached out my hand toward the bag. Detective Chase just looked at me.

"I can't let you touch this, not even the bag. Is this your husband's ring?"

"It could be. Not one hundred percent sure but it does look like his and he does have large fingers. You found it on the beach?"

"Yes. About ten feet above the high-water mark. Close to your sitting area and the kayak rack. Speaking of which, there was only one kayak on the rack. Did you only have one?" He asked. I was certain he knew we had more than one kayak.

"We have two kayaks."

"You bought them this week I understand."

"Yes. We picked them up on Monday. How do you know when I bought them?"

"I'm a detective, part of the job. When we walked down to the water on Wednesday afternoon, I recall only seeing one on the rack. When did you notice one was missing?" He was leading me.

"I don't know."

He looked at me with great skepticism. "Lastly, tell me about the knife."

"The knife?" I asked, feigning innocence. It might be time to dial a lawyer.

"Yes, the knife."

"I don't know what you are referring to."

"You have a set of Henckels knives, and the five-inch utility knife is not in the block."

"That set was a wedding gift. Last I noticed, all the knives were there. I didn't know there was one missing. It must be somewhere in the house, but you have searched and have not found it, I presume."

"That's correct."

"The party on Tuesday night... maybe one of the people hired to help took it accidentally or it was thrown away or something. I can't help you there."

"Do you have an attorney Mrs. Woodley?"

"I don't."

"You're going to be needed at the station in the next day or so for some additional questions. You might want to consider obtaining counsel at this point."

"Noted." I said, hiding my fear.

Maybe it was related to my medical situation or state of mind, but I had an impulse to tell him everything. The lies and deceit were hurting every fiber of my being and I wanted it to end. I couldn't go on like this. I wanted to confess to everything but realized that I didn't know what exactly I'd be confessing. When did my life twist into so many complicated facets?

As I was about to tell him everything, a slight woman in a white coat walked in the room. She looked at my visitor and then over at me. She walked over to the computer monitor while putting on her reading glasses. Trying to read her body language, I was aware of her frowns as she scrolled through my chart. Something wasn't right.

I turned to Detective Chase and said, "I'd like you to leave now."

It was after ten that night before I was able to convince the hospital to discharge me. Patience is not my virtue, and with everything happening right now, I couldn't take another minute of listening to the monitors. During the last twelve hours, in between the battery of assessments and staff checking in on me, I had nightmares. Visions of splattering blood filled my aching head. The doctor reported that there was no indication of serious head trauma, and I passed all the neurological tests. They did load me up with massive quantities of intravenous fluids including potassium. They asked that I wait to speak with the hospital social worker, but that request was denied. The doctor was kind to me and one of the nurses used the Uber app on my phone to get me a ride home. The discharge process was slow but before eleven I was wheeled out to the parking lot and clumsily entered the back seat for the quick ride home.

During the ride, I realized that I felt better, at least physically. The lower body pain had dramatically subsided, and my vision was improving. The driver left me at the top of the driveway as instructed, and I walked over and grabbed the mail from the box. Crunching down the seashell driveway, it took everything in me not to walk over to the shed and see for myself what happened. *Don't look in that direction, Em.* In my mind, Detective Chase and other police were hiding in the bushes over there, waiting for me to do something stupid. Not today. It was another dark, moonless night and I was relieved when I got halfway down the driveway and the motion detecting light turned on and lit up the front of the house.

Keying into the house, I dropped the mail on the foyer table and walked to the alarm panel. I was about to press the passcode to disengage the alarm when I noticed that the keypad indicator signaled me that the system was DISARMED. Not knowing if I was angry or scared, or a combination of both, I pulled my phone from my pocket. I had saved Detective Chase's contact information the other day and decided to call him even though it was late. I didn't feel safe.

After four rings, his groggy voice answered.

"Detective Chase, it's Emerald Woodley. How are you?"

Silence.

"I'm sorry for calling so late but this is important. Did you activate the house alarm last night? The reason I'm asking is because I'm back from the hospital and, when I got home, the alarm was not on."

"I did as you instructed and held the alarm for three seconds and it beeped twice, and the screen said ARMED. No question that it was set."

"Well, the alarm is off."

"Who else has the code?" He asked pointedly.

"No one else that I'm aware of."

"You and your husband?" He uttered.

"Yes, no one else other than me and Samuel, that I know of. The alarm was installed only a few months ago."

Detective Chase sighed heavily into the phone. "What about the father, would he have the code? And whoever accessed the house would also need a key, correct?"

"Yes, and I'm not aware of his father having the code nor a key, but not sure."

"Maybe you should ask the father. You could also call the station if you want an officer to come down and look around."

"Okay. Sorry for waking you up."

After a strong cup of coffee that went down rough and gave me intense heartburn, I spent the next hour in the study peering out the window. Physically, I was exhausted, but my head was spinning with questions. Who broke into the shed after I was there? What happened to the bag with the knife and my clothes? Did someone enter the house while I was in the hospital? Shortly after Samuel and I were married, we contracted with a security company to install the alarm system. I wanted to include cameras, but Samuel didn't like that idea, and we never had them installed. He won that battle.

Courage was never my strong suit. *Poor little Emerald, paralyzed by fear.* I could taste the bitter combination of coffee and morning breath and it was fogging up the windows in the study. *Brush your teeth Emerald, then go back to the shed. If the police are there to arrest you for killing your husband, at least you will have clean teeth.* After dressing in black leggings and a matching windbreaker, I grabbed an old pair of black sneakers and a lightweight set of running gloves from my closet. In my hand was a small flashlight. I turned off the switch for the outside motion sensor lights and slithered out the door like a cat burglar.

The silence seemed deafening to me as I walked up the driveway veering left through a row of Norway spruces that Harold had planted years ago. I wondered if the police even needed to be there to ambush me, maybe they set up video cameras to watch my every move. In a strange way, the thought of being hunted made me smile. *Get it together Emerald.*

When I was about ten feet away from the shed, a crunching

sound nearly caused me to scream. It was coming from the right side of the shed, and I froze in place for several minutes, moving only my eyes to scan the area. Then I saw it. The black and white creature waiting for me. A skunk.

Clicking on the flashlight, I pointed the beam directly at the oversized rodent until it turned, and the light reflected from his dark eyes. After a brief stare down with the weak flashlight beam shining directly at him, he turned his shiny head and slowly scampered away into the dark night. Exhaling in an overly dramatic way, I moved the beam toward the base of the shed, illuminating the bottom section where I had placed the bag. The area around the base seemed much cleaner than I recalled from the other night. In my mind, there were years of accumulated rust-colored leaves that I remember scooping away and then pushing back to make it less obvious. As I moved the flashlight along the bottom trimline, I saw that there were very few leaves on the ground.

Recalling that there was a large knot in the pine board above where the bag was hidden, I saw where I needed to go and mapped out my strategy. Placing the flashlight in my mouth, I confidently strode toward the spot and before reaching the shed, I dropped down on all fours and lowered myself to the ground further until I was low crawling like a soldier. Timing it perfectly, my right arm went under the trim to the exact spot where I had placed the bag. I desperately wanted the bag to be where I left it and not in an evidence lab being forensically tested. I reached in and touched something. I pulled my hand out quickly, alarmed by the unknown object. It felt different. Reaching back in, I felt for the taped surface of the bag and realized, even with the thin gloves on, I was touching something else that was thinner and smaller. I pulled it out and used my face to swivel the light toward the object. It was a small white package with my name on the front. In smaller letters under my name were four words that sent a chill up my spine.

~

In one hand, was a glass of straight whiskey. In the other, I held the package. I was afraid to open it. One of my Harvard professors overused the phrase, "words matter," which I was very distinctly reminded of in this moment.

'We need to talk.'

It was disturbing and deeply thought provoking at the same time. It led to so many questions. *Who is 'we' and what do we need to talk about? Why am I being tortured?* Taking a deep breath, I opened the adhesive-sealed package and dumped the contents on my lap. It landed with a soft thud. Inside was a sealed plastic bag with a clunky flip phone and a small piece of paper. I unzipped the bag and retrieved the thick sheet of paper with typewritten words.

Tomorrow morning. Precisely 8:45 a.m., turn on the phone. And don't be in your house or in your car. They may be listening. Answer my call.

The whiskey had completely taken over my mouth and my brain. Getting oxygen into my lungs was a struggle. I needed answers to these questions. *Okay Emerald, use your high-priced, Ivy-league education and start figuring things out. Who could have written this?*

The first answer was obvious. Samuel. He disappeared, created chaos and drama for almost one hundred hours, and now, finally, he wants to talk. Talk about what? And if he wanted to talk, he could just come home. Did I even want that?

Then, my thoughts slid to Detective Chase. He or another one of the officers that searched the house had to have found the garbage bag under the vandalized shed. So, who took the bag with the bloody dress and the knife and replaced it with the package with the phone and the note. And, why? If it was the police that did this, why did they do it? The disorganized thoughts running through my brain were endless. But before I could attempt sorting things out, I needed some sleep.

~

SINCE MY BIRTHDAY MORNING, each day starts off worse than the day before. I had fallen asleep in the chair, and my glass had tipped over during the night and smashed on the floor. I squinted against the bright sun rays that were cascading through the open blinds in the room as I moved around the broken glass and into the kitchen. I stopped at the refrigerator and opened the door, its handle cool in my grip, as I retrieved a bottle of cold brew coffee that I began to chug. It was a little past seven according to the digital display on the stove.

After a breakfast of scrambled eggs and pita bread that was even more stale than the day before, I took an excessively hot shower and felt a surge of energy while I dressed. The bright early morning sunshine had transitioned to Cape Cod grayness by the time I peered out the bedroom window at eight. The ominous message on the note tugged at me and I set a plan in motion. I would take the call down by the water behind the house.

Coltrane jazz was echoing from the fire pit area, as I stood on the rocky beach near the water, and at precisely 8:45, I opened the flip phone and pushed the power button. It was odd looking at the tiny gray display window with the raised numbers on this phone. I had never seen a flip phone in real life, only in the movies. The device felt clunky in my palm. After a minute, the phone emitted a retro ringtone that was out of place. Nothing came up on the small screen. I answered without saying a word, holding the phone tight to my face. After a few seconds, a man spoke.

"We need to talk." The voice was gruff, and the man sounded older, unfamiliar. I couldn't tell if the connection was staticky or if he was intentionally muffling his voice.

"You said that in the note. I get it. So, talk."

"First, I told you not to do this from home. Tell me you're outside at least." *Was he watching me?*

"How do you know where I am?" I asked, panoramically swiveling my head to see if I could see someone watching me.

"Don't answer my question with a question. Are you outside of the house?"

"I'm down by the water, and I have music playing between the house and the beach."

"Okay. We are in a situation here and I'm considering helping you, but I haven't decided yet."

"What is the situation you are referring to?" *Be smart Emerald.*

"The situation is complicated. There are three things that you need to understand. First, this situation has been in the making for hundreds of years and I can't get into the unabridged version, at least not right now. Second, you can't trust anyone. No one. Not even me. Third, they are going to bring you in for questioning today. Don't say anything. No lawyer. Just say nothing."

After a few moments of more static, I spoke. "Who are you?"

There was a pause. "Better you don't know right now."

"Are you watching me?"

"People are watching you. There are things that you don't know and can't begin to understand which is why I said, trust no one."

"This is confusing. I've already tried to find a lawyer. I feel like I need one."

"You will need one at some point. You might need a full legal team. But not today. When the time is right, I'll let you know."

My head was spinning. I felt like I was in a bad *Lifetime* movie.

"You know my name. Can I have yours?"

"Not now. Maybe later." He responded with a weird tone.

"How will I hear from you?" *Do I want to hear from him?*

"Same process every day. Like today. Turn the phone off after each call. Turn it back on at 8:45. If I have something to tell you, I'll call. If not, you won't get a call from me."

"Okay."

"Before I hang up, what are the three things."

"There is a long story behind what is happening. Trust no one. I'm going to be questioned and I don't talk or get a lawyer."

"Remember these things." He said with urgency. "Find a place to hide the phone and turn it on tomorrow morning. And don't hide it under the shed."

"One question. Am I in trouble, did I do something?"

There was a pause. "It would be better for you to understand that you are in danger. And have been since you were born. Things are happening now, the situation is escalating, and you need to watch your back." The phone went dead.

STANDING IN THE GARAGE, I surveyed the area thinking of a good place to hide the secret phone. My gaze landed on the mangled bike as pain shot through my body when I looked at the severely damaged frame. It was lucky I wasn't more seriously injured. I focused on the bright yellow water bottle that was attached to the part of the frame that had remained intact. Unscrewing the cap, I slid the flip phone into the bottle, replaced the cap, and slid it back into the holder. That was the best I could do.

I stood frozen once again, as thoughts swirled through my mind like a tornado. *The phone call, my missing husband, the bloodied dress and knife.* The sound of tires rolling over the shells in the driveway interrupted the series of questions in my head. I peered through the side window of the garage that faced the entryway to the front door. As it was early in the spring, the hydrangea bushes were not in bloom, and I could see two men striding up the walkway to the door. I started to panic until I recognized the confident gait of Detective Chase. Here we go. The knocking persisted as I entered the house through the garage entryway. Making my way around the corner to the front door, I opened it up and smiled.

"Detective Chase, you should have called." He looked sharp today in a cross-stitched brown jacket and tan pants. His gray hair shined in the early morning sun which had reappeared.

It was then I noticed the other man standing behind Detective

Chase was the guy with Bill Crossman from the other night. Guy Simon. *Trust no one.*

"What are you doing here Mr. Simon?"

Detective Chase shot a look at him before speaking. "This is my partner, Detective Simon. We would like you to come down to the station for some questions."

"Are you arresting me? I mean, do I have to?"

"No, we're not arresting you." Chase replied. "We do expect your cooperation as we continue to follow leads on the disappearance of Samuel."

"Your husband." Simon added curtly.

"If you are not arresting me, I'm not going with you." I said in Simon's direction. "I'll drive myself there after I have lunch. I have nothing more to say to you. So, it will be a waste of your time."

Simon stepped forward. "Are you refusing to cooperate? Not a good idea."

Detective Chase looked at him again and spoke softly. "We need your help. We have follow-up questions and new information."

I appreciated the politeness and was conflicted by the random stranger's instructions to not talk during questioning.

"I'll be there at one this afternoon."

"Fair enough." Chase nodded. He walked past his partner toward the car. Simon glared at me until I shut the door.

Although my appetite had been nonexistent and the queasiness hadn't dissipated, I forced myself to eat a salad of arugula, onions, sweet peppers, avocado, and tofu. I drank two bottles of sparkling water left over from the party. I was alone and scared as reality was setting in around me. Samuel was a distraction from my sadness after the accident with Harold and Mary. He suddenly appeared in my life when I was all alone and said all the right things and made all the right moves to comfort me. And then we were married. It all seemed surreal.

During the ride to the police station, I continued the internal debate about the random stranger making demands that I remain quiet during questioning. *Was I stupid for obeying this anonymous, unsolicited advice?* I didn't want to seem uncooperative and, although my feelings for Samuel had certainly changed over the last four days, the need to understand what happened that night was gnawing away at me.

THE NEWLY RENOVATED police station had a busy vibe. I stood in the cold vestibule and fifteen minutes passed before Detective Chase opened the door and nodded for me to follow him. We casually strolled down the hallway and entered a small and even colder space. My years of watching detective shows led me to believe that we were in an interrogation room. I never thought I'd see the day. I expected there to be a two-way mirror with other police staff watching the interview, but instead, I found myself in a room covered in perforated white tiles, centered beneath a ceiling camera. I sat in a cold, metal chair and the entire situation made me feel as if I was on the set of a movie.

"Thanks for coming in Em." Detective Chase was trying to be friendly, and I nodded. He took a seat directly in front of me on the other side of the fake wood table and pulled a fancy looking black portfolio from his laptop bag. He placed it directly between us and a small notepad on top, each movement intentional.

"Do you want to have counsel present?"

I shook my head.

He paused. "Have you heard from Samuel? Anything new on your end?"

I shook my head, again indicating a negative response. Maybe I can cooperate and fulfill my promise to the anonymous man providing me with instructions.

"It is better if you answer the questions directly Mrs. Woodley."

I just stared.

"Okay. Here is where we are." Detective Chase recited my rights and then consulted his notepad, speaking slowly. "Working on a timeline from the day that your husband was last seen. You met with a psychiatrist and mentioned violence against your husband. After that, you drank beer and whiskey at Captain Kidd's, proceeded to your attorney's office and told people that you wanted to not be married anymore. You went to the market and purchased more alcohol which you drank in public...a half-pint of Jack. You drove impaired and had an accident. It was a bike, but still against the law. You admit to taking unknown medications without a prescription. You told us you were at your party and had a great night. That, it turns out, was a lie. And then your husband went missing. And then you told the attorney that you did not need a recommendation for a divorce lawyer. We are here trying to put the pieces together and find out what happened. And there are people frustrated and thinking that you are holding back information."

I couldn't help myself. I needed to defend his assertion. "I made a comment, in jest, with a doctor, who appears to have violated my right to confidentiality, and misrepresented my comment. I went to my attorney and vaguely discussed my options to annul my marriage. I was angry and hurt. Then, I was drugged by my husband and confused by what happened. I made mistakes that day. The bottom line is that I don't know what happened to my husband."

"Do you have an anger problem? A drug problem?"

I stared at him and shrugged.

"It is preferred that you speak."

I glared.

"Dr. Crossman believes that you did something to his son."

There was awkward silence.

Detective Chase looked up. "Any comment on that?"

"No comment." It came out louder than intended.

Detective Chase continued to look at me with his dark green eyes. I couldn't tell if he was frustrated or sympathetic. He finally spoke.

"During the search of the house, we found blood in multiple places."

I continued my pattern of glaring and shrugging.

"Do you want to know where we found the blood?" He prodded.

"Listen, Detective Chase. I'm losing patience here and ready to walk out. I have told you everything I know.

"*Everything*?" He seemed to know something as his question included a tone of disbelief.

"Just tell me what you want me to know and ask questions. I'll answer them if I have any. I'm getting tired of this charade."

"Our techs found blood in your bedroom suite shower, in the sink in that bathroom, and in the kitchen sink and drain."

That shook me. "Samuel's blood?"

"Lab is still working on that, but we should have the analysis in the next day or two. Our IT techs are working on getting into his phone to see if there is anything of value there. One question though... back to the drugs. Do you have an opioid problem?"

That made me laugh out loud. "Of all the problems I have, opioids, or any drug for that matter, is not one of them."

He looked and me and did that annoying thing of tilting his head sideways. "Dr. Crossman showed me recent text messages that he had with Samuel. Your husband told his father that he believed you were addicted to some type of opioid and was inquiring about setting up an intervention for you and different treatment options. He wanted to help you."

That statement had the same effect, I imagined, as a dull, rusty knife ripping through the soft skin of my back. *What the actual fuck is going on?*

He continued. "For the record, you are denying illicit drug use?"

I paused, and almost grabbed the water bottle but had second thoughts. "Yes. For the record, I am denying any use of drugs. I have never used, or even seen, an opioid before. This is insane."

He gave me a look and flipped open his portfolio. I looked down at an evidence bag with an unlabeled, zinc-colored pill bottle. There appeared to be a dozen or so white pills inside.

Shrugging, I nonchalantly asked, “What do you have there?”

“Fentanyl. Found under shirts in your dresser drawer.”

“Not mine. I have never seen that and have never taken fentanyl.”

He pulled a piece of paper from the portfolio. I could see the Falmouth Hospital logo on top and suddenly knew where this was going.

“Toxicology screen from the hospital. You tested positive for fentanyl when they ran your panels.” He placed the paper on the desk in front of me, flipping it so the report was facing me. I refused to look down.

“Can I see the pills?” I asked meekly.

“Absolutely not.”

“Just hold the bag up. I want to see if they look like the pills that Samuel gave me that night.” Detective Chase complied, and I looked at the pills. It was hard to see through the plastic bag and protective coloring of the bottle, but they looked like the pills Samuel gave me. I nodded and felt a wave of nausea crash over me.

He pointed at the hospital toxicology report on the table. “See what else was found in your system?”

I finally looked down at the report and said aloud the word listed under fentanyl. “Naloxone.”

He nodded.

“What is naloxone?” I fearfully asked.

“Narcan, it is an opioid antagonist. They give it to people to reverse overdoses.”

“I overdosed?”

“You had Narcan in your system.” He said with an even tone.

“I think this is enough for today.” And I walked out of the room.

~

Back at *Indigobird*, I sat in the car for a long time and cried. I was so confused by what was happening. The pills. The Narcan. The bloody dress and knife. Samuel telling his father that I had a drug problem. Nothing made sense. I prided myself on being logical and resilient, but I was falling apart and had no one to help me. Except for an anonymous voice on a burner flip phone who likely had the bloody dress and the knife.

Entering the house, I turned off the alarm and went into the kitchen. My first instinct was to pour a glass of wine or something stronger but held off and brewed coffee. It was closing in on four in the afternoon, and I was hoping the caffeine would help me sort through the many questions bubbling in my head. Entering the study with an oversized mug of coffee, I sat at Harold's desk and opened the drawer. There was a stack of unused legal pads and a package of ballpoint pens. For the next hour, I sipped coffee and furiously wrote down everything that could possibly help me understand what was happening. The sound of the iPhone ringtone from the kitchen interrupted my thoughts. Ignoring the phone call, I continued to get everything down on paper. After more than eight pages of semi-legible notes, I ripped the pages out of the legal pad and started a fresh page, looking to legibly narrow it down to the most important questions. This brought me back to my studying strategy during my Harvard days, which seemed so long ago.

1. *What is missing? Samuel (presumably), the second kayak, bag with the knife and dress*
2. *Was someone (Samuel) trying to kill me (fentanyl)?*
3. *Who shot me with Narcan? (I could not have done that myself.)*
4. *Who is watching me? For how long? How many people? Are they connected?*
5. *Who is the anonymous burner phone guy?*

6. *Why was the basement in disarray and who was looking for what down there?*
7. *Who is Samuel Crossman? What do I really know about Samuel?*
8. *Was it a coincidence that Dr. Ferguson also had my mother as a patient?*
9. *If I'm in danger, what should I do to stay safe?*
10. *Can I run away?*

It made me nervous to have all my random musings written down on paper. I kept defaulting to feelings of guilt which didn't help. I keep feeling that I did something, but I don't know what. After reading aloud the ten questions, word by word, ten times with a soft whisper, I brought the pages from the legal pad into the kitchen. Finding a long candle lighter in the drawer next to the sink, I burned each page, one by one, until there was a pile of charred paper smoldering at the bottom of the deep stainless-steel sink. I flipped on the faucet and washed my thoughts down the drain.

After foraging through the cabinets and forcing down crackers, Gouda cheese, and a protein bar, I walked out to the brick patio, settling into a chair facing the water. The sun was hovering over the waterline, soon to be lost for the day, and I thought about the last five days. My mind kept replaying the ominous and bizarre, in retrospect, statement from Samuel. *"Tonight, everything changes."*

Gazing at the ocean and sipping on a glass of lukewarm water, I had the thought of switching to whiskey, or brown water as Harold liked to call it, but was enjoying this period of clarity and mental focus. The last five days have included head trauma, deadly narcotics, Narcan, fainting, intravenous fluids, and excessive alcohol. I was starting to get back to a level of normal, whatever that meant. Between the bike accident and the fentanyl, I could be dead or severely incapacitated right now. This thought rushed adrenaline through my body.

My serenity was interrupted by the sense that someone was watching me. *Paranoid much, Em?* The sun had set below the water, and darkness transcended abruptly. Swiveling in the chair as much as my still sore body would allow, I saw him standing at the corner of the patio, arms crossed and daggers in his eyes. Bill Crossman.

"You can't take my call or call me back?" He barked.

"My phone is in the house. What are you doing here?"

"I want to talk. I need to find my son. You were the last one to see him and I want answers."

Thinking about the burner phone guy's voice in my head, I didn't respond right away. Instead, I motioned for him to sit in the chair across from me.

"How do you know I was the last one to see him?" It seemed like a good question.

He sat and furrowed his brow. "It's only logical. The party ended, everyone left, he and I spoke in the driveway, and then I saw him walk into the house. You were the only one left in the house."

"If that is the case, it seems like *you* might have been the last person to see him." *Nice comeback Em.*

"What do you mean?"

"You just said that you saw him walk into the house. The last time I saw him was through my bedroom window when you were arguing with him at the beginning of the party." That caught him off guard.

"We weren't arguing." He said in an escalated voice.

"It seemed like you were. Your body language. And his."

"Listen, we're getting off track here. Something happened that night and you know more than you're telling me and the police."

I thought for a minute. "I really don't know anything. I drank too much on Tuesday afternoon. I was angry and hurt. Then, I had an accident on my bike because someone was following me. Your son gave me fentanyl, and I overdosed. Someone gave me a Narcan shot.

I'm lucky to be alive. I heard the cars leave the driveway. Your son never came into the house."

It was a bold statement that I free versed for two reasons. One, I wanted to see if he responded to the part about someone following me, and if he had any reaction when I mentioned the fentanyl and Narcan. The second piece was fiction, but also a test. I could tell he knew more than he was telling me. He was silent and I spoke again.

"If he walked into the house, he did not come upstairs. I was alone, in bed, waiting for him to come in and help me understand what had happened. He never came in. I laid in bed, awake all night, and came down in the morning to find the house empty."

"Why did you not tell the police this?" He asked.

"How do you know what I told the police?" I countered.

"Simon is a family friend. He is trying to help me locate my son. I... they think you did something to him."

"Did what? That makes no sense. I was drunk, severely injured, poisoned by your son, given Narcan, barely alive. What could I have possibly done to him? And why?"

He gave me an incredulous look. "So, *you* are the victim here?"

"That is the way I see it. Now get the fuck out of my house and don't come back."

My words were calm, yet firm and direct. I don't know where it came from, but it did the trick as he sprung to his feet, and I watched him disappear around the side of the house.

Shortly before eight the next morning, I took a walk down the bike path towards the village of Woods Hole. It was an unusually warm and humid day for this time of year. Opting to sleep in the first-floor guest room, I had enjoyed a peaceful and deep sleep. After a hot shower and carefully wrapping my injured knee with a compression bandage, I dressed in off-white tech pants and a matching short sleeve shirt. My iPhone fit neatly into the pocket of the pants, and the burner flip phone was zippered inside my jacket. Strong sunlight radiated through the trees and a pair of sunglasses gave me protection from the rays and provided me with a cover-up for my swollen eye.

The timing of the walk allowed me to duck off the bike path and access Nobska Road and make it to the lighthouse ahead of my deadline to turn on the burner. Access to the top of the lighthouse started at eight in the morning on Sundays and, surely there would be limited tourists this time of year. As expected, the small parking area below the lighthouse was vacant and the chain lock to the entrance door was open. I ascended the steps to the top of the lighthouse, flipping open and powering on the phone at the designated time. Enraptured by the scenic view of the glistening ocean, the obnoxious old school ring of the burner ruined the moment.

"Good morning." I spoke first. There was silence on the other end.

"You sound better today. Tell me about yesterday. Don't spare any details."

I walked through the entire day from memory. Detectives Chase and Simon appearing at the house. The interview at the police station. The toxicology report indicating fentanyl and Narcan in my system. The pills found at the house. Detective Chase's statement that Samuel and Dr. Crossman had a text discussion about my drug use. My abruptly leaving the police station. I ended there to take a breath, when I noticed that a black Chevy Tahoe with tinted windows had pulled into the parking lot below.

"Tell me something." I said while watching the SUV. I realized that I may be trapped at the top of a lighthouse with only one way out.

"What do you want to know?"

"Are you watching me now?" I asked, my eyes fixed on the Tahoe. As I said that, a large man exited the driver's door of the SUV. He had a cell phone pushed against his face.

"Not at the moment. Where are you, by the way?"

The man with the phone was talking but I couldn't tell if he was the one talking to me.

"Nobska Light. At the top."

"Interesting." He offered.

At that moment, the man below opened the rear door of the SUV. My body tensed. I stepped back from the dark, metal railing and surveyed the area. There was no way out. I looked down again and saw that two children had jumped out of the back seats. My breath returned.

"Why is that interesting?" I said breathlessly.

"We'll get to that later. Anything else from yesterday? Last night?"

I hesitated. "That's about it."

"Tell me about the visit from the father."

I quickly recounted the visit and conversation while wondering how he knew about this but afraid to ask. I spoke quickly as the man and his children were entering the lighthouse below. As I ended with my final statement to the father, including the expletive, the group had reached the top of the lighthouse and one of the kids shouted.

"You are not alone anymore, I take it." Burner man stated.

"No. Headed back down the stairs now." Walking past the man and children and offering a courtesy smile, I eased down the steps carefully. When reaching the bottom, I kept walking onto Church Street, veering left toward *Indigobird*.

He finally spoke. "At six tomorrow morning, someone will come to your house to provide security upgrades and some protection for you. I know I said to trust no one, but things are escalating, and you need to be safe, at least in the short term. The police are not prepared for what is happening. This situation is spiraling, and you are caught in the crossfire."

"You tell me to trust no one and now I'm supposed to trust a stranger in my house, upgrading security systems. You're all over the place."

"I realize that. Things move fast. Your trepidation is reasonable. I don't see an alternative."

"What if I say no?" I asked. "I am not comfortable with that."

"You won't." He replied with pronounced assuredness.

"You sound confident."

"This is going to sound like extortion but hear me out. Plan B is to give the bag with the bloody clothes and the knife to the police. You would be arrested and held on assault, and most likely murder charges. There is no body which would be a problem for them, but you would be held for a while and likely safer than you are right now."

"Fuck. I don't understand what is happening right now." I suddenly felt lightheaded and on the verge of a full-blown panic attack. I leaned against a wooden fence and stared at the patchy weeds below.

He broke the silence. "As I said before, it's a long story. In time, things will make sense. But we need to keep you alive or this whole thing is pointless."

"Give me a reason to trust you. Tell me something that will help. I have a PhD from Harvard and am a very analytical person. I need something because none of this makes sense."

"Technically, you are PhD ABD." *All but dissertation.*

"How do you know that? I mean... that does not prove much. Anyone could find that out these days."

There was a long pause before he spoke. "I have known Harold for more than thirty years. He shared his secrets with me. He was a good man, but you don't know everything about him. There are things he did not want you to know."

I was speechless and struggling for words. Waves of nausea rippled through my body.

He spoke again in a demanding tone. "We need to move on here. Six in the morning tomorrow. Open the door and let the man do his thing. Today, spend time digging into Samuel's past. Don't talk to anyone, but search through his things at the house. Look for any work records, tax filings, skeletons in the proverbial closet. You must understand that you know little about him. Learning more will be shocking but will also help with seeing what is going on."

"What does his past have to do with what is going on?"

"Like most people, they are not who they appear to be... trust me on that. Also, a so-called journalist is going to reach out to you today. Bill Crossman is in contact with a major media outlet, and they are working the story. Ask the person for their email address and tell them that you will email a written statement."

"How do you... I mean... what should I say..." Words were a challenge today. Ducking off the paved road, I eased down the dirt trail toward the bike path as the gravelly earth crunched with each step.

"Your statement should indicate that you have not seen Samuel since Tuesday night. There was your birthday party at the house, and you have not seen him since. You are concerned for his well-being and cooperating with his family and the police in their missing person investigation. And if anyone has information that might be helpful, direct them to Lincoln Chase at the Falmouth PD. Thank the department for their work in trying to find your husband."

"That is my statement?" I asked.

"Yes. Keep it simple. When the reporter emails you back with more questions, and they will, don't answer the questions. You got all this?"

"Let the stranger in my house tomorrow morning, look through Samuel's belongings to find information, follow your instructions on the reporter, watch my back, and answer your call tomorrow morning, as always. Those are my instructions, correct?"

"Yes. Good—"

I interrupted him. "Wait. How do you know they are working on a story?"

"The reporter has been reaching out to people who were at the party for comments and verification that you were not there."

I was back on the bike path about a quarter mile from the house and breathing heavily. My knee was throbbing. "And you know that how?" I asked.

"They reached out to me. I was at the party."

As I stepped down the bike path toward the house, processing yet another deepening twist to the ongoing saga that my life had devolved into, I stopped quickly and stood silently, coming across a car parked on the road next to my mailbox. *Watch your back.* I listened as two men argued. They were arguing about whether I was at home or not. Their words about me were not kind. I recognized one of the voices as an angry Bill Crossman, seated in a freshly detailed, black Mercedes convertible. There was another man in the passenger seat that I did not recognize. Both had binoculars pointed toward the house and they didn't see me coming from behind. We exchanged some harsh words as it freaked me out that he was spying on me with a stranger assisting the surveillance. He introduced the other man as Marcus, a recently retired NYPD police officer that was now a private detective. They requested access to the house to look for anything that might help them find Samuel.

Even seated in the convertible, Marcus was tall, and looked like a heavyweight boxer, replete with a nose that had been broken many times and a long, thick scar that ran from his sideburn down his neck. He was wearing a faded Gold's Gym tank top that provided little coverage for his large, muscled frame and his oversized trapezius muscles. He scared me, and I wondered if that was the point. Crossman was wearing a navy blue sportscoat, white button-down shirt, and aviator sunglasses. He looked ready for a business meeting or yacht club brunch. As the conversation got more heated, I told him that I needed to think about allowing them into the house. Going back and forth between "trust no one" and my statement that I'd be emailing to the reporter that I was cooperating with the family, I was conflicted, but I did not want them in my house. Marcus finally spoke in his thick New York accent.

"We just want to look around a little. The local yokels might have missed something."

"I'll call you later Bill, after I think about it. Now please leave my house."

Bill did not look at me and the other guy continued the conversation.

"We are not on your property unless you own the street. We can sit here all day and night if we want to. I like the view."

"Fuck you. Get the fuck out of here." I was losing it.

"Easy lady. That language. Me and Bill, we are just here as ornithologists enjoying the view. You know what that means?"

"Go watch your birds somewhere else."

"I like the view from here. Looking for that elusive indigobird. Heard there might be one around here."

I turned away and walked down the driveway. As I reached the house, my iPhone started buzzing in my pocket. The call was from a blocked number, and I pressed ignore. Entering the house and disengaging the alarm, I prepared a leisurely Sunday brunch of tasteless oatmeal and cantaloupe that bordered on being inedible. Meanwhile, five more calls came in from a blocked number. After the sixth call, a voice mail was left from a woman stating that she was a freelance reporter for several media outlets and needed to talk to me. She gave me a deadline of calling back in fifteen minutes if I wanted to be on record related to 'my husband's disappearance under mysterious circumstances.'

Waiting fifteen minutes, I called her back. In my mind, it was going to be a difficult conversation, but I had no idea. She answered the phone and told me that the story was with her editor and would be posted online in the next hour and likely above the fold on Monday morning's print edition. It seemed like a veiled threat.

She proceeded to share that the story was going to include eyewitness accounts that my husband painstakingly planned an elegant birthday party for his wife, me, and that I was too intoxicated to attend. She recounted details of my drunken afternoon with quotes from the server at Captain Kidd's, a client from the waiting room at the Law Offices of Leonard Fiore, information from the Falmouth police, and statements from Dr. William Crossman, the father of the missing man. The story, she continued, was going to include indication that I was either too impaired or too ungrateful to attend the lavish party. She closed out her tabloidesque rant by saying that there are reports that I'm hindering the matter and that 'the missing man's father was forced to hire a private investigator due to Ms. Woodley's lack of cooperation.' The last part was a quote from the story she gleefully offered.

Saying nothing but biting my tongue to the point of tasting blood, which was becoming a habit, I made the offer to email her a statement which she scoffed at, but did, begrudgingly, provide an email address. She indicated that it might be too late to get it into the story. I didn't like this bitch. Within five minutes of the call, I emailed my statement to her and then sauntered into the living room.

I spent the afternoon stressfully tossing and turning on the couch, and finally dozed off before being interrupted a little after three by the sound of the iPhone chirping. There was a text message from Bill Crossman. No words, just a link to a New York City newspaper article titled "Man Missing After Throwing Lavish Party for Wife." The article was worse than I imagined. It did not include my statement and toward the end indicated that the reporter reached out to me for comment but did not hear back before deadline. For the next few hours, my iPhone, on silent mode since I knew what was coming, buzzed every few minutes. I had more than thirty text messages and forty phone calls before I completely shut the notifications off. Multiple communication attempts from Detective Chase, the other detective, Bill Crossman, other media outlets, long-lost classmates, and other random numbers I didn't recognize.

After periods of uncontrollable sobbing and bouts of self-pity, I regrouped, and stress ate a pint of gourmet chocolate coffee ice cream. I turned back on my notifications and within minutes the phone buzzed. I picked it up and answered.

"Hello." I answered somberly.

"It's Detective Chase."

"Hi."

"I wanted to check in. I tried earlier."

"I was just about to return your call. Wanted to stop crying first."

That created silence. He finally spoke.

"I take it you have seen the article."

"Yes. Crossman sent me a link."

"I figured. Wanted to check in about it."

"Listen, I feel like we have gotten off on the wrong track here. I respect what you are trying to do and have profound respect for police and people that help others. I'm only twenty-eight years old, alone in the world, and really struggling with everything. In the article... this notion that I'm uncooperative is not fair. And the statements from quote, unquote unnamed sources from the police department, that is not fair either."

"Just so you know, I never talked to the reporter. I never do."

"Then who did?" There was silence, and I figured out the unnamed source.

"No comment." He offered.

"I'm being harassed and tormented. I do want to know what happened to Samuel, but I did not have anything to do with him being missing or whatever."

"Or whatever?" He asked.

"Is it possible that he just took off? Maybe took my money. You know, we sold the boat and got cash for it. More than fifty thousand. I have no idea where that money is." That just came to me, but it was true.

"That is interesting. You didn't mention that before."

"I hadn't thought about it until now."

"Listen, it is late on a Sunday. Can we connect tomorrow? I have

court in the morning but could stop by on my way, around 8:45."
Was that specific time a coincidence?

"Maybe later in the day would be better. Also, earlier today I had a verbal altercation with Samuel's father and a private detective named Marcus. Retired from New York City, or so he said. They were at the end of my driveway, on the road, watching the house with binoculars."

"Binoculars?" He asked. "What did they want?"

"They wanted to search the house again. I obviously didn't let them. I just don't know who to trust anymore."

There was a long pause before he spoke. "Trust no one."

CHAPTER 4

COLDER WATER

Shortly before five on a dark, dreary Monday morning, I sat at the kitchen table with a steaming mug of black coffee. Scrolling through my phone, I checked the weather app and saw an alert for severe storms that were moving across the Atlantic seaboard and would hit Cape Cod this morning with the main impact striking later today. Coldness was present in the house, but the rain had not started. The calm before the storm.

Distracted by my mess of a life, the once steaming liquid was now lukewarm. I had been awakened before daybreak by car horns blasting from outside the house. Although *Indigobird* was set back from the road and the bedroom was on the ocean side, the blaring horns sounded through the entire house. I had thrown on a fuzzy bathrobe and grabbed my phone, traversing the stairs with the same agility I had prior to the bike accident. I reached the foyer just as the motion-activated lights flickered off. Checking that the inside alarm was armed, I crept to the door and looked outside. It was still dark but the dim moonlight cast rays of ambient light into the front yard. I looked down at the iPhone to see what time it was, but the screen was dark, the battery dead. *Nice job, Em.* Manually turning on the outside lights, I saw a stack of newspapers on the front steps. Someone was taunting me.

I felt helpless. I thought about last night's conversation with Detective Chase. Was it coincidence that he offered to come by at 8:45 this morning or did he know about my daily call with the anonymous man? And his statement of 'trust no one' was the same advice from the voice at the end of the old school burner phone. Is Detective Chase the anonymous burner man? On some levels, it made perfect sense. On others, it made no sense at all. For some reason, Detective Chase was starting to grow on me. He seemed by the book and there was no reason for him to play this game. I recalled that the anonymous man told me that he had been at the party. There was no reason Detective Chase would have been here, and my experience as a frequent forensic television expert told me that would have come up at some point by now.

In my mind, I went through the people that Samuel had invited to the small gathering. Most of the guests were friends of the Crossman's or local celebrities associated with the Woods Hole social scene. Samuel had talked about some important people from the Woods Hole Oceanographic Institution. Known as WHOI, it is the world's most prominent organization dedicated to ocean research, exploration, and education. They had researchers, scientists, and engineers that studied the ocean to understand how it impacted the planet and our lives. I remember almost falling asleep as he went on and on about WHOI. He also mentioned a well-known Boston restauranteur that was opening an intimate, high-end seafood restaurant in town, and primetime reservations were booked for most of the upcoming summer season. That piqued my interest a little as I love seafood and I do remember saying that if he attended my birthday party, I should never have to wait for a table.

Because of my elevated level of impairment that night, recall of the people that I watched from the window was fuzzy at best. I now remember that Guy Simon, Detective Chase's partner, might have been mingling on the patio. I remember vague familiarity when I first met him the following night. Was he the burner phone man?

To distract myself, I ventured into the basement with dread and fear. The security guy would be here in less than an hour. As I began sorting through the nondescript boxes that contained items moved from Samuel's apartment, my mind was flooded with thoughts on what would be found. Most of the items seemed to have no value, boxes full of work clothes with blue paint stains, cheap kitchen utensils. He hadn't moved much of his personal belongings into the house. Most of the things from his apartment were donated to a local homeless shelter. For some reason, his lack of personal items created sadness in me. After each box was meticulously scoured for anything helpful, I slid them over to the corner of the basement. Seven boxes of nothing of importance with two more to go. I thought about burning the useless belongings, wanting to get rid of any reminder of him. Just a week ago I had been in love with him, or so I thought.

Thirty minutes in, I had nothing to show for my efforts. In the second to last box, I picked through another stained work shirt wrapped around sad looking Christmas ornaments. One of the ornaments stood out to me and I remember Samuel displaying it in the living room last Christmas. It was a small, ceramic Winnebago about five inches long with a Christmas tree on top and a wreath on the door. There were multicolored lights on the roof and on the tree and I recalled with a smile when he first displayed it, flipping it over and sliding over the power button which illuminated the lights on top and an interior light inside the ornament.

Curious to see if it still worked, I flipped it over to turn on the light and something rattled inside. I looked in the window, which was no wider than an inch, and could see the tiny bulb shining incandescent light that made me look away. Next to the bulb was a dark cylindrical object. Shaking the ornament made the lights flicker and the object moved. Unsuccessfully trying to tilt the ornament at the right angle to extract the object, I gave up and threw it against the cold concrete wall. The decoration splintered into jagged slivers of ceramic. I walked over to the wall and picked up the object. It was a thumb drive.

Sitting at the kitchen table, I dramatically pushed the dull, black object into the USB port of my MacBook. As surreal as the past six days have been, plugging in the drive sent chills down my spine. The sense of dread encompassed my body. On my screen, a window popped open with a singular folder labeled *Travel Photos.* Holding my breath, I double clicked on the icon and hundreds of jpeg files were listed on the screen. Sorting the files by date, I could see that the oldest ones were from more than four years ago and, scrolling to the bottom, the most recent image was from about a year ago. I debated where to start, and although I wanted to start with the most recent images, I opted to start with the oldest. Stalling.

Clicking on each picture, one by one, it started off with boring photos of Samuel and his father at a golf course. The palm trees and other backgrounds told me they were not taken in Cape Cod. Much more tropical. Going in sequence, I clicked on each of the images, racing to finish before my guest arrived. I wanted more coffee and realized that my blue light glasses would be welcomed by my weary eyes as they were starting to burn. I was about to get up to find the glasses and brew coffee when a picture of a group sitting at an outside table with a golf course backdrop caught my interest. Zooming in on the image, my eyes widened. The picture was of a younger Samuel and his father with two other men. Samuel's dark beard was much thicker in this picture, and he looked to be sporting a man bun. *Gross.*

One of them was clearly the retired NYPD Detective, Marcus, who was watching the house the other day. He was sitting next to Samuel wearing a dark golf shirt two sizes too small that clung tight to his massive torso. The other man had a golf hat with a visor pulled far down over his forehead. I continued to zoom in until the photo became grainy, but it resembled Detective Chase's partner, Guy Simon. As thrown as I was with the picture, I quickly realized that maybe there is nothing here. Samuel and his father liked to play golf and it was clear that he was friends with Marcus. But where did the Falmouth police officer fit in?

Giving up on my need for caffeine and disregarding the eye strain, I continued frantically clicking on the images in the folder. Many of the pictures were taken without anyone in the frame, just amateur photos of different backdrops. Some included what looked like tropical oceans and there were a series of mountainous shots, but for the next few dozen images, there were no more people in the photos. Then I found an icon with a movie file and clicked on it. A shaky, poorly focused video of Samuel's father and the NYPD guy trudging through white, sandy dunes framed by tall seagrass and deep blue ocean popped on the screen. The camera followed the two men until they came to the edge of the dunes over churning, blue water. The wind seemed to be picking up as crackling sounds emanated from the MacBook's speaker. Marcus was looking over at the ocean and I could hear him say, with his thick and obnoxious New York accent, "That is where they found her. Just a few miles out and buried in the sand. Why the..." He was cut off. Bill Crossman was next to speak. "They found some of it, but not all of it. Not all was on her." He looked back toward the camera and spoke again. "Samuel, are you taking pictures of us?" The camera panned to Marcus. "Yeah, Blackbeard, turn the fucking camera off you stunad."

The short video ended, and I watched it three more times. Paying attention to the background during my last viewing, it reminded me of the Cape Cod National Seashore. It was somewhere in New England, I was sure of that. Deciding it was time to take a break, I went upstairs to my bedroom to retrieve my glasses from the nightstand. Back in the kitchen, I dropped a pod into the Keurig and once the hot liquid finished dripping into my cup, I splashed in almond milk. I peered outside through the early daylight, and I took in the building seas and the crashing of waves against the rocky shore. Ten minutes until six. My heart filled with dread.

~

THE SHOCK of seeing Samuel in over a dozen images and the one video with the two men that have caused anxiety and consternation in my life over the past week was nothing compared to what I'd see over the next sixty images. Beginning almost exactly one year before I met Samuel according to the file data, these images were haunting. It began with photos that appeared to be taken from a boat with easily recognizable Vineyard Sound landmarks. The Aquinnah cliffs, the steamship boats that travel back and forth between Woods Hole and the island, the jetties outside Falmouth Harbor. As I continued clicking, I came across a dozen photos of my house taken from the ocean. These images were from different days and taken at different angles. In one of the pictures, Harold and Mary could be seen sitting on Adirondack chairs on the rocky beach with *Indigobird* in the background. They looked oblivious to the photos being taken.

The next series of images were of a sailboat. Harold's boat, the *Woodley*. There were images of the sailboat sitting at her dock in Woods Hole, taken from multiple angles. Additional photos of the *Woodley* sailing through the sound. Some were far away, and others were within twenty or thirty feet of the boat. There was one picture of Harold and Mary seated on the rear deck of the boat, posing for the camera. They were both smiling. It was obvious they knew the person taking their picture.

The last ten images were inside the *Woodley*. The engine compartment, the cabin, the generator, the galley. These photos were all taken on the same day, a month before their final voyage. I ran to the kitchen and vomited in the sink. After trying to compose myself and sipping tap water directly from the faucet, I grabbed my phone and started to call Detective Chase but stopped before pressing his number. Something hit me. The work shirts in the boxes, stained with paint and grease, had the logo of the same marine company that serviced the *Woodley*. Samuel had worked there.

Back at the kitchen table, I copied all the images in the folder and uploaded them to my iCloud account. Fear and confusion enveloped my body. Samuel, who would eventually become my husband, had been stalking my grandparents, the house, and the sailboat. I tried to recall in my conversations with him if he ever mentioned working in the marina. I ran back downstairs and placed the thumb drive back into the shattered Winnebago ornament and wrapped it up in one of the work shirts along with as many chards of ceramic that I could collect without drawing blood. Stuffing the shirt in one of the boxes, I headed back up the stairs filled with confusion and anger just as the doorbell rang.

PASSING the mirror in the foyer on the way to the front door, I stopped for a moment and did a doubletake. Between the sobbing last night and the new information I came across this morning, I looked like hell warmed over. Swallowing in disgust, I tasted acrid bile and realized I had not brushed my teeth after vomiting in the sink. Not sure if I cared at this point. Peering through the sidelight, I saw a tall, thin man standing on the front steps. Behind him was an upright, convertible hand truck that had white boxes and a bright yellow toolbox. The man was wearing a thin, black wool cap and a rugged looking work jacket. He looked to be in his fifties with longer locks of silverish hair framing his tanned face and a matching goatee. He looked like a retired surfer that was now installing security cameras on cooler days when the surf conditions were not ideal, offering me a slight bit of reassurance. He pressed the bell again.

"Give me a minute." I yelled through the door.

"No problem."

Grabbing a gray three-quarter down jacket from the foyer closet, I put it on to greet the man. Deep breaths.

"Good morning." I said, opening the door.

He looked down at a tablet strapped by Velcro around his left arm. Between his right arm and chest, I could see the folded-up newspapers that I had forgotten about from this morning.

"Good morning. I'm here to upgrade your security system. Also, here as your paperboy. It brings me back to my youth." His smile was of overly whitened teeth, and he handed me the stack of papers. I wondered if he had read them and if he knew that he was doing this job for an ungrateful wife who was refusing to cooperate with the police. He didn't look like a guy that paid attention to the news but what did I know? Conscious of my vomit-flavored morning breath and yellowing teeth from too much coffee and not enough Crest, I took a step back and waved him into the house. He peered in the foyer looking down at the light colored, Italian marble flooring.

"The wheels on the cart are dirty from the driveway. Perhaps you could open the garage and I can set up in there."

"Perfect. I'll meet you by the door."

After letting him and the chilly air into the garage, he looked over at Harold's work bench and asked if he could use that area for his equipment. When I obliged, he began to unload the boxes. I noticed that there was no vehicle in the driveway and asked him about it.

"This job is high priority, a covert operation. Having a van in the driveway for the next few hours would interfere with that objective. I have specific instructions and timelines and would like to get right on it if that's okay with you." He spoke quickly, and with precision. Military?

"Okay. Can I get you a coffee or water or something?" I politely offered.

"No thank you. I have my thermos and have everything I need."

"I never got your name."

He looked at me. "No, you did not." He turned his back and went to work.

RETURNING INTO THE HOUSE, I went upstairs to my bathroom and brushed, flossed, and gargled with all-natural mouthwash for at least two minutes. I kept thinking about the word trust, and how it had been interweaved in so many of my conversations and thoughts over the past week. I trusted Samuel and realized that, at best, he was never looking out for my best interests, and he likely facilitated our relationship for sinister reasons. The pictures of the sailboat haunted my thoughts which were now spiraling out of control. Speaking of trust, in the middle of all this trauma and confusion, there was a strange man in the house installing cameras and upgrading the security system based on the advice of an anonymous man that talked to me on a burner. Stripping out of my clothes, I turned on the shower.

After the long shower, I dressed in deference to the weather report, and put on black nylon running pants and a matching tight, long-sleeved black rash guard. A white windbreaker with a wide black zipper and white running sneakers completed my outfit. After putting my hair in a tight ponytail and throwing on a thick white flyaway tamer headband, I looked in the mirror. *Em, if you were going to audition as an extra in Star Wars, you nailed it.*

Descending the stairs with a little bit of life, the security guy was mounting a small camera that faced the front door. I nodded while walking toward the kitchen. The digital display on the stove told me that it was 7:49. I brewed coffee and grabbed the almond milk out of the refrigerator. As a drill whirled in the distance, my last conversation on the burner phone came to mind and I thought about the exact words the mystery man used to detail what was happening today. Something to the effect of security upgrades and protection but that was all. That led me to my next little dilemma. If the security guy was still working inside the house which I imagined he still would be, where was I going to make the call?

Walking to the back of the house, I watched the dark skies sliding across the horizon and hovering over the sound. Just as I came up to the window, the sky opened, and sheets of rain began pounding off the clapboard siding and ricocheting off the brick patio. The noise and distraction were so intense that I hadn't noticed the security guy had moved into the room.

"Supposed to be a rough storm for the next day or so." He spoke as he moved to my right and looked out the window.

"I heard. Gale force winds, heavy rain, high surf. Got to love these Nor'easters."

"Classic Miller Type A."

"What?" I was confused.

"A nor'easter is an extratropical cyclone and considered unique for their combination of northeast winds and the intense amount of moisture found in the swirling clouds. The Miller Type A is a subclass that forms in the Gulf of Mexico and travels up the eastern seaboard, intensifying along the way. There is also a Type B."

"You a meteorologist or something?"

"I used to do a lot of surfing and you become pretty well versed in weather knowledge."

I knew it. "Interesting."

He went back to work, curiously moving through the downstairs with a small, black electronic device that he strategically waved around the walls and furnishings. It was surreal but this is how messed up my life has become. Moving into the living room so he could do his thing, I took a seat in Harold's favorite chair that directly faced the large painting over the fireplace. Within a few minutes of a staring contest with the bird, the man entered the living room continuing to wave the device. It beeped a few times near the painting, causing the man's face to crumple in confusion. He looked at the device and waved it around the painting and the beeping continued. I held back from asking what was going on. After he finished going through the entire room, he spoke.

"I'm planning to take a break and have a coffee. Maybe we can sit down and talk for a few minutes about the security system specs and the plan?"

Looking down at my watch, it was twenty minutes until the call would come in, and I realized that I needed to get the burner from the hiding spot and find a dry place outside the house to wait for the call. I hesitated until he spoke.

"Is that a problem?"

"I need to take a phone call soon. How long will it take to go over the security stuff?"

"Today, you don't need to take the phone call. We can talk in person."

~

He walked back toward the garage and returned a minute later with a silver tumbler that I assumed was coffee and made himself comfortable in the love seat to my right. After he took a sip from the cup and placed it on a coaster on the side table, he looked directly at me and spoke.

"You look scared Emerald. And I understand that. I'm here to help you, but I get that your instincts are telling you to run out of here. They should be." He waited for me to nod before he continued.

"If you want to leave right now, I won't stop you. I'll finish installing the equipment and leave the user manual for you to learn the system. I'm hoping that you will decide to stay and talk with me. There are things, as I have told you before, that you don't know and need to know. At this point, your life depends on it. I never thought it would come to this, but recent events have led us to this reality. Escalation is the key word here. There is one way out, and I'd like to get you there."

"I'm so confused." I meekly responded.

"That is understandable."

"Where do we begin?"

He pointed to the painting above the fireplace. "That is where this begins. That oil on canvas. The title, this house, and that bird, are the first pieces of this puzzle."

"*Indigobird*? What are you talking about?" I stammered.

"Any idea where Harold got the name for this house?"

"No idea. I always found it strange and never understood the name. A bird from Africa."

"Right. But it has meaning. Look it up." He pointed to my iPhone.

I complied and typed indigobird into the search bar. "Small songbird...part of the Viduidae family... also known as the steelblue widowfinch."

"Keep reading." He ordered.

"Other species include the Cameroon indigobird, Wilson's indigobird, pin-tailed whydah..."

"Stop there."

"Pin-tailed whydah?" I asked.

"Do you know about the *Whydah*?"

"I don't know anything about birds, sorry." I thought about the comment from the guy in the Mercedes. It was all starting to feel like a Hitchcock film.

"We're not talking birds anymore." He said with a slight chuckle. "The *Whydah* was a ship. From more than three hundred years ago."

"Okay. Still not following."

He nodded. "What do you know about the Woodley family?" He paused to clarify. "Your ancestors?"

"Harold told me the family traced back to the early 1600s. They came in on a small ship from England. Gosnold was the captain. They settled around here and were active in maritime trade and shipping for many centuries. They owned a fleet of ships and were whalers, caught and traded fish, and so forth. Over the years, the family had setbacks, and many were killed by the Spanish flu, including his grandparents. For centuries they were wealthy and legendary in the area, but the family fortune dwindled and really all that is left is this house."

The man nodded. "What did he tell you about his life and your life?"

"I grew up here, in this house. For most of my life I thought that he was my father. When I was ten, I learned that he was not my father, and that my mother, their only child, had died while giving birth to me. That he was my grandfather and Mary was my grandmother. My mother died, I have never met my father, and I'm thinking that my husband may have had something to do with my grandparent's death."

His blue eyes looked deep into mine. "We will get back to that later. I want to fill in some of the blanks. Back to the *Whydah*."

For the next thirty minutes, he chronologically detailed the story of the *Whydah*. He explained that the proper name was *Whydah Gally*, and it was a fully rigged galley ship that was built in England as a passenger, cargo, and slave ship. In 1717, on the return leg of her maiden voyage, the ship encountered pirates near Cuba and surrendered a few days later near the Bahamas. A pirate named Bellamy took over the ship and continued to pillage and plunder along the east coast, taking more ships along the way, as he headed toward the coast of Maine. He described the *Whydah* as a solid, reliable vessel that was over one hundred feet in length and held up to thirty cannons. While he spoke, I did an internet search for images of the *Whydah* and was impressed by the craftmanship and size of the ship. The image helped me better understand this tale and confirmed that this story was not just the disorganized thoughts of a madman. Dropping the phone on my lap, I took a sip of barely warm coffee.

The tale continued to fascinate me as he described the pirate life and how these men stole ships along the way in their journeys. He knew a lot about this subject. Two things dawned on me as I multitasked between listening to him and trying to make sense of how this had anything to do with my current situation. To me, pirates were fictional characters in stories. Murals on the walls of seaside restaurants. Johnny Depp movies and rides at amusement parks. I could rationalize that there were people on boats back then, and even today, that rolled up on other boats and stole from them. But, in my mind, pirates were fairy tales. The other thing that I thought of, which caused my blood to pulse heavily through my body to the point that I looked at my smartwatch to check my resting heart rate, was the frequency of which Harold told pirate tales to me as a child. My bedtime stories were never of princesses or animals, they always featured pirates and buried treasure. The endless stories he told while pointing at the picture in this room. Probably why I saw pirates as fictional characters. He must have noted my distraction and stopped his story in the middle of describing the weather issues that impacted the *Whydah* along the east coast.

"You still with me? We are getting close to the most relevant parts here."

Shaking my empty coffee cup, which I now realized had the *Indigobird* logo on it, in some weird level of déjà vu, I responded. "Yes. I need a refill. How about you?"

He pointed to his tumbler and shook his head. "All set. But be quick."

IN LESS THAN THREE MINUTES, I had returned to my seat ready to hear more.

"I was distracted before, thinking about all the nights that Harold told me pirate stories to put me to sleep. He would never read books to me, but now I'm remembering all the nights that he would regale me with stories of pirates and treasure. He had a vivid imagination and told the stories with conviction."

He nodded. "They may not have been imagined stories, but we will get to that. In April 1717, the *Whydah* suffered extreme weather damage somewhere off the east coast. There were mixed stories that the ship berthed at Block Island and possible other ports for repairs. She continued toward Maine and, much like today, ran into another violent nor'easter, which forced her off course and dangerously close to the shoals in Nantucket Sound. The *Whydah* was driven aground at what today is now Marconi Beach in Wellfleet. Not sure how they could calculate this, but the legend is that winds of over seventy miles per hour and forty-foot waves snapped the main mast. She violently capsized in about thirty feet of water. Over a hundred people went overboard. The *Whydah*, its cannons, everything aboard, sunk quickly to the ocean floor."

Some level of clarity entered my mind. "Everything aboard?"

"They looted dozens of ships along the way. Captain Bellamy was fierce, and probably the most notorious and successful pirate of all time. He was up there with Edward Teach, also known as Blackbeard. Captain William Kidd was another one. And, in an early example of breaking the glass ceiling, an Irish broad named Anne Bonny was also a legendary pirate."

"Irish broad?"

He smiled. "Just checking that you were still paying attention."

"And Captain Kidd, they named the restaurant in town after him?"

"Yes. That ties into the story, and I'll get to that in a minute."

"And when you say everything aboard, they must have had some good loot?"

"It was estimated that there was more than four tons of gold and silver on the *Whydah*."

"Whoa. They ever find it?"

"Not long ago, 1984 to be exact, a local guy and an expedition found the ship, the cannons, and some of the treasure. There is a museum down in Yarmouth that has most of the salvaged wreck and artifacts."

"Some of the treasure?" I asked.

"Understand that almost two hundred and seventy years had passed. Lot of shifting sand and geological activity."

"There is something else to the story. I can feel it."

He smiled. "Yes. This is where the Woodley's get involved."

"Involved how?"

"By the early eighteenth century, the Woodley family was firmly settled in the area. Some in Woods Hole, while others were down the paths in Falmouth. Most of the settlers from the family were into the typical activities of those days. They were farmers, raised animals, caught, and sold fish, bartered with the Indigenous people. On a good day, when a whale beached on the shore, the Woodley's would be right there to harvest the dead mammal. The whales were valuable commodities, even before whaling became a more common trade."

"Sounds like a good day. Where is this going?"

"One of the Woodley men deviated from the more traditional route and engaged in the burgeoning slave trading that was happening at the time. James Woodley. He and his two sons assisted the slave trading ships, helped with making repairs and supplying the ships. People described the three as wanna-be pirates. Over time they were cut off from the family, as much as you could back then, and somewhat shunned by both the colonists and the local Indians. But they prospered over time and others joined them. Another settler that had moved up the coast from Long Island got friendly with the Woodley crew, and they became thick as thieves as the legend goes."

He paused and sipped from his steel tumbler, peering over the top at me before speaking.

"By 1710, that Woodley crew had money and two small ships in Woods Hole. Their primary purpose at that time was aiding and abetting the pirates and the slave ships. By 1717, they were also involved in wrecking."

"Wrecking?"

"Today it would be known as marine salvaging. When word came of a shipwreck, they would search for the lost cargo which was often gold and silver."

"So, the Woodley crew found some of the *Whydah* treasure?"

"That is a good question. The legend is that either the Woodley crew was able to steal from the *Whydah* when it ported for repairs in Woods Hole the previous day or they salvaged some gold after she sunk. I have also heard that both are true. The story gets more interesting. The settler who was part of the Woodley crew never made it back from Wellfleet. Four set out, and only Woodley and his two sons returned. It was a big deal."

"I'm lost. So, three hundred years ago, they stole and found a few gold bars. Why is this relevant today?"

"Legend has it that they made off with four or five hundred

pounds of gold coins. Worth about ten million today. And the loot, as they say, disappeared and has never surfaced. And trust me, people have been looking for it for three hundred years. It is relevant because Harold told people he knew where the gold was hidden."

"Come on. Harold liked his whiskey and liked to talk. That was Harold. It can't be true."

"Right. People dismissed his decades of drunken treasure stories until he showed off a gold coin that had an inscription on it that someone linked to the *Whydah* coins." He shrugged and looked intently at me.

"Wait, what? When?"

"About a year before he passed. He was into a few drinks at Kidd's and passed the coin around the table. A waitress took a selfie holding the coin and posted it on social media. Word traveled fast."

"Are you fucking kidding me?" I said, shaking my head.

"I'm not. There is one more thing which complicates this situation."

"What is that?"

"The settler from Long Island who was part of the Woodley crew, and never returned from the *Whydah* wrecking trip...his name was Elias. Elias Crossman."

My brain was swirling with questions and the rest of my body shook with palpable anxiety. He went into the kitchen and returned to the living room with a large glass of ice water. Eerie silence filled the room. I didn't know where to begin. As I continued to process this information, random thoughts and questions pinballed underneath my headband. The first question came out of nowhere.

"You said that you were at my birthday party?"

"Interesting segway." He raised his eyebrows. "I did not see that question coming. But yes, I was."

"Why were you here?"

"Fair question. I have been on and off the Cape all my life. One of the hustles in my earlier days was working parties in the Woods Hole social scene. I was asked to cook for your party. I have a secret way of making spatchcock chicken that people seem to like. It is really all about the brine but—"

"You were the chef? Spatch?" I interrupted him.

"Yes."

"But how?"

"One of the invited guests is a department head at WHOI. He has an in-law suite above his garage that I have rented from him for the past few decades. Every summer, he has parties at the house, and I indulge him by cooking the chicken. It's part of the rental arrangement. He must have told Samuel and they asked me to be here to cook for the party."

"Tell me what happened that night."

He paused for more than a minute. "I'm not ready to tell that story yet. In time, I'll eventually tell you everything. But for now, we need to focus on the present. I need to install a few more cameras and change the locks. And we have other things that need to get finished today. We are on the clock."

I didn't want to accept his answer and shrugged. "Follow me. I want to show you something."

We went into the kitchen, and I powered up the laptop. Accessing the saved images, I clicked around while explaining how I found the hidden thumb drive. To be efficient, I clicked on the images that were most relevant to our current conversation. The golf photos with the father and Marcus, the images taken of the back of *Indigobird*, the pictures of the *Woodley* on the water. Then I clicked on the video. We watched it, and he asked me to play it again. He translated for me the line from Crossman when he said 'that is where they found her a few miles out and buried in the sand.' I had originally thought that he said, 'why the' but listening again, it was clear now that he said '*Whydah*.' Things were starting to make a little more sense.

Next, I showed the picture of the interior of the sailboat. The cabin, the generator. He shook his head while looking at the images. I assumed he was thinking the same thing as me. Then I told him about the soiled work shirt found in Samuel's belongings that had the logo of the marine company where the sailboat was serviced for the final time. When I said his name, he informed me that it was also the same first name as Captain Bellamy. *Was that a coincidence?* My stomach somersaulted when he reminded me about the part of the video where Marcus referred to Samuel as "Blackbeard."

It was shortly after noon by this time and while he went back to the camera installation, I went into the kitchen to find something to eat. I had offered to make lunch and he responded with a nonchalant nod. In the freezer, I found a frozen container of chicken soup that I had made over the winter, and I defrosted it slightly in the microwave to the point where it could be slid into a large saucepan to reheat. We sat at the kitchen table, slurping the soup while listening to the building rain and the booms of thunder that shook the house. I finally asked him how he fit into this picture, other than being the chef at my birthday party.

"I was born in 1965 in town and was an only child. My father was a lobsterman during the season and did odd jobs around here in the winters. He had built a small house over by The Knob. My mother taught English at the high school for a while. I finished the maritime academy in 1986 with a degree in maritime business. Then went into the Marines and was stationed out in Oceanside, California. Served our country, surfed when I could, and enjoyed it out there. Eight years of active duty and then I moved back to Woods Hole. My father fell off the boat and drowned in 1994, after I had been home for less than two weeks. I took over his lobstering business for a while and took care of my mother. After she passed away, I sold the boat and the house. I traveled for a while chasing the waves, and did consulting in the maritime business space, got another degree, and had a few other jobs. But I always ended up back here."

"You mentioned that you knew Harold?"

"I have been somewhat of a loner my whole life. Never really connected with anyone. I don't drink much, but I'd often pass time at the bars and restaurants in town. When I had a good week of lobstering, I'd bring a large sack of them into some places and give them to the locals. Harold asked me for a ride home one afternoon and I gave him a bag. You were coming home from school or something and he wanted to have a nice dinner. He said lobsters were your favorite. In fact, I had dinner with you on more than one occasion. Right here at this table."

"I don't remember." I said thinking that Harold used to have many people over the house throughout the years and I didn't remember anyone.

"You were a kid. More fascinated by the lobster than anything. Anyway, Harold and I became friends over the years. Mary would not let him drive after drinking, so I became his designated driver on occasion."

"Mary liked to keep him in check."

"It was a full-time job. He could get wild. But he had a big heart. He really cared about you and talked about you all the time."

"With all your maritime experience and what you know about the missing *Whydah* gold, is that what this is all about?" I asked in an accusatory tone. "Are you just another person in my life focused on finding the buried treasure?"

"I was hoping that you would ask that question. And the answer is yes. But not for the reasons you think."

"That makes no sense. What are your reasons then?"

"As long as the gold is out there, you are a target. Crossman and his crew are not going to stop until they find it. And I don't want the gold. Far as I'm concerned, that gold is like a blood diamond. Slaves, murders, treasure hunters. I'm far from rich but have more than enough money to support my simple life."

"Crossman has money. He is a big doctor in New York, must make a ton of money."

"Turn your computer back on." He pointed at the screen. "Access the board of registration in medicine for New York."

"Okay, I'm here. What am I looking for? Wait, you want me to run his name through the database."

"Yes." He nodded.

I punched in the name. "What the...his medical license is inactive? Says that he voluntarily surrendered his license to practice. Two years ago."

"I heard he got caught up in an insurance fraud scheme. He made a deal to avoid charges if he paid a small fine and gave up his license. He flipped on other doctors that were doing the same thing." He said, rubbing his fingers through his goatee.

"Even if that is true, he had been a doctor for a long time. He has the house here and a penthouse in Manhattan. He has money."

"The penthouse in the city has two mortgages on it. Even in this market, he is underwater. It is also my understanding that he got caught up in the crypto fraud. He is leveraged and likely broke."

"So that is why he is trying to find the gold?" I pondered.

"That is a likely reason. But he had been looking for the gold for a long time, even before his financial situation became an issue. I think it is a weird revenge or principal thing."

"Revenge for what?"

"For James Woodley and his sons killing Elias Crossman to keep the gold for themselves."

After the soup, I watched intently as he began changing all five of the exterior locks. While he managed that, I downloaded the software that would allow me, retrospectively and in real time, to see what was going on throughout the house. There was a motion activated feature I could enable that would alert me of any breaches of the system. It was too much information for me to handle. I sipped warmish water and did some internet sleuthing while he wrapped up. Shortly after three, the set up was complete and we convened at the kitchen table once more. We each ate an orange and sipped on more water. He grabbed the orange peels and went into the kitchen, returning with the Maker's Mark bottle and two highball glasses. He gazed intently at me as he poured a splash in each glass.

"Now, the hard part. This might help." He said with apprehension.

"Okay." He did not need to twist my arm too much. The brown water warmed my mouth and burned slightly as I emptied the glass. He took a small sip and then spoke.

"You never asked me my name."

"I did earlier, and you wouldn't tell me." I countered.

"Fair enough. We'll get to that. For now, if you want, you can call me DW."

I pushed my glass toward the bottle. He poured a healthier amount this time.

"Those are your initials." I glared at him. "I know your name. You're not the only one that has sources."

"You looked me up?" A wry smile crossed his face.

"I did."

"Smart. Listen, the next part of this is complicated." He looked down at his watch. "We met nine hours and twelve minutes ago, but we have covered a lot and some of the puzzle pieces have been connected. I need to tell you a few more things and outline the plan to keep you safe and protect you from these people that will harm you if they think it will help them find the gold. We both know what they are capable of, correct?"

"Yes."

"And before you ask, going to the police is not an option. I don't know if they can be trusted. Especially Guy Simon, but it might run deeper."

"Tell me the plan." I said as lightning flashed behind him, and thunder shook the house. I drank my whiskey.

For the next forty minutes, he outlined the series of steps that needed to happen today, thoroughly explaining the rationale behind each one. As he went through them, my tongue tightened, and my body became powerless. He waited for a response, but I had none. As he finished, my brain could not compute how insane the whole thing sounded. I looked at my watch and it was 3:57.

"And he is going to be here in three minutes." I stated with disbelief.

"Yes. I took the liberty of setting the meeting with the mindset that you would be on board. There are risks in the plan and if I had a better idea, I'd certainly share. I have taken lengths to protect your interests and hope that you can see that. It is entirely your call. He was instructed to ring the doorbell once, precisely at four, and wait for exactly one minute. If the door is not opened, he will walk away, and the sit down does not happen. I don't have a back-up plan right now but if you choose to go in a different direction, I'll try and come up with something."

I looked down at my watch and saw that it was four.

"He is late." I said, just as the doorbell rang.

SHORTLY AFTER SIX, I was seated in the uncomfortable chair in Doctor Ferguson's office. I had no intention of keeping this appointment and was not there for therapeutic reasons, but I had an agenda. I needed information. Ferguson smiled at me like he was pleased that I showed for the appointment. He was wearing a dull outfit of tan khaki pants, a light blue button-down shirt, and the same jacket as the first appointment. No tie tonight. His legs were crossed, and the notepad was resting on his knee. I spoke first.

"The last thing you mentioned, doctor, when we met last week was that you knew my mother. I want to know in what context you worked with her?"

He paused. "As you know, Emerald, doctor patient confidentiality continues in cases of a deceased patient."

"Listen, I'm not asking for her records or diagnostic information. I just want to know what she was like and, maybe if I understood what troubles she presented with, it could help me with my issues."

"Last week you indicated that you did not believe you had issues."

"A lot has happened since we met last, as you are aware. My husband is missing, there are people that think that I had something to do with it, things are not going well for me right now. I'm in crisis."

We went back and forth about the benefit of my desire to understand my mother's problems versus his ethical considerations. For every reason he provided that precluded me from information, I presented a thoughtful rebuttal. With his light eyes, he looked at me pensively, scratching his gray beard with the pen. I sensed he was close to talking.

"Dr. Ferguson, how old was my mother when she was a patient? Surely you can tell me that."

"I treated her when she was ten, and then again when she was around sixteen."

"She was a minor. Did her parents authorize her treatment?"

"Of course, I'd not have..." His voice faded as he realized where this was going.

"Then you can tell me why my grandparents referred her to you for treatment without violating her confidentiality. Or I walk out of the door, and we never speak again."

He nodded, "Very well. The first episode of care, when your mother was ten, related to her admission to a psychiatric hospital in Boston. They had brought her in to see a specialist. Your mother had stopped eating and was reporting night terrors. I remember looking at the records from that hospitalization. There were... auditory and visual hallucinations. Men dressed in black, chasing her with swords. It was extreme. She needed to be restrained for most of her stay there. That is why she ended up seeing me."

"How long did you see her for?"

"We met weekly for about three months, and she made progress. Mary homeschooled her during this period and by the start of the following school year, she was back with her peers like nothing had happened. It was an odd, short-duration psychotic break. Honestly, I was a little shocked at her strength and progress. And I won't say anything else about my work with her at that time."

"But you treated her again?"

"The day before her sixteenth birthday, she ended up in the emergency room for... stitches on her wrist. The doctor at the hospital found that she had healed... healed cuts on her arms and legs, so she was involuntarily admitted. I was an attending psychiatrist at the hospital and consulted on the case. I reconnected with your grandparents and started working with her again. This time, she continued to spiral and was going through... other problems. There was indication of self-medicating. Alcohol, pills. She was paranoid and delusional. We worked together for almost a year. She went through periods of doing well but would relapse and decompensate."

"Then what happened?"

"It was around that same time that I had a sabbatical planned. I transferred her care to one of my colleagues, another local psychiatrist. I left the area for over a year. When I returned, I heard about her... passing after having a child."

The thumping of my heart echoed through the room as my soul continued to weaken. My life had been carefully sheltered from lies and secrets that never ended. Shattered, I sat in silence. Dr. Ferguson changed the subject and asked pressing questions about Samuel's disappearance and the night of the party. It felt as though he was asking questions in an interrogatory, non-therapeutic way. My limited responses to him were weak and short. It was clear that he had sources beyond the town gossip and media coverage. He continued to scratch his sorry beard with the pen, and in that moment, I noticed it was a thick ballpoint pen. Temptation to rip the pen from his fingers and stab him through the face kept surfacing. As the session was concluding, he tried to set another appointment. Being direct this time, I told him that it would not be necessary as I was not coming back. As I walked out the door, I asked a final question.

"Your sabbatical, where did you go?"

He stood and shrugged his weak shoulders. "A secluded villa in the Florida Keys."

AT EXACTLY ELEVEN THAT NIGHT, I went into the garage and opened the door to my car, Harold's old Jeep Cherokee. It was dark green, an older model with high miles but well taken care of by Harold, and then by Samuel. The almost empty bottle of whiskey fit nicely in the console. Slowly backing out from the garage, I encountered the continued deluge of rain that pounded the windshield as I navigated out onto the driveway. The wipers, flipped on their highest setting, did not help with visibility. As I turned on the radio, the local station provided an urgent weather update about continued heavy rain, high surf advisory, and gale force winds. It was April 1717 all over again. The shell driveway was flooded where it met the road. This storm was a perfect metaphor for my life right now and the symmetry did not escape me. Like the *Whydah* right before sinking into the icy ocean, the driving wind was violently shaking the Jeep. I took a sip of the whiskey, heading right along the road toward the harbor. I needed this pain and misery to end. While taking another sip of whiskey, someone pulled out behind me and sped up, almost hitting my bumper. The amber liquid escaped my mouth and sprayed on the steering wheel and dashboard. Tossing the bottle to the passenger seat, I opened my phone, scrolled my recent calls, and pressed send on a name. He answered right away.

"Emerald. Another late-night call. I was about to—"

I interrupted him. "I need help. Where are you? It's an emergency!"

"I'm at the police station. What's going on?"

I could hear him moving. "I'm driving, and someone is following me. I need help!"

"Where are you exactly? Give me details."

"On the road by the harbor, I don't remember the name. I'm by the marina, headed toward the motel on the corner. A light-colored van is on my bumper and just nudged me!" As I spoke, the lights behind me faded away. Or did the driver turn them off?

"Drive to the station, you are close. 750 Main. I'll meet you out front."

"No. Whoever is following me will know where I'm going. I want this to stop, I want this to end." Over the speaker, I could hear an engine start and what sounded like tires chirping.

"Stay on the phone with me Em. What are you driving? I'm five minutes away."

"Jeep Cherokee. Green. I'm going into the parking lot by the motel. He might have me blocked in!" I screamed.

"Stay on the phone. Don't get out of the car!"

I jumped out of the Jeep, raising the phone to my ear and yelling over the wind. "Too late. I'm trapped with no way out of this." I headed toward the beach.

Running down the beach, I stayed as far from the water as possible for better footing. I never looked back.

"Emerald, are you with me? I'm three minutes out."

I kicked off my sneakers before reaching the pile of rocks. Before ending the call and slipping the phone into my jacket pocket, I said one last thing while climbing up the jetty.

"You are too late. If he does not get me, I'm going to end this myself. Bye Chase."

PART TWO
CHASE

CHAPTER 5

TRADING PLACES

I jammed the cruiser into park while still coasting through the lot, as my body, free from the restraint of a seatbelt, jerked forward and hit the steering wheel. The cruiser was inches away from the running Jeep, fully illuminated by the interior lights, with the driver's side door wide open. The parking lot was pitch black with dark clouds hovering low, fighting with the dense fog that covered the beach and the water. Jumping out of the cruiser, I opened the trunk to grab a large spotlight and swapped my thin windbreaker for a heavier blue raincoat that had POLICE emblazoned in yellow lettering on the back. Estimating that Emerald was five minutes ahead of me, I could not wait for the back-up that I called in during my ride here. Her call was frantic, someone was chasing her in a white van, and she was headed toward the harbor. I ran toward the beach swiveling the spotlight from left to right. The condensation in the air was so thick that the beams of light decreased visibility. My police cruiser lights were still flashing behind and swirls of blue light cut through the fog.

Training the light on the rocky jetty to my right, I saw something moving toward the glowing red channel marker that signaled mariners to the right entrance of the harbor. The jetty was less than a hundred yards away and I made my way toward the rocks, trudging through the flooded sand on the beach and struggling to maintain my footing. I yelled her name and shined the light directly on a figure, and then swept the light across the beach to determine the best path to the rocks. It was her. I was sure of that. *Why was she running?*

I yelled her name again and moved away from the crashing waves for better footing. Suddenly, a gunshot rang through the air, and I dove to the ground for cover. Was she shooting at me? I stayed down, tasting the gritty sand that splashed into my mouth during my fall. I was still close to the shore and the incoming tide was crashing onto my legs. The spotlight was a few feet in front of me, face down and illuminating a puddle of saltwater. Behind me, I heard sirens approaching and cars coming into the parking lot. Another gunshot crackled through the air. I grabbed the gun from my holster.

"Stay back!" I yelled toward the parking lot, not convinced that anyone could hear me over the violent winds.

Seconds later, I was lit up by multiple beams coming from behind. Someone barked loudly.

"Stay on the fucking ground! Don't move!"

A third bang ripped through the dark air.

Then I heard a female voice. "Is that a cop?" She must be able to see my jacket.

I rose to my feet and yelled as loud as my lungs would allow. "It's Chase. Don't shoot me. Someone else is shooting. Not sure where the shots are coming from. The girl, she is down toward the end of the jetty."

Two uniformed officers crept down toward me with their guns drawn. I recognized the officers as Mark Harris and Jenelle Keith. Harris was an old-timer, in decent shape mentally and physically for his age, but counting down the days to end of watch. He was a good cop for most of his career but seemed to be mailing it in as retirement loomed. Keith was a recruit or 'boot' that was teamed up with Harris for training. I remember scoffing at the idea of setting up the boot with an old man that had mailed it in. I walked toward them and they shielded themselves behind me, still crouched down. They both looked terrified, and I was thankful that neither of them shot at me. Harris spoke first.

"What the fuck Chase? The girl set you up?"

I shook my head. "She called me at 2310, about twenty minutes ago. Frantic. Said that a white van was following her. I left the station and kept her on the phone. She said she was pulling into the parking lot. The Jeep was still running, and the door was open. I went to check on the beach and saw her running down the jetty toward the end."

As I spoke, we cautiously moved away from the beach and regrouped behind a concrete retaining wall. Harris shined his spotlight up and down the jetty and the beach. Keith was completely crouched behind the wall. Harris spoke as he continued to move the light back and forth.

"I don't see anything. There is no one out there."

"I saw her." I said and pointed. "She was at the end of the jetty under the channel marker. I saw her in the red light."

"Well, she is not there now." Harris proclaimed as he shined the light on the channel marker. "And there is no way out from there. She would have had to walk right past us."

I shook my head. "Right. Call the cavalry."

Over the next hour, the parking lot filled with law enforcement, first responders, and Coast Guard personnel. Additional boats from the harbormaster and sheriff's office navigated the choppy waters looking for any sign of Emerald. In the parking lot, a pop-up tent was set up to provide shelter from the torrential rain and I stood over a table across from my chief, Tony Charell, and a captain from the state police that I did not know. He introduced himself as Thomas. Charell directed his first question at me, and it related to procedure. The guy always did things by the book.

"Chase, you responded alone, no backup?"

"I was finishing some work at the station. She called my cell. My partner Simon is off until Friday. I made the call to try and intervene. I radioed for patrol response after she hung up on me."

"I see." He said with a nod. "You may continue."

Charell knew the details of the ongoing investigation into the disappearance of Samuel Crossman but asked that I start at the beginning for the benefit of the state police captain. It was made clear that there would be cooperation between the law enforcement agencies on the scene. He was all about not ruffling feathers.

Starting with the phone call from Dr. Crossman, I concisely recounted the series of events that transpired over the last week. Samuel Crossman missing. Questions about his wife's behavior and potential role in his disappearance. The searches of her house. The questions about her drug use and the toxicology report from the hospital indicating fentanyl and Narcan in her system. Her behavior with the psychiatrist and the attorney. The blood found in the sinks and shower at the home, indicating that the blood in the bathroom sink and shower were from Emerald and the blood in the kitchen sink was neither Emerald's nor Samuel's. Nothing of forensic value was found on Samuel's phone. Emerald's question of whether Samuel took the cash from the boat sale and fled for some reason. We all agreed that we had nothing and seemed to be at a dead end.

Charell looked intently at me when I spoke. He was a tall, African American man in his early sixties. He was thin and wiry, with a shaved head that glistened. Prior to being appointed as chief, he had a distinguished career in the military and the Boston FBI. After retiring from the bureau and moving to Scottsdale, his wife died suddenly, and he found himself bored and alone. He came back to Massachusetts, and within a few months was given command for our department after our previous chief resigned under murky circumstances.

He finally spoke in his polite yet firm manner. "Tell me what happened tonight. Don't spare any details."

I paused and sipped some water. "I was at the station doing some paperwork, about to call it a night, when Emerald called. She said she was in her car, the Jeep, and there was a white van following her. She said she was scared, and people have been following and harassing her. I told her to drive to the police station and I would meet her out front and talk to the driver of the van. She said no, that if she went toward the police station, the driver would likely peel off and she wanted to know who was following her. She demanded that we meet here in this parking lot."

The state police captain held up his hand. "She asked you to meet her at this spot?"

"Yes. By that time, I had already left the station and was out front. I jumped in a cruiser and started heading here. She then screamed, and said the van just nudged her from behind and was pulling into this parking lot. I heard a scream, some muffled words, and then the phone went dead."

This was not entirely true. I clearly heard the muffled statement that she made but wanted to keep that to myself for now.

"I decided to not wait for backup and saw her running down the rocks. She got to the end, and I pursued. I didn't see anyone following her. Someone fired two shots and I went down for cover. Then there was a third shot. Backup arrived, she was no longer visible, and we made the calls."

For the next thirty minutes, the three of us stood holding umbrellas on the beach as we watched the boats navigate in specific patterns at the mouth of the harbor and to the left of the glowing red channel marker. The dense fog had lifted, and visibility had improved since first arriving here, and the ocean water was calmer than it had been a few short hours ago. The rain had tapered off for a brief period but was back with a vengeance. The whirling of a Coast Guard chopper circling above echoed through the night.

During this time, we were briefed on the search. The Coast Guardsman explained that the tide was rolling in strongly from the northeast, and it was likely that the subject would be found in the waters in front of us or in the shallows off the beach. In the distance, divers were working the water.

"Search or recovery? Any chance she will be found alive?" I asked.

He looked at his watch. "At this point, the likelihood decreases by the minute. But we never give up hope."

After an awkward pause, Charell spoke. "Let us see what they found in the car."

We walked over to the Jeep, which had been cordoned off by police tape. As we approached the vehicle, a short man with glasses and a state police baseball hat walked slowly toward the three of us. He carried a police-issued flashlight.

"Jacobs. Find anything in the Jeep?" Thomas asked as he motioned for the man to hurry over.

"Hey Captain. Nothing yet. Going to have it towed to Bourne and set up in the garage so we can look for prints. Too wet to do on the scene. Nothing else of interest at this point."

"Did you find a phone?" I asked.

"No phone. There is an empty bottle of whiskey on the passenger side floor and the car reeks like alcohol. Maker's Mark. Other than that, the vehicle doesn't have much inside it. Box of tissues, a few loose coins in the glove compartment. Been a while since I have seen a car that was so void of... anything."

As if the thought crossed our minds at the same time, Charell, Thomas, and I walked to the rear of the Jeep. I motioned for Jacobs to hand me the flashlight and he complied. I crouched down and shined the light on the bumper. Running my finger across the faded black plastic covering, I could see a symmetrical line of darker black along the entire bumper.

"Thought she said it was a white van." Thomas scoffed.

Charell looked at him and shook his head. "White van with black bumper makes more sense. Not many vehicles have white bumpers."

Jacobs bent down next to me and called over another tech, asking for the plastic sheathing.

"I'm going to cover this up, so the rain doesn't wash away anything of forensic value. My tow truck is here, we need to get this to the garage, and we'll start working on it tonight."

The uniformed officers moved some vehicles around to allow the flatbed to load up the Jeep. The three of us stood there and watched the flatbed exit the parking lot. Charell looked at me and spoke.

"Chase, any chance she set you up? Lured you down here to take you out?"

I immediately responded. "That doesn't make sense. If she wanted to ambush me, why would she take shots from the end of the jetty? She has no reason to kill me."

"You think she took out the husband? The article... it made her look... culpable." Charell offered.

I paused before speaking. "Honestly, at first, I had my suspicions. But when you break down the evidence, we got nothing. None of this makes sense to me. Husband goes missing and a week later, the wife is running from someone she claims is following her and she takes a header into the ocean. Something else is happening here."

As the night progressed, the number of people on the scene fizzled out to the point where it was just me, the Coast Guard, a state police tech, and the crew from the harbormaster's office. At around three in the morning, I was awakened from a quick sleep in the cruiser by commotion at the water's edge. *They found something.* Rubbing my eyes as I descended toward the beach, I shined my backup flashlight on the small Coast Guard boat that was idling ten feet from the shore. The rain had stopped while I was napping, and I felt a rise of humidity in the air. One of the crew members held up a dripping wet object that looked like an article of clothing.

The man yelled from the boat. "Found this at the bottom in five feet of water. Women's rain jacket. White. Size medium. There's a phone in the pocket. We're going to keep searching."

I walked down the beach toward the jetty and reached the spot where I had fallen earlier and saw the now dead spotlight in a puddle of water. Walking past it, I continued toward the jetty. The tide had gone out by at least ten feet, and I saw something floating in the sudsy foam at the corner of the water abutting the rocky seawall. Running toward the jetty and careful not to fall again, I waded through the shallow water. Shining the light down, I saw them. Two white sneakers being dragged back and forth by the meek tide. I took off my jacket to scoop up the shoes. Jacket, phone, shoes. No body.

It reminded me of a story from a few years back. An empty boat was found one morning beached about ten miles away from where I stood. They identified the boat owner and learned that he had departed from the Vineyard the previous night after an argument with his wife. Coast Guard boats and helicopters searched the waters for the man. They searched six hundred square miles for three straight days. They never found him, but did find, drifting aimlessly in the rips, an empty beer can in a white Koozie with the name of his boat. His body was never recovered.

I lumbered back to the parking lot and found the state police tech and gave him the sneakers, relaying where they were found. Watching the boats crisscross the area, doubt crept in that they would find her alive. There was less than thirty minutes between the last time that I saw her on the jetty and when the first boat arrived on scene. In another five minutes, a Coast Guard cutter and two other boats arrived. The quick turnaround and the location were all in favor of finding her tonight, either alive or deceased. I knew that in most marine rescue situations, the person being searched for was usually in the water for many hours, sometimes days, before the search began.

My small house in the Teaticket part of Falmouth was ten minutes away but I stayed in the parking lot until the sun crept over the horizon. After bouts of interrupted sleep in the cruiser, I woke with a stiff neck and back. My ribs were throbbing from my hasty driving maneuver last night. At seven in the morning, the search continued, and I munched on an egg, cheese, and avocado sandwich that the boot from last night had handed to me. She had also brought a large Styrofoam cup which I assumed was coffee. After taking the first sip, I opened the car door and spit the white liquid out onto the pavement below. She was sitting in the car next to me and looked bewildered. Keith was not in uniform this morning and was wearing tight olive-colored pants, black field boots, and a shiny black jacket. Her highlighted blond hair was pulled back in a ponytail and her dark complexion matched her pants. I noticed her oversized greenish eyes that sparkled when she spoke. Her voice was warm.

"Too hot?" She politely asked.

"What did they put in this?"

"Extra cream, extra sugar, decaf. Harris told me that is how you like it." Her voice faded toward the end, and she could tell by my facial expression that he intentionally misled her. Today's version of hazing a boot.

I poured the rest of the coffee out the door.

She sighed and motioned at the sandwich. "I get it. You're not a vegetarian either. Damn. Why do you all have to be this way?"

"You all? I have nothing to do with this." I responded with a smirk. "I'm not a vegetarian, but the sandwich is good. Thanks."

"Right. Sorry for generalizing. Why did they pair him with me?"

I ignored her question and there was silence until she spoke.

"Listen, I hear that you are the best detective in the unit. I want to be one someday and hope to learn from you. Harris does not teach me anything and hardly talks to me. He calls me Keith and says it roughly like he is speaking to a male. Why won't you just call me Jenelle or Officer Jenelle?"

"Not the way it works in the department, even these days." I took another large bite of the sandwich.

"Messed up." She sighed. "But whatever."

"Thanks for the sandwich and terrible coffee, Jenelle. Next time, get me a cold brew with light ice. That is what I drink from May through the first frost. Then it is hot coffee with nothing in it."

"Noted. I can run back to Dunkin' right now if you want?" She offered with enthusiasm.

"I'm good right now. You on shift today?"

"At 1600. I came down to bring you breakfast."

I smiled at her. "I appreciate that. Want to take a ride?"

"Yes sir, Detective. Where are we going?"

"You can call me Chase." I said while starting the engine. "Going to her house."

"Emerald Woodley's? Let me grab the backpack out of my car."

WITH LOCAL TRAFFIC building and after getting stuck behind a school bus, the ride to the house took ten minutes. An overcaffeinated Jenelle dominated the conversation, talking about her first few months as a police officer. She went through the roster and gave me a rundown of her interactions with various people in the department. I was impressed by her intuition and reads of people and was interested in her assessment of my partner, Simon. She said that he gave off a 'slimy vibe' and that she didn't like him. As we rolled down the road toward the house, I motioned for her to stop talking. Through the partially leafed trees, I could see down the driveway that there was a large vehicle backed up to the garage. I stopped the car and pointed. Jenelle opened her backpack and pulled out a pair of binoculars. Adjusting the lenses, she motioned for me to pull forward a little.

"Take a look, can you make out the license plate?" She handed me the binoculars.

"Mass plates. Charlie, India, Mike, five, one, zero." As I recited the plate information, I watched her enter it into the laptop affixed inside the cruiser.

She spoke. "RV registered to a... first name Donovan, last name Williams, age 56. Address in town. No priors. Nothing in the system."

"What is he doing here?" I asked rhetorically. "Pull up the reports from last night on Emerald. Did anyone come by the house?"

Jenelle manipulated the mouse pad with her unmanicured fingernails. "Patrols stopped by at 0214, 0422, and last one about an hour ago at 0638. No reports of anyone on the property."

"Have your gun on you?" I asked.

"No, it's in the safe at my house... I didn't expect... Chase, behind us!"

I looked in the rearview mirror and saw a man standing directly behind the cruiser. He wore a medium-weight green jacket and a baseball hat. We made eye contact through the mirror, and he slowly raised both of his hands in the air while backing away from the cruiser. I pulled out my gun and opened the door keeping my eye on him the entire time. He stopped moving and kept his hands up. As I exited the car, he spoke.

"Detective Chase. My name is Donovan Williams. Call me Donovan. I'm not here to cause any problems. I'll keep my hands in the air and do exactly what you tell me. Let us all be safe here."

I slowly approached the man noting his rugged face and neatly trimmed silver goatee with matching strands of longish hair flowing under the hat.

"You have a weapon on you?" I barked.

"Yes sir. Loaded Sig Sauer." He said loudly. "Tucked into my belt in the back. I have a concealed carry permit. At no point will I make a move for the gun. You are welcome to take it while we sort this out."

By this time, Jenelle had exited from her side of the cruiser. I looked over at her.

"Keith, get back in the car. Donovan, on your knees!"

The man looked down at the wet ground and shrugged. He complied with the order. I had him interlock his hands behind his head and move to a position where he was face down on the ground. I walked to him and swiftly put on handcuffs, taking the gun from the swell in his back. Holstering my gun, and placing his in my jacket pocket, I walked him to the trunk of the cruiser and searched him for other weapons. He was silent and completely cooperative. The only thing on him was a set of keys.

"As I said, Detective, I mean no harm. I can explain when you are ready."

Saying nothing, I placed him in the backseat of the cruiser and returned to the trunk to store his gun. Back in the car, I turned toward him and spoke.

"Is there anyone else on the property?"

"No. Just me. Can we go down the driveway and talk." He said with a head nod toward the house.

I looked over at Jenelle suddenly wishing that I didn't offer to bring her along. Her olive skin had faded three or four shades. She was looking down at her phone.

"I'd rather go to the station and talk." I said firmly.

He looked at me. "It would be better to talk here. I have documents in the RV that I'd like to show you and will straighten this out. I've done nothing wrong here. We can quickly clear up this matter."

"You are trespassing at a potential crime scene."

"I'm an invited guest by the owner of this house, retained by her to provide services. I have a contract in the RV."

"Retained? You're a lawyer?"

I looked over at Jenelle, and she nodded while covertly flashing her phone in my direction. On the screen was an image of Donovan in a light suit that matched his hair and goatee. Shaking my head, I pulled down the driveway.

To my surprise, Donovan did not object to a warrantless search of the RV but requested that we take off our shoes. I laughed with no intention of meeting his demand. The smell of fresh coffee hit my nostrils when I opened the door. I saw that the interior of the newer model RV was meticulously maintained, and it looked like it was driven right off the showroom floor. I looked down at my muddy boots, gazed back at him, and slowly took them off. Jenelle did the same. Inside the van, there was no clutter, no dishes in the sink, nothing out of place. There was a safe in the bedroom closet, and he had told us that there were two other handguns and ammunition locked in there. It was a biometric safe that required both a fingerprint and a key to access, and he pointed out that I had his keys. He asked that we bring him a pair of sweatpants and a Mass Maritime Academy sweatshirt that were folded on top of the pillows of the neatly made bed. Letting him out of the cruiser, I uncuffed him so that he could change out of his muddy clothes. Without a second thought or any shame, he stripped down and changed into the clean outfit. Wrapping up the dirty clothes into a tight ball, he placed them on a drier area on the shelled driveway. He motioned to the RV, and I put my hand on his shoulder and spoke.

"I don't know what is going on here but for everyone's safety, I'm going to put the cuffs back on you."

"Normally I'd object, but given the circumstances, go ahead." He put his hands out. "But can you cuff me with my hands in the front? I was brewing coffee before you got here, and I'd like to drink a cup. And I have papers inside that I want to show you. It would be much easier if I had use of my hands."

The three of us sat at the dinette in the RV. Donovan poured coffee in two paper cups and offered one to me and ignored Jenelle.

"No coffee for my colleague?" I asked.

"Your colleague? She's a cop? I thought she was your daughter or something. Bring your kid to work day. And she would not dare drink this strong, black coffee. Probably prefers that poison from the over-priced coffee places. Right, Officer?" His words were sympathetic and condescending at the same time.

I was losing patience and exhausted. "She's not my kid."

He looked over at her. "I got a kid around your age. Enjoy your youth. Can I pour you a coffee?"

Jenelle shook her head. "I'm all set with caffeine for the morning. You two can have your old man drinks. I'm good."

Emitting a small laugh, Donovan spoke. "This kid is going to be a great cop someday. Cheers." He held up his cup and took a measured drink of the hot liquid with the metal bracelets dangling in front of us.

"Listen, it's been a long night. Tell us why you're here." My patience was waning.

"Ms. Woodley reached out to me and retained me for my services. I have a contract."

"Why does she need a lawyer?" I asked, looking directly at him.

"In addition to being an attorney, I'm a licensed and bonded private investigator. She retained me to provide protective services for her. She's in fear for her safety. We executed an agreement yesterday afternoon with the job starting at seven this morning. My first hour on the job and a suspicious car was stopped at the top of the driveway. I flanked you by walking through the trees. I recognized you in the cruiser, she told me about you, Detective Chase. Her description was spot on. Which is why I backed away and kept the situation from escalating. She trusts you a little bit but doesn't trust anyone else. As I said, she's afraid."

I thought for a minute as it was not adding up in my head. "She retained you last night and asked you to start this morning?"

"Yes. We met here yesterday and took care of some security items, signed some paperwork, and she gave me payment. I asked when she wanted me to start, and she said today worked for her. She's not on the property right now. When she returns, she'll be able to tell you herself."

"So, she is afraid for her safety, contracts with you, and tells you to come back in the morning?" I said with a clear tone of skepticism.

"Yes. When she told me that the job would be around the clock, I needed to square away a few things. I told her I wouldn't stay in the house and needed to get the RV ready. She said that it would be fine if I showed up this morning ready to go. I can show you the contract which specifies a start time of 0700 today."

Donovan slowly rose and went into the front compartment, returning with a single piece of paper. He spoke while handing me the paper which was a straightforward contract specifying the scope of work and the terms of payment for said services related to his professions as a licensed private investigator and as an attorney-at-law.

"Your questions... something is off here. What are you not telling me? Is Emerald okay?"

I looked over at Jenelle, sensing that she was ready to say something, and I shook my head and quickly spoke.

"Donovan, where were you last night?"

"After we finished meeting here, I went to the market to get supplies. Loaded up this van with what I needed and then I was at my apartment. Getting ready for this job."

"Where is your apartment?"

Donovan provided an address which I recognized as near the biological labs in Woods Hole, close to the aquarium. He told us that he lived in an in-law apartment on a property owned by a WHOI employee and that the employee just left for Coronado, California for a marine biology course and was not due back until the end of the month. He had no real alibi other than offering to dig up the receipts from the market. He complained of spending more than one hundred and fifty dollars for two bags of groceries and three cases of water.

I finally spoke. "I need to get into the house and to determine if Emerald is in there."

He responded quickly. "Nothing happens here until you tell me what is going on."

This caused me to pause and look over at Jenelle who, busy scrolling through her phone again, spoke for the first time since declining the coffee.

"The story is online but nothing specific. Only a matter of time though." Exactly what I wanted to know. She had good instincts.

"A woman matching Emerald's description went into the harbor last night. Off the channel marker rocks. We found her car in a nearby parking lot." I said peering directly into Donovan's eyes.

"Went into the harbor, as in *jumped*?" Donovan asked in an even tone.

"Something like that." I responded.

"You sure it was her?"

"Pretty sure. You got the keys, let us in the house." I demanded.

"I do have the keys but need to show you another document."

Donovan walked to the front compartment again, returning with another piece of paper. I scanned the brief document, dated yesterday, signed by Emerald, and notarized by a local attorney. The legalized context of the document authorized Donovan Williams to have unrestricted use and care for the property. One clause immediately caught my attention which was written in lawyerly language. It outlined that Mr. Williams, if Ms. Woodley was not on the premises nor available, had the sole discretion for authorization to access the property and the dwelling. It included additional language about legal permissibility and in accordance with local, state, and federal law.

"What the fuck is this?" I scoffed.

"You can read. It's a document that clearly and legally outlines her wishes related to the property. Based on that, and in alignment of my conversations and understanding of my client's wishes, I'm denying your request to access the dwelling. However, I will enter the house and conduct a review according to any reasonable specifications."

"There are exigent circumstances here." Jenelle interjected, and I winced.

"Exigent circumstance relates to the imminent threat of bodily harm to a person or destruction of property. Neither apply here." He offered sympathetically, speaking in her direction like he was trying to be helpful. "But I do want to cooperate here."

We agreed that Donovan would enter the house and look for any signs of Emerald. He was also instructed to verify that the Jeep was not in the garage. I removed the handcuffs and Donovan walked toward the house. After he entered through the front door, I went over to the kitchenette and grabbed a paper coffee cup from the counter and poured Donovan's coffee into the new cup and carefully dropped the used one into an evidence bag taken from my pocket. Looking at Jenelle's wide eyes, I spoke.

"You never know, and you did not see this."

"What do you think?" She asked while nodding.

"Not sure what to think at this point. In the last week, Samuel goes missing without a trace. There are things that happened that make Emerald look culpable, but it is all circumstantial and there is no tangible evidence that she did anything. She calls me throughout the week, telling me that people are following her. She sounds paranoid and unwell. She is so fearful that she hires this guy to protect her. Last night she called me and said she was being followed. I saw her jump into the harbor. And then Donovan shows up today."

"Nothing is adding up." She offered.

"Yep. The math is off. To solve a murder or find a missing person, the last twenty-four hours of the subject's life and the first twenty-four hours after are the most important hours in the investigation. I want to know what happened yesterday, and today is going to be a long day."

We exited the RV and walked over to the cruiser. After ten minutes, the mechanical churning of the garage door opener grabbed my attention and Donovan was standing at the edge of the concrete floor. There was a black sedan in the garage but no Jeep, as expected. Jenelle and I exited the cruiser and walked toward him.

"House is empty and, as you can see, the Jeep is not here."

"Nothing amiss in the house?" I asked.

"Looks the same as it did yesterday. Detective, may I have a word, without your colleague?"

I tilted my head toward the cruiser and Jenelle walked away. I entered the garage and faced Donovan, looking at him eye to eye before he spoke.

"There are things that I want to share with you from yesterday that came up in my conversation with Emerald. Might be helpful for you."

I nodded. "What have you got?"

"What do you know about the death of her grandparents?"

"Carbon monoxide poisoning. Down in Tarpaulin Cove. They went to sleep and never woke up."

"Was that ever investigated to rule out that it wasn't an accident?" He asked.

I shrugged. "Not sure. Out of our jurisdiction. I don't recall hearing about anything suspicious about the incident. How is this relevant?"

"Emerald... she told me yesterday that she recently found pictures that were taken shortly before the incident. Pictures of this house from the sound, pictures of the sailboat taken on different days and locations, pictures of the interior of the sailboat and the mechanical components of the boat, including the generator."

"And?" He was leading me.

"She found these in a thumb drive hidden in a box that contained Samuel's stuff. All the images were taken before she met him. She believed that he was watching or stalking her grandparents." He paused.

"What else?"

"The boxes had shirts from a marine company in the harbor. Work shirts, stained with boat paint and grease. She thinks he might have worked there. It's the same one that serviced the sailboat within weeks of the incident. She was on edge about it."

"How on edge was she?"

"She seems like a tough kid, but it rattled her. There's more."

"Keep going." I stated.

"You have been in this area for a long time, you know about the *Whydah* gold and the stories?"

"I do."

"You know that Harold talked about knowing the location of the gold." He said looking directly into my eyes.

"He had been talking about that gold for years. My father knew him. When Harold drank, he could spin tales with the best of them. In the seventies, he would be drinking at the bars, draw on cocktail napkins and send tourists off with handwritten maps. He carried a red sharpie in his pocket to mark where the treasure was buried. People would show up all around the Cape with metal detectors and shovels, digging around until they realized they were being punked. The guys at the bar thought it was funny. But it was all a joke."

"What about the coin he flashed around? You know about that?"

"I do." I said while shaking my head. "We, including the feds, went to the house and talked to Harold. It was a real gold coin, and it had an inscription that looked just like the coins from the pirates."

"Looked just like?"

"It was close. Really nice work. The jeweler from town, the guy that melted scrap gold into a coin and made markings that vaguely resembled treasure from the *Whydah*... he did a respectable job. Harold certainly got his money's worth on that joke. He thought it was funny."

"Are you sure it was a replica?" Donovan asked with confusion in his voice.

"Positive. The jeweler had payment receipts, before and after pictures. And the FBI analysis confirmed it. It was fugazi."

"Harold playing games. Interesting. Listen, when Emerald and I spoke yesterday, we didn't have that information. I told her the story and we both believed that Harold had a piece of the gold and may have known the location of the buried treasure. And that it might have gotten him killed and put Emerald in danger. We were thinking that everything that happened was related to the gold."

"Anything else?" I asked impatiently.

"You know about her family, the early settlers that were here in colonial times? Her family has been here before the Mayflower."

"Why would I know about that? What is the relevance?"

"Some of the Woodley's were wreckers in the early 1700s. They had an outsider that joined their crew. The legend goes that the crew went on an expedition to salvage treasure from the *Whydah* after word spread that it sunk. The three family members returned but they came back a man short."

"Get to the point." I barked, my patience wearing thin.

"The guy that did not return with the crew. His last name was Crossman. That rattled her even more."

Goddamn. "Rattled enough to take a header into the ocean?"

After my conversation with Donovan, Jenelle and I headed back to the harbor, riding in silence. Donovan had asked for my phone number and said that he would call me if he remembered anything else. He begrudgingly gave me his number which I programmed into my phone. As I was backing out of the driveway, he ran over and asked for his Sig back as I had forgotten that it was in the trunk of the cruiser. I had no legal reason to not return the gun.

Rolling into the parking lot, it was back to business as usual. The storm's crippling front edge had passed and all that remained were dark gray skies and choppy waters. The lot was open for public use while a solitary state police cruiser sat quietly idling. The helicopters were gone but I could see boats continuing to circle the area, looking for the body. Jenelle thanked me for the opportunity to ride along and said that she needed to get to a local farm to get a ride in before her afternoon shift. It was then that I realized she had on equestrian clothes.

Later that afternoon I was back at the station, reading reports from the Coast Guard and other law enforcement entities. I made phone calls and scrolled through work emails. My mind kept going back to the conversation with Donovan. The locals in town talked about the *Whydah* treasure for as long as I could remember. As a kid, the three television stations that we had access to occasionally had news reports about developments off the coast of the National Seashore. Even before the confirmed discovery in 1984, there were treasure hunters that would occasionally descend into the area to look for the gold. My father used to tell me that the local restaurants and hotels used this as a marketing tactic for business purposes, particularly in the offseason.

The need for a shower and bed was calling my name. About to close my computer and stop for the day, I recalled something that Bill Crossman told me during one of our earlier conversations after Samuel went missing. Extracting my note pad from the black portfolio, I flipped back the pages and saw the note that had popped into my head. During that conversation, he demanded that I arrest Emerald and charge her with harming his son. Politely explaining that there was no evidence of foul play, and it was an ongoing investigation, he made a comment that stuck in my head and was worthy of a quoted note. He had said that she would not get away with harming his family like in the past. The statement made no contextual sense to me at the time but now it made me pause.

Thinking it was going to be an exercise in futility but plodding ahead anyway, my fingers clicked slowly on my keyboard, internet searching for Elias Crossman. The search produced results of a person with the same name but having a life span about one hundred years after my targeted timeframe. More clicks took me to names of his parents and then grandparents, and I located a Jonathan Crossman born in September 1717. Five months after the *Whydah* wrecking expedition, and I noted that it was possible that

Elias Crossman could have impregnated a woman prior to his reported death in April. The site had cursory information on Jonathan, and his family was noted to have lived in Barnstable, not too far from here. The records did not go back any further, and as I was about to go down the Woodley family rabbit hole, I sensed someone standing over my desk. Charell looked down at me.

"We need to talk. My office." He ordered while walking away from my desk.

His office was orderly and well-decorated, aligning with his magnanimous personality. He was wearing a tailored blue suit and silver tie that perfectly fit his frame. It had been thirty-six hours since I put my clothes on. Sand was caked on the lower part of my pants, and the remnants of saltwater stains were visible on my shirt. He looked me over and then spoke.

"Press conference scheduled in twenty minutes. Going to inform the media, and the public, that we believe Emerald is the person that entered the harbor and is currently unaccounted for. Bring me up to speed on anything I need to know."

"As expected, no sign of her at the house. I understand they have not recovered a body yet. Interesting situation at the house but it should not be part of your communication."

"I'll make that decision." He scoffed. "Tell me what happened there."

Avoiding the subject of buried treasure, I detailed my visit with Jenelle and the interaction with Donovan Williams. Charell spoke.

"This Mr. Williams is camping out in front of the house, providing protective services for a client that you saw jump into the harbor and is allegedly missing and presumed dead pending recovery of the body?"

"Something like that." I said shrugging. "That is how he framed the situation."

"Any legitimacy to his story and his position here?"

"Not sure. In addition to being a PI and providing security services, he is also an attorney. He had papers that outlined the scope of his work and a document that he contends authorizes him to remain on the property and make decisions if she is unavailable."

"Convenient. Legally binding?" He asked.

"The contract looks legit. Emerald and a public notary signed the other document. Seal, stamp, and everything."

"And this was all done yesterday? Who notarized that document?"

"Attorney in town, Leonard Fiore. I called and emailed him. He was also the guy who I spoke with early in the investigation about the husband disappearing. Emerald went to his office the day of the party and caused a scene there."

"I recall. Asked about a divorce or annulment." Charell leaned back in his chair.

"Right."

"You haven't heard back from him?"

"Not yet."

"Let's pause on that," he suggested. "What else?"

"If you are going to name Emerald as the jumper, I advise that we set up a patrol car outside, on the street, to keep people away from the house. There will be people that go there, and with Donovan camping in the driveway, it might be best to avoid the drama."

After giving the address of the house to Charell, he used his office phone to call his assistant to set up an around-the-clock detail starting at six this evening and going until further notice. He provided the necessary details. After carefully cradling the phone back in the receiver, he looked at me.

"Give Donovan a courtesy call. I'm sure he'll appreciate both gestures. Now, for the attorney."

Charell extracted a cell phone from his pocket, clicked a few buttons and placed the phone on the desk. Ringing tones sounded from the speaker.

"Chief Charell. To what do I owe this pleasure?"

"Len. Good evening. I'm here with one of our detectives, Lincoln Chase, and you're on speaker. We have a few questions. You have five minutes." He had a way of inflecting his tone to make questions sound like statements.

"Go ahead. I'm in my car heading downtown to meet a client. But I have time for you, Chief."

"You may have heard the news that a person was seen jumping into the harbor last night. Detective Chase witnessed the incident. They are still searching for a body."

"Yes. I have seen the news reports. The person has not been identified as far as I know. How can I help?"

"Chase got a call last night from Emerald Woodley. She told him that she was being followed. He responded and found her vehicle in the parking lot adjacent to the harbor and believes that she is the person that went in the water. She was a client of yours, we understand."

There was a slight pause. "Yes. She is a client."

Charell continued. "As we are in the process of investigating and ascertaining what happened, we understand that you had a meeting with her yesterday. And before you give us any privilege nonsense, we are not asking for protected material, just confirmation relating to our investigation."

"Understood. I'll tell you what I can. A third party reached out to me and retained me for legal services related to Emerald. These services included the review of legal documents that had been drawn up by this third party, and to witness and notarize said documents. I met with Emerald and the third party yesterday afternoon. We met for about an hour."

I spoke. "The third party is Donovan Williams, also an attorney from the area. I ran across Donovan today and he showed me a document. That is why we are reaching out to you. He is camped out at the house and showed the document that she signed, and you notarized."

"And she is now missing. Presumed dead." Len spoke slowly.

There was silence before I spoke again. "How did she seem yesterday in your office? Any indication that she was under duress?"

"First, the meeting was at her house. At four yesterday. She did not seem under duress. She was shaky for sure but there was no indication that she was under duress or forced into signing the documents."

"How do you know that this Williams did not force her to sign the document?" Charell interjected.

Another pause, longer this time. "Hold on, I'm parking the car."

Charell looked down at his watch and held up his large hand. He mouthed 'five minutes.' *Right, the media.*

"I'm back." Fiore said. "Williams left the room, at his own suggestion, and allowed me time to speak alone with Emerald. I had questions. Obviously, this was an unusual situation. She did tell me that she was scared for her safety during this conversation."

"So, she was scared, and you signed and notarized the document. It sounds like she might have been under duress from Williams," I added. Charell's icy eyes met mine and he used his hand to signal me to tone it down.

"I did not believe, at the time, that she was under duress. You keep talking about a single document. There were documents, plural, which were reviewed during our meeting. Which document are you referring to?"

"The document that authorizes him to access and have control of the property if she is not there to make decisions. Is that legally binding by the way?" I asked.

"If it were not legally binding, I would not have signed it. She has the right to assign that type of authorization to a third party. It does not occur that often, but I have been involved in other legal matters of a similar vein. That was just one of the documents. There was another one that we reviewed, and I signed as a witness. That document... was filed at the probate court today per her instructions."

"What document was that?" Charell demanded.

"It was... her revised will which named Williams as the executor of her estate. Listen, I advised her against that, but it is ultimately not my call."

"Wait. She signs paperwork that authorizes his control of the property and makes him in charge of her estate in the event of her death, which may have happened seven hours later. There is no duress there?" My statement sounded like an accusation.

"She was not scared of Williams. She made that clear. And there was something between her and Williams, some level of familiarity. Again, I advised her against executing the documents or at least taking time to reconsider. But, at the end of the day, I'm obligated to follow her instructions, even if I don't agree. That case law is clear, Detective."

"If she was not scared of Williams, who was she scared of?" Charell said, as he picked up the phone and stood.

"She was scared of the Crossman's."

An unruly gaggle of local media members were gathered in our largest conference room at the station. I also recognized faces of Boston television and crime beat reporters that had graced the Cape with their presence, and other media looking people. It was clear to me that word got out that the incident in the harbor was related to the story of Samuel Crossman's disappearance, a sensationalized story that captivated people's attention. There was something about the framing of the story; a kind-hearted man plans a thoughtful party for his new bride, she does not show up to the party, and then he goes missing. Then the internet sleuths start questioning her role in his disappearance.

As much as social media and other technology goes against my values of simplicity, morality, decency, and justice, it also makes the job of detective much more difficult. The station had been flooded with useless tips from people over the last two days. Samuel sightings in Nantucket, New York, and even Falmouth. Our department was small and consisted of fourteen leadership personnel including the command staff, lieutenants, and sergeants. There were currently four detectives with one vacant position and about forty patrol officers at this time of year. Simon was on vacation until Friday, and the other two detectives were running around chasing their tails on the ever-increasing dead-end leads from the keyboard detectives.

Charell marched into the room with his assistant, walking up to the podium. While he adjusted the microphone to account for his height, the murmuring in the room slowly subsided and he waited until there was complete silence before speaking. Standing at the far back of the room near the closest exit, my plan was to head home after he spoke. As I settled in, using the wall to hold up my weary body, I noticed Bill Crossman sitting in the room next to a large, muscled man that towered over the much smaller doctor. It looked like the retired NYPD officer based on Emerald's description.

Charell was a direct and charismatic man, with years of experience speaking in public and skilled at commanding an audience. He had an iPad propped on the podium but spoke directly to the crowd without ever looking down at his notes. He greeted the audience with a friendly tone, said that he was going to provide an update on the incident at the harbor but was not entertaining any questions at this time as this was a fluid and ongoing situation. In less than three minutes, he provided the details of Emerald's frantic call to a detective that was at the station. He included that she reported being followed and was in fear for her safety. He stated that the detective ascertained her location, responded to the scene to assist a resident reporting distress, had followed departmental procedures by calling in backup, and briefly recounted that the officers heard multiple gunshots, and that a detective surmised that she had jumped into the water. He briefed the group on the coordinated search and rescue efforts, reminding everyone that the incident occurred during severe weather. He closed by saying that there has been no recovery of a body and acknowledged that this incident was also being reviewed in coordination with the missing person investigation of Samuel Crossman.

He smiled and wished the crowd a pleasant evening and

concluded with the statement that he was returning to work and that sufficient departmental resources were being allocated to this effort. As he walked away from the podium, the barrage of inaudible questions from many in the audience talking over each other was my cue to slither out the door and head home. I had strategically parked my personal SUV, a dark blue Toyota Highlander, on the side of the building to be able to coast unscathed out of the rear of the parking lot. The digital clock on my dashboard flashed 5:55 and reminded me that I needed to do one more thing before calling it a day. Using the navigation screen on the Toyota, I made a call. He answered after three long rings.

"Chase. Any news on Emerald?"

"Good evening, Donovan. Heads up. I'm stationing a patrol car up on the street next to the driveway. Two uniforms will be sitting there for at least the next day. The chief just had a presser, and the media has confirmation that Emerald is... unaccounted for. I'd expect there may be people that come to the house, and I have instructed the patrol officers to deny any unauthorized access down the driveway."

"Okay. Thanks for letting me know."

"Dr. Crossman and another party were at the station when the chief made the statement. I suspect they may make a visit and will not be permitted down the driveway."

"Two things," Donovan said. "The guy, you probably know, is retired NYPD. Some musclehead that was watching the house with binocs and made some vague threats toward Emerald."

"I'm aware. She told me about that. The other thing?"

"You should check into Bill Crossman." He paused. "Not sure if you should still refer to him as Dr. Crossman."

"What are you saying?"

"Better if you Bing him."

"Bing him?"

"Internet search engine. Look up his name in the New York state board of medicine database. Dig around, it's interesting." My navigation screen flashed to signal another call coming in. I expected this one.

"Okay. I'll give you a call tomorrow. Got to run, another call coming in."

I clicked the screen to take the other call and spoke first.

"Bill, what can I do for you?"

"Detective, it's *Doctor* Crossman. You skipped out of the circus back there before we could speak."

"I haven't been home for days. I'm off duty. Can we set up a time to talk tomorrow? Unless you have something urgent."

"Something urgent? Are you fucking with me? My son has been missing for a week and you are no closer to finding out what happened. And now you're going to be distracted trying to find out what happened to the girl. This is bullshit."

"You heard the chief. Appropriate departmental resources are being deployed on both cases."

"Meet me at the house right now. I demand to look around there. I have hired a private detective who is committing his full resources and expertise to find out what happened to Samuel. He is with me now and we're headed to the house. You can meet me there if you want. Or not. I have a key and will let myself in."

"There's an alarm." I replied.

"Big deal. I have the code. It is my son's house. I have the right to enter his home."

"Not going to argue legality here. But listen carefully. There is a marked police car at the top of the driveway. Two officers are there, and under my order, they will not allow anyone on the property."

"What about that fucking RV that has been sitting there all day?"

Debating on how much to share and distracted to the point of driving past my house, I sighed loudly.

"Am I boring you detective? What is with the RV?" He asked with an agitated tone.

"The RV and the occupant have legal access based on an agreement with the property owner. That's all I'm going to say about that." Channeling a line from a movie in my top five.

"Well, I'll talk to the so-called occupant, Donovan Williams. I'm sure he will understand the situation." *He knew about Donovan. But how?*

"Where are you now?" I asked casually, having turned the SUV around and pulling into my driveway.

"Grabbing food at the Mexican place downtown. Then headed to the house. I'll bring guac and chips for Williams."

I sighed again, louder this time. "I'm going to call the unis right now. Hey, how do you and Marcus take your coffee?"

"Okay, that is more like it. About time you did something here. Both of us like extra cream and no sugar."

"Great. When I call the officers, I'm going to tell them that if you take one fucking step on that property to arrest you and your private detective. I'll bring the coffee to your jail cell in the morning. The stuff at the station sucks. Good night, Crossman."

LABORED BREATHING WARMED MY PILLOW, and my chainsaw-like snoring jolted me from deep sleep. Within an hour of shutting off the purring SUV, I had ravenously consumed leftover Thai take-out, taken a quick shower, and cocooned in my blankets before eight. The digital bedside clock told me that I had slumbered for nine hours, and the tell-tale noise of the Mr. Coffee machine served as my alarm clock. The rhythmic sounds of percolation reminded me of the ebb and flow of the ocean, and coupled with the pleasant olfactory sensation, this was much preferred than the blasting of synthetic noise. You can't hit the snooze button using this method.

Sipping the fresh brew at the desk in my study, I opened my laptop, logging in to the department's intranet. Scanning the overnight reports, there was documentation of some activity at the house. One report indicated that Crossman did stop by the house at around eight and spoke to the patrol officers who had been forewarned by me that this was likely to occur. The detail of the report read that Crossman spoke briefly with them, offered them guacamole and tortilla chips. An offer that, according to the report, was politely declined. At my request, the license plate numbers of each car that drove by the house were taken down and entered into the system resulting in multiple pages of data relating to the registered owners of those vehicles. It was overkill but I prided myself on the details of detective work.

During my second cup of coffee, I scribbled priority follow-up items, formulating my plan of attack. These primarily focused on the Crossman family, checking in on the information from Donovan about the connection between Samuel and the marina that serviced the sailboat. That information piqued my interest. Breakfast was an overtoasted bagel, so large that it barely fit into the heating slots, and filled with perfectly ripened avocado, Havarti cheese, sea salt, and tomato. While enjoying the sandwich, I accessed the public database for New York medical doctors, and nodded my head while reviewing his profile. The license for William Crossman was listed as inactive, and further defined that the licensee voluntarily surrendered their license. Searching further on the reason for the voluntary surrender yielded nothing. It struck me that Donovan seemed to be always one or two steps ahead.

Wearing khaki-colored pants and my customary dark, side zip boots like the old school detectives, I stood shirtless while ironing a white button-down, when I heard my phone ringing from the study. After a quick debate on whether I should answer or let it go to voicemail, I placed the iron upright on the board and went to the study. The caller ID indicated it was Donovan and I answered right before it went to voicemail.

"Donovan, it's early."

"Chase. How soon can you be at the house? I'll alert the officers up top but wanted to call you first. Or you can call them and have them come down. Your choice."

"What's going on?" I asked.

"Someone accessed the property just now. I have the person detained for safety reasons." His words were carefully crafted.

"What? A person got by patrol? How?"

"The subject accessed the property from the rear." Donovan replied. "From the ocean."

"How do you know that? Your RV is in the front of the house. What are you doing, rounds?"

"Not really the point here, Chase."

"Right. I can be there in ten. You all set, or do you need the someone to come down?"

"I got this under control." There was confidence in his voice.

"Who is it?" It was more of a rhetorical question. I knew the answer.

"Crossman." He responded. Bingo.

"I fucking told Bill to stay away from there."

"It's not Bill." He countered.

"What?"

"Samuel. My man says his name is Samuel Crossman."

CHAPTER 6
FACE TIME

Deciding against wearing a partially ironed shirt, I hastily threw on a gray cashmere sweater, secured my holster in my belt, and ran out to the Toyota. I kept Donovan on the phone during this process and started speaking again while I was backing out of the driveway.

"What do you mean 'he says his name is Samuel'? You know what he looks like, right? Can you confirm that it's him?"

"Chase, you need to come down here and see. He has something covering his head, secured by heavy-duty tape. I can't confirm it's him, but he says it is. He wants to go into the house and see his wife. The man is crying."

"Did he say anything else? Tell you anything?"

"No. He won't talk to me. I found him down by the beach. He's disoriented. There are small openings for his eyes but whatever the material, it's going to take sharp scissors or a knife to get it off his face. That is not something I'm willing to do. I zip tied him to one of the chairs in the back."

"Zip ties? Are you fucking kidding me?"

"There was a masked trespasser on the property. Not taking any chances. I called you right after restraining him. Everyone is safe and we will sort this out."

"I'm there in five." Ending the call, I went through my phone contacts on the screen. Scrolling to Charell's information, I pressed the button. He answered quickly.

"Detective, good morning. I'm on a run and speaking to you through my ear buds, so please bear with me."

"No problem, Chief. Got a call just now from Donovan. I'm headed to the house. He reports that Samuel Crossman is on the property. Don't have all the details but wanted to let you know right away."

"Samuel is back. The prodigal son has returned. What the hell is going on?" His labored breathing and heavy strides echoed through my speakers. "Keep me apprised."

As I approached the property, the marked cruiser was idling near the crest of the driveway. Rolling up slowly, I pulled close to the passenger side, and Jenelle lowered the window at the same cadence as the Toyota.

"Morning Jenelle. Didn't expect to see you here this morning."

She yawned and looked over. "Good morning. Worked patrol until midnight and took this shift as a detail. Ten minutes to go."

Over the next minute we spoke through the windows, and I briefed her on the situation. The plan was for her to join me, and the other patrol officer was going to stay in the cruiser until the next shift arrived. I made it clear that no one was to access the driveway or property without radioing me first. After parking my SUV, Jenelle and I began walking to the right side of the house to access the back area. She spoke quietly on the walk.

"We didn't hear or see anything. The previous shift report had Donovan entering the RV at nine and in for the night. We saw nothing until Donovan walked up the driveway and gave us a wave around six this morning. He has been in the RV since then, as far as we could tell. He said Samuel Crossman accessed the property from the ocean?"

"That is what he said, and we're about to find out."

As we rounded the edge of the house. Donovan motioned us over to him, where he stood over the restrained, masked figure. Surveying the scene, I could see a bright yellow kayak beached on the rocky surface near the water. Donovan saw me looking in that direction and shrugged his shoulders. The figure in the chair was squirming and yelling. Jenelle stayed flanked to my right, and I spoke in the direction of the man on the chair.

"Sir. My name is Detective Chase, Falmouth PD. You're Samuel Crossman, correct?"

"Yes. This is my house and this man attacked me and tied me to the chair. What the fuck is going on?" He yelled while continuing to thrash in the wooden chair.

"Samuel, I need you to calm down." I said, placing my hand on his knee. "I'd like to remove the mask, but I need you to relax so it can safely be cut off. Understood?"

"Fucking untie me too." He exclaimed loudly. "And where is my wife, what has this man done to her?"

"One step at a time. The first step is removing the mask. I have a knife in my pocket and will take that covering off your head when you relax and stay still. The police are here, and we will work through this situation. You can let me know when you are ready."

"I'm ready. Get this off me." His body leaned back in the chair, and he tilted his head back.

Motioning Jenelle to come over, we surrounded Samuel and she spoke.

"My name is Jenelle with the Falmouth police. Detective Chase and I are going to work together to take the covering off your head. The knife is sharp as a razor, and if you move abruptly, it will affect our safe removal of the mask, so you better stay still."

The masked man nodded. The sharp knife entered the black synthetic material that I now noted was secured to a black rash guard shirt by an excessive amount of heavy-duty adhesive tape. The mask and the shirt appeared to be made of the same material.

Flicking the sharp edge of the knife like I was fileting a fish, and directing the blade away from his neck, I cut through the section of shirt and mask under the thick tape. Jenelle stood over him, pinning his shoulders to the chair to prevent any sudden jerk-like motion. Once I cut through the thick tape, the mask loosened. With the knife back in my pocket, I spoke.

"Almost there, Samuel. I'm going to pull the mask over your head. Continue to stay still for me."

At that point, the mask came off easy except for a strand of tape that stuck to his beard. He yelled when I ripped off that piece of tape, and his dark eyes pierced mine when it was all over. No question that the man was Samuel Crossman.

"Now cut me loose." He demanded.

"I'm going to cut you free but, for everyone's safety here, I'm going to ask you to stay seated in that chair while we talk. But first, do you need any medical attention or water?

His face looked gaunt and reddened by either the sun or from the tight-fitting mask. One of the challenges of being a detective was the delicate balance between empathy and suspicion, and this situation was hard to read. This seemed to play that he was the victim here, but the information gathered over the last days created shades of gray.

"I don't need medical attention and if I want water, I'll go into my house and get it. Now let me loose."

I looked at Jenelle, and her eyes were on Donovan, who was standing toward the back of the patio behind Samuel. She nodded her head toward the front of the house, reading my mind that we needed to extract Donovan from the situation to prevent escalation. There was no telling what Samuel would do once free of the restraints. Things would go better without Donovan on the scene. He sensed that as well, and nodded when Jenelle approached, following her to the corner of the house. Softly, I spoke.

"When the officer comes back, I'll cut the zip ties. One minute or less."

"Tell me what is happening here." Samuel replied.

"We'll get to that when she returns."

Jenelle was back in less than a minute carrying a large bottle of water and a gray wool blanket. She placed the blanket and bottle on the table next to Samuel, and I extracted the knife and sliced off the plastic ties. Samuel gingerly stood up on the patio and quickly sat back down on the wooden chair. He looked at me and spoke.

"I have been through hell."

I nodded. "Tell me what happened."

He shook his head. "You start. Tell me what is happening? I'm not talking until you tell me what the fuck is going on."

Pondering the ultimatum, I bit. "You were last seen over a week ago on Tuesday night after the birthday party. Today is Wednesday. You were considered a missing person for the past eight days and the department has been looking into your disappearance."

"Where is Emerald? Why is she not out here? I want to go in the house."

"It is better that we talk out here. I'll explain."

"Then explain." He demanded.

"Two nights ago, she called me at the station. She reported that someone was following her and when we responded to her location, by the harbor, she... went into the water. They have searched for her, but she is unaccounted for at this point."

"Went into the water in the harbor... what do you mean? She is... gone?"

I reviewed in more detail the circumstances of the situation including Emerald's fear for her safety and subsequent engagement of Donovan to provide security services. Snickering and stating that it was obvious that the hired man was useless, Samuel pounded his fist on the chair and again demanded to enter the house. Placing my hand on his broad shoulder, I spoke directly about his request.

"There may be a problem with you accessing the house. When Emerald engaged with Donovan for protective services, she entered into an agreement that authorizes him to make decisions on access to the property if she was unable to do so."

"Fuck Donovan. This is my house. I have rights."

By midafternoon, the chaos at the house had settled down slightly. Charell had ordered a continued police detail because of the media presence, increasing it to four officers and two marked cruisers. There was a line of media vans and other parked cars winding down the secluded and narrow dirt road. Samuel was permitted to enter the house and had angrily collected bags of clothes and other items, the whole time threatening to sue the department. On more than one occasion, he told me that he would have my badge. His father made veiled threats as well while standing on the driveway with Jenelle, who later told me that he was speed dialing local attorneys. We sat in my Toyota which was parked halfway down the driveway, strategically positioned between the patrol cars and the RV.

"Bill is pushing for an emergency court hearing. Heard him talking to a few lawyers about getting in front of a judge as soon as tomorrow to get them to void the agreement between Emerald and Donovan for authorization and access to the property. Think that will happen?"

"Not sure." I replied. "Lot of odd circumstances here. Knowing the politics, it is likely that a lawyer would get some type of emergency hearing to review the agreement. Not sure how that will go though. Seems legally complicated, particularly with Emerald missing."

"What did Samuel say about being missing for over a week?"

Pondering my response, I saw that Donovan had stepped out of the RV and was walking toward my car. As he approached the door, I slid my hand over to lower the window. He spoke first.

"Wild day. What is the deal with the police detail? How long are they going to be out there?"

"At least for the next twenty-four hours. Maybe longer."

"Where was he for the last eight days?" Donovan repeated the same question as Jenelle.

"No comment." I said shaking my head. "This is an active investigation with lines that are already blurred."

"Understood. And thanks for having the detail to keep out the family and everyone else. I'm guessing that this will not be the end of it for the Crossman's."

"Unlikely." I replied.

"Okay. Well, if there is nothing else, I respectfully ask that you leave the property. I'll continue to be here as contracted and be in touch if anything goes sideways."

Making a three-point turn in the SUV, I headed through the scrum at the top of the driveway and took a left toward Woods Hole. Rounding the lighthouse, I spoke to answer Jenelle's question.

"Fucked up story from Samuel. He claims that after his father left the party, he went to check on Emerald, but the bedroom door was locked. He went down into the kitchen to find a screwdriver to pop the lock and when he entered the kitchen, he heard a noise in the garage. He said that the lights in the garage would not turn on, but he went in there anyway and was subdued from behind. According to him, there was a struggle, and a masked man placed a knife into his ribcage and forced him back into the house."

"A masked man?" Jenelle asked.

"Yes. He went on to say that he was forced through the house and out the rear doors toward the beach. Down by the water, Samuel said that there was a small gray dinghy beached on the rocks and a larger boat was anchored or floating about fifty feet from the shore. Claims that one of his kayaks was next to the dinghy. He said that he was able to break free from the masked man and they fought on the beach. Said he lost the fight and was knocked out and the details were fuzzy. He said he didn't remember much."

"You found Samuel's ring on the beach?" She asked.

"We did."

"Maybe he lost it in the struggle."

"Possible. Samuel is a big guy. Said the masked man was wiry but strong. When we checked his body, Samuel did have cuts and a partly healed gash on his stomach near his rib cage." By this time, I had pulled into the public boat launch beyond the downtown area.

"You believe his story?" She asked with appropriate disbelief.

"Not sure yet. That part seems somewhat plausible. Part two is much less believable."

"What is part two?"

"Claims that when he woke up, he was tied up on a boat, with his head covered. He described being on the water, and while going in and out of consciousness, was on a boat the entire time. He said he had no idea where he was... just that he was tied up and secured in a cabin. Says that he was given food and water at times, and it seemed like he was in there for a month."

"Then what happened? How did he escape?"

"Samuel said that he was on the water during the storm that blew through, and then, maybe the next day, the boat started moving again. Said he was placed in the kayak, pushed out the tuna door, and the kayak was tied to the side of the boat. He said his hands were wrapped in rope and it took about an hour to untie his hands and release from the boat. He couldn't get the mask off and then paddled with the current and somehow landed on the beach."

"That does seem weird, right?" She asked.

"Some parts of the story make sense. He had the cuts and what looked like a stab wound on his stomach. Confirmed bruises and ligature marks around his wrists and ankles. He refused to go to the hospital for medical treatment. I wanted them to run some panels to see if he had anything in his system."

"What happens next?"

I shrugged. "Not sure. With Emerald missing and her body not recovered at this point, I don't know what the chief will want to do. Everything is messy."

Jenelle looked around the harbor. "Why are we here?"

"Practically or existentially?"

"Practically. Wait... you want to look around and see the boats, and which ones have tuna doors."

"Right. The slips in the harbor and moorings look about half full, as it is early in the season. Going to get a list from the harbormaster and see if we can learn anything. Let's take a quick look around while we're here."

BACK AT THE STATION, with a half-eaten Rueben with extra sauerkraut laying on my desk, I went through the list of boats and their owners provided by the diligent harbormaster, who had done me a solid, and highlighted the boats with tuna doors already in the water. The good news was that there were only eleven boats in the harbor that met the criteria. The not so good news, which I should have considered, was his reminder of the fourteen total harbors, seventy miles of coastline, and three thousand moorings in town. Realizing this might be another exercise in futility, I plodded along while finishing my late lunch.

There was one boat owner in the harbor that caught my attention. Nathan Ferguson. Flipping through my notepad, I found his name. *Emerald's psychiatrist.* I met with Ferguson two days after Samuel went missing. Bill Crossman had provided me with his name and address, indicating it was someone that was treating Emerald for her issues, and he understood that Emerald had an appointment with him on the day of the party. Recalling the brief conversation between his sessions, he danced around the confidentiality issue and willingly confirmed Emerald was a patient and he had seen her two days ago. Ferguson said he was an acquaintance of Bill Crossman and aware of the Samuel situation and wanted to provide any information possible within the confines of confidentiality law. I had taken the opportunity to ask if he thought that she might have had something to do with his disappearance, but he deflected that question and would not give a straight answer. Looking down at my notes, I had quoted him as saying 'anything is possible, the family has had their troubles.'

The dots were difficult to connect. Even if I believed Samuel's story, Ferguson did not match the limited description of his assailant, and there was no motive that I could determine for him being involved. He knew the Crossman's and they referred Emerald to him for the help that she needed. I kept going back to my early conversations with the elder Crossman and thought about his persistent attempts to let me know that Emerald was unwell, struggling with addiction and mental health problems. He was hostile and spoke poorly about Emerald. I ran Ferguson through the system, and, as expected, his record was clean.

It seemed like a dead end, but the connection still intrigued me. Checking the registry of motor vehicle database, he had a white Land Rover and blue Lexus convertible registered at his home address. When comparing the plate numbers to the now computerized list of vehicles that passed the house the night after Emerald went missing, his Lexus plate matched a vehicle that drove by twice in the same hour. I took down his home and office addresses.

The phone in my pocket vibrated with a text from Charell summoning me to his office in five minutes. I closed my files and walked into the tiny kitchen area that was thankfully empty. The coffee pot was warm, and I filled my FPD mug halfway up and watered it down with hot water from the faucet. The chief liked to tell his command that early was on time, on time was late, and late was unacceptable, so within four minutes I was seated across from him in the office. He was wearing a light seersucker suit over a dark blue button-down with a bowtie that matched the ensemble.

"Nice suit." I offered.

"I'm the keynote speaker for a charity event for a local nonprofit tonight. It's derby themed, and this was the best I could do."

"That works." Nodding my approval.

"Where are we with the cases? Be straight with me."

"Always. Emerald is still not accounted for. Surprised she has not... surfaced for lack of a better word. Donovan continues to be camped out at the house and the detail out there was a good move."

"Glad you approve. It was your idea by the way. And a good one."

"When I left there today, there was a line of vans and cars down the street." I reported. "Somewhat controlled chaos as far as I can tell."

"And Crossman?"

"His story has some... plot holes and I'm working on it. Things don't add up."

"I read the reports. You seem skeptical. He took the denial of access to the house poorly, I understand."

"As I'd expect, but I don't blame the guy. Complicated situation. There is more to the story if you have some time."

He consulted his watch. "I have fifteen."

"What do you know about the *Whydah*?"

Over the next ten minutes, I outlined the information we had related to the Woodley's, how the Crossman's were involved, and the possible connection of the sailboat incident to Samuel. His normally affable smile was noticeably absent as I continued about the missing gold and Harold's trickery over the years. Charell was not a local and seemed to have no idea about the urban legend of the gold. I wrapped up with my plan to keep an eye on Samuel and his father and look more into the connection with Ferguson.

"You think that Crossman killed the grandparents and then married the girl, and this is all part of this treasure hunt for the missing gold and to avenge a murder from three centuries ago?" He asked while rubbing his large hand across his chin.

"Admittedly a stretch. There are three connected cases here. One, questions on the death of the grandparents. Two, the alleged abduction of Samuel. Three, the missing and presumed dead Emerald. I don't think investigating a death from 1717 is relevant."

"And where does this Donovan Williams fit in?"

"That is a good question." I shrugged.

"When is your partner back?" Charell asked.

"Simon is supposed to be back Friday. I heard he was marlin fishing down in Florida."

Charell rose from his chair. "Things are going to get interesting over the next few days. Heard from a source at the courthouse that Crossman filed a petition to be able to return to the house and have the agreement related to the property voided. There will be a hearing this week, likely on Friday. Papers will be served tomorrow." He moved to exit his office and I followed.

"Any chance that works?" I had wondered about the legal implications.

"Honestly, I'm not sure. Complicated legal matter with conflicting case law I'm told. These things, depends on the quality of the arguments and the unlucky judge that gets entangled in this mess."

"When I told Samuel about Emerald jumping into the harbor during the storm, he did not seem fazed. In fact, for the next few hours I was right by his side, and he never asked another question about it or showed any emotions."

"Supports your theory that he married her as part of the treasure hunt." Charell nodded.

"Not really my theory, but it is odd that he did not show any concern about his wife being missing. At first, I thought maybe he was just in shock, but I'm not sure anymore."

"Well, if they recover her body from the sound or she is not found, then he might get the house anyway."

"That's the thing. Emerald changed her will the day she went missing. Donovan is now the executor of her estate. We don't know what she included in the will."

THURSDAY WAS SUPPOSED to be an off day for me. I had been on for twelve straight on account of the Samuel-Emerald situation. The long days were taking a toll on my sleep, and this morning, I struggled to get out of bed. The Mr. Coffee alarm had woken me up at five as planned, but it was after eight before I made it to the kitchen and was forced to heat the now cool coffee in the microwave.

I thought about last night. After leaving the station, I had taken a ride into Woods Hole, driving to Ferguson's office on Gardiner Road. The blue Lexus was in the driveway of the small house where he practiced. I had watched as a younger woman walk through the side door shortly before six, and a few minutes later, an older man exited through the front door, jumped on a loud motorcycle, and audibly polluted the quiet neighborhood heading toward town. After an hour, the woman walked out the front door. Five minutes later, Ferguson had walked out the front door, locked the dead bolt, and jumped in his convertible. I had followed him through town, and he had taken Nobska Road onto the street toward Emerald's. He had sped by the house without looking over, and I had breezed by the detail without stopping. I then took a circuitous route to buy a few minutes, drove by Ferguson's house, and saw the Lexus parked in the driveway. *Brilliant detective work.* I had decided to call it a night.

Once the coffee was sufficiently warmed, I took it outside to the small porch that overlooked my backyard. Spring was evident today, with bright sun and little wind. A thin layer of green dust coated the outdoor patio set and small gnats were buzzing around, so I retreated into the house. Breakfast was another oversized bagel and smeared with avocado past the perfectly ripe stage but not too brown. As I was cleaning up in the kitchen, I heard loud banging at my front door and a familiar voice.

"Chase, you in there?"

I walked to the door, opening it for Simon. He was wearing a Hawaiian shirt, light colored shorts, and sandals. His face was deeply reddened by the sun, except for the distinctive lighter areas around his eyes from sunglass stenciling.

"Morning." I offered.

"Just back from the airport in Boston. What the fuck, partner? Lot of stuff went down when I was away."

I nodded as he walked past me into the kitchen and poured coffee into a white mug. Simon and I had been partners for the past three years, and this was the first time he was at my house. Trust, critical for police detectives, had never really formed between us. We never socialized, and I realized that I didn't know much about him. He took a sip from the mug, frowned, and opened the microwave above the stove.

"I need to heat this up." He muttered with slight agitation.

"No problem."

We were seated at the kitchen table. Simon wanted to go outside on the deck, but I mentioned the pollen and May flies, so we opted to stay indoors. He looked around and then spoke.

"Fishing was epic. I'll have to show you the pictures. We got marlin, sailfish, and mahi. What can you tell me about the Crossman thing? I was off the grid until getting to the airport this morning, got a bunch of calls from Bill."

"How well do you know the Crossman's?"

He looked curiously at me. "Why does that matter?"

"It matters to me. I know you went to the house with Bill the day after Samuel went missing and did not identify yourself as a police officer. That is some cowboy stuff right there."

"I went there with a friend who was concerned for his missing son, I was not there in any official capacity." He glared and slurped from the mug.

"Still fucked up. Answer my question."

He glared. "I have known Bill for a long time. We met at the Golf Club back in the eighties and have played on many occasions. Been friendly for a long time. I don't see how this is relevant to this case."

"Well, you know that Samuel is back and now Emerald is missing. Nothing seems to be adding up."

"And you saw her take a dive into the harbor. You sure it was her?" His voice registered skepticism.

"One hundred percent. She called me, told me that she was being followed, and we found her car in the parking lot. I saw her on the rocks and then she was gone."

"Damn. That is messed up. And they never recovered the body. Any chance she made it out of the water?"

"We investigated that, and it is doubtful. There was a nor'easter blowing through and the winds and the tides were all over the place."

Simon continued to ask questions primarily focused on Emerald and the situation with Donovan. It struck me as odd that he never asked me about Samuel's reported abduction and the holes in his accounting of what happened. My low level of trust for Simon continued to decline during the conversation. As he asked more questions to get up to speed on where the investigation stood, I made the decision to throw a wild curveball, and interrupted his incessant questioning.

"Think this has something to do with the gold?"

"The gold? What are you talking about?" His acting skills were poor.

"There are people that think this is related to the *Whydah* gold. The treasure that Harold liked to talk about. Emerald thinks that her grandparents were murdered by people looking for the gold and are now after her."

"That is crazy. Her grandparents died of carbon monoxide poisoning in that old sailboat. Murdered? By whom?"

"Treasure hunters. People looking for the gold."

"That girl watched too many movies. Treasure hunters. That's a good one." He laughed.

"The pirates of Woods Hole." I shot him a look and made a mental note of the disturbed expression on his face.

SIMON LEFT the house with some awkwardness, saying that he was going home to clean up and then would head to the station to get more up to speed on the cases. He seemed rattled by the mention of the death of the grandparents and my connection of this situation with the *Whydah* treasure. My call to update the chief went straight to voicemail. Puttering around the house doing chores, primarily to distract my ruminating about these cases, I acquiesced in my pursuit of work life balance. Working on the case sounded better than mowing the lawn, particularly with the temperature climbing to the mid-eighties. Dressed in blue khaki pants and a white golf shirt and my standard issue boots, I holstered up and jumped in the Toyota. Taking the scenic route to the station, I passed by the south facing beaches and saw that the parking lots were filling up and the sand was crowded with people getting a jump start on the summer given this hot, humid day. Other than in a professional capacity or surfcasting for dinner, I have spent extended time on a beach exactly twice in the last ten years, failing to understand the fun of roasting in the sun surrounded by loud people. Stopping by early in the morning or late in the day for a saltwater cleanse was one thing but sitting in a chair next to throngs of strangers did not seem like my idea of a fun time.

Simon was at his desk when I entered the detective area, and he barely looked up as I sat in my chair. If he was surprised that I came in on my day off, it did not show on his face. I looked over at him.

"Howdy partner. What are you working on?"

He cleared his throat. "Thought you were off today."

"And I thought you were in Florida until Friday."

"Listen, Lincoln. I don't understand why there is tension between us. Your style makes it difficult to collaborate with you. We don't get many big cases in this tiny town, but now we have one, and we need to work together."

"Fair enough. Where do you want to start?"

"You tell me."

I thought for a moment. "Coast Guard."

"They called off the search for Emerald yesterday, how are the Coasties going to help here?"

"I'm planning to investigate the death of the grandparents." I said then paused. "See what they can tell me."

"Sounds like a good place to begin. You don't think it was an accident?"

"No offense, Simon, but if we are going to partner on this, I want to get clearance from the chief. You know the family. If this was not an accident, then Samuel is suspect one. I don't want your involvement to mess this up."

"Are you fucking kidding?" He yelled and stood, menacing above my desk. His words had echoed through the unit. I looked over as Charell stepped out of his office.

"Detectives, in my office, now." He commanded with a slightly elevated voice.

Seated in his office with the door shut, he asked what was going on and why his two lead detectives were devoting their energy to arguing with each other instead of making headway on the intertwined cases that were plaguing the town and casting a poor reflection on his department.

"I hear there are Times reporters, and not the Cape Cod one, coming into town because of this mess. Chase, tell me why you are arguing with your partner in the middle of the unit."

"Chief, I want to look at the carbon monoxide incident and told my partner that I wanted to check with you to see if he should be on the investigation given his connections with the family. I want to avoid any appearance of any type of conflict of interest or anything that taints the case."

"Conflict of—" Simon started before he was interrupted by the chief.

"I'll let you speak in a moment. You will wait your turn." His tone was condescending. He looked down at his vibrating cell phone on the desk and answered it.

"Chief Charell... I see... I'm sending one of my detectives down. He will be there in ten."

He looked me dead in the eyes and spoke.

"They found a floater down in Little Harbor by the Coast Guard station. Chase, head down there now. Simon, you stay in that seat."

LITTLE HARBOR WAS outside of the downtown area of Woods Hole and the location of the New England Coast Guard Southeastern Sector. It was a small harbor framed by a massive USCG Cutter Tybee. The bike trail ended near the spot, and it provided sweeping views of the harbor. It was less than two miles from where Emerald lived, and around seven nautical miles from where she jumped. My mind was twisted during the quick ride, and feelings that I let the kid down were weighing on me. I followed Crane Street down to Cowdry Road to the scene. State police cruisers had cordoned off the road and the medical examiner van was backed up in front of the Coast Guard station. Badging my way through the crowd, I saw a statie that I knew, and he waved me over.

"Chase, how's it going brother?"

"Garcia, doing well. Lot of chaos over the last few weeks. How are you?"

"Man. I was seven minutes from clocking out and jumping on a fishing boat with some guys from the unit. They are crushing big bass down in Quicks and Robinsons. You tell me how I'm doing."

"Sucks. Fish will be there tomorrow."

"You never know but one can hope." He responded with a smile. "You want to see the body before it goes into the van?"

"Sure thing." The tension inside was building.

Seeing dead bodies was not a common occurrence for a detective in this small town, but I'd seen just enough of them to get used to it over the years. In cases where you know the person, it's more challenging. My heart filled with dread and sadness as I walked toward the van. The body was on the stretcher, enveloped in the standard maroon cover. When I looked down, something seemed off. As the medical examiner slowly unzipped the cover, shock waves spiraled through my body. Garcia seemed to notice.

"You good Chase? You look like you seen a ghost."

"Yeah, I'm okay." I nodded. "You know who this is?"

"Negative. No identification, nothing."

"Name is Marcus Amato. NYPD, retired." His face was bloated but I recognized it from the station. The sideburn scar, although caked with salt, helped in my identification, as did the distinctive features of his face. The broad shoulders and muscular frame matched my recollection of him.

"Shoot. You knew the guy?" Garcia asked.

"I did not. But I knew *of* him. Related to a case I'm working on. Gun shot death?"

"Yeah. Two to the back of the head. Dude was executed. Big man, must have been taken by surprise."

"Or he knew his killer." I suggested.

"Anyone we should be talking to?" He asked. "You know something?"

"Bill Crossman."

"Crossman? The guy whose son was missing and just surfaced the other day?" Garcia whistled.

"That is the one."

"You got that case. And the girl that went into the harbor. Wait... you thought this was her, right?"

"I'm not sure what to think anymore." I pointed toward the harbor. "Where did they find the body?"

"It was floating up against the cutter. New ensign was looking down and saw the body. Third day in the Hole. Welcome to Cape Cod."

Garcia and I watched the body being loaded into the van. I provided relevant details about Crossman, and how Marcus intersected with my cases. He made me commit to at least one spring fishing trip with him, and we shook hands before parting ways. On the way back to the car, I called the chief to give him an update. There was silence when I told him that a retired detective had taken two in the back of the head before being dumped into the harbor. I briefed him on the connection to the Crossman's. He was silent for a minute before telling me that he put Simon on leave for insubordination. The conversation after I left did not go well and the chief put him on ice until next week. That was good by me. Just as Charell ended the call and I slipped the phone into my back pocket, it vibrated.

"Donovan. What can I do for you?"

"Process server just came by with a notice to appear at Falmouth District Court in the morning. I expected it."

"If you expected it, why did you not duck it? You seem like you got skills in that area."

"Saw the guy from a mile away and, you're right, I could have ducked it. But why delay the inevitable." He chuckled.

"You know any good lawyers?" I asked while jumping in the car.

He laughed. "I know one. He is expensive, but brilliant."

"You know the saying."

"Yeah, yeah. A lawyer who represents himself has a fool for a client. But I'm not really representing myself. Just trying to do right by Emerald."

I thought for a second. "It is curious to me that you never ask for updates on the search for her. I expected a few calls a day from you."

"Detective, if you found something or had something to tell me, I know that you would. By the way, are you investigating the sailboat incident?"

"No comment. But I do have something to tell you. They just fished Crossman's friend, the NYPD detective, out of Little Harbor."

"Marcus. What happened?" He asked matter-of-factly.

"No comment. But thought I'd let you know." I suddenly wished I had asked him in person to gauge his reaction.

Donovan changed the subject. "You going to be in court tomorrow? You won't want to miss my performance."

THAT EVENING, I met Jenelle for dinner in downtown Falmouth. I had run into her at the station late in the day. She had been picking up daytime details at Emerald's and was not back on patrol until tomorrow. She suggested that we catch up on the cases and asked if she could take me out to dinner. The question if this was a good idea crossed my mind, but I was hungry and, when she mentioned wanting to go to a new Greek restaurant in town, the decision was easy. She showed up fashionably late and sauntered over to my table. Over spanakopita, grilled octopus, and lamb kebobs, paired with sparkling water, we made small talk about the warm weather. She had wanted to order a bottle of wine, but I dissuaded her by saying that we were going to do a little reconnaissance after dinner. She seemed thrilled. As the sun faded behind the shops on Main Street, we exited the restaurant and jumped in her car. Too many people knew mine. Our first stop was Ferguson's house. I suspected that he would no longer be at his office, but when we circled his house, the blue Lexus was not in the driveway. She asked about my interest in him, and I could only shrug and say I had a hunch.

The next stop was the Crossman house which was going to present more of a challenge. Unlike Ferguson's, this house had a long, winding driveway, and the house was not visible from the street. After a drive-by, Jenelle parked her car a few streets down and used her phone to pull up a map that provided street and satellite views. She pointed to where she could drop me off and detailed how to wind down the neighbor's property and cut through to the side of the Crossman driveway next to a structure on the satellite that looked like a detached garage. Her guidance was helpful, but as I stood on the edge of the property line, no cars were in the driveway and the house was pitch black.

We ventured to the harbor where Ferguson kept his boat. As we entered the marina parking lot, I instructed Jenelle to loop down the access road where boat owners could temporarily park their cars to drop off supplies before heading out on the ocean and, at the end of the day, load up their cars. As we glided down, dueling music from the boats and voices of laughter and conversations drifted through the humidity. Checking my notepad, I confirmed that Ferguson had a thirty-five-foot Boston Whaler assigned to slip A-7. When we rounded the corner, I noted that the slip was empty. I directed Jenelle to park at the far end of the lot which was raised above the marina and had a straight-line view to the boats in the A slips.

"What do we do now?" She asked.

"We wait. Give it a few hours to see if he comes back."

"Just sit here?" She groaned while putting in ear buds. "Boring, but I guess it is part of the job."

"You can watch a movie or MTV or something. I'm going to rest my eyes."

"MTV. Are you serious with that?"

Being close to the harbor and breathing in the warm salt air through the partly opened window must have influenced me, as I was dreaming of fishing when I felt a thump on my arm. I opened my eyes.

"Boat backing in." She said with binoculars pressed over her eyes.

The digital display on her dash told me I had been asleep for more than an hour. It was after ten, and the boat bumped backward into the slip. During my siesta, a thin layer of marine fog had drifted into the harbor, and visibility through my unfocused eyes was limited.

"Tell me what you see." I asked.

"Three men... no make that four. I got an older guy up top driving the boat. Three guys down below. Father and son, it looks like the Crossman's. Yes, definitely them. Another guy went into the cabin. No visual on him."

"What are they doing?" I asked.

"Drinking beers and having fun it looks like. The father just pulled a fish from the cooler and is showing it off to a person on another boat. One of those big fish with the stripes on the side. Tuna or something."

"Striped bass."

"Whatevs. The other guy is coming out of the cabin. Reaching in the cooler for another tuna. No, he reached in for a beer. Damn. I know that guy."

FALMOUTH DISTRICT COURT was frenzied on Friday morning with media vans filling up the parking lot which forced me to park in an auxiliary lot down the street. The heat and humidity had broken overnight, and I trudged up Jones Road enjoying the perfect temperatures of the morning. My gray court suit swished in the light breeze, and I walked up the steps into the courthouse. The media members in front of the building started fervently buzzing as I strode by, and I heard my name called as the requisite 'care to comment on' went in one ear and out the other. I just smiled at the cameras and entered the front door. The media comments were for the chief.

The hearing was in the courtroom of the Honorable Lucinda Whitten, a fair and reasonable judge that I had been in front of on occasion. The room was packed when I entered, but I was able to find a seat in the back row next to a group of reporters. One looked over at me, proffering a pen and small notepad with 'Any Comment?' written in oversized letters at the top. I shook my head up and down, and she handed me the items. With the pad tilted toward me to obscure my comment, I wrote something down and continued to smile as I held it tight to my chest. As the judge entered the room and the order to 'all rise' was given, I handed the pen and pad back to the anxious reporter. She looked down at the pad, saw that I had only written 'no' on the page, and shook her head. I smiled at her again.

The judge was in her early sixties, with perfectly dyed black hair without any graying at the roots. Although hard to tell with the puffy black robe that pillowed her body, she competed in local fitness competitions and her pink Hummer was a fixture outside of the gym on Main Street. The light, wooden paneling behind the bench made her look large and powerful, which was likely the intent of the courtroom design. United States and Massachusetts flags stood stiffly to her left. A large screen was mounted on the wall to her right. She greeted the audience and spent two minutes outlining the housekeeping rules of her courtroom. She thanked everyone, in advance, for following the rules and made it clear that any disruptive behavior would be grounds for removal from the building. Looking down at the bench, she continued by reading the court docket numbers and other legalese relating to the motion filed by the plaintiff, Mr. Samuel Crossman. She asked the plaintiff table to introduce themselves for the record. A tall, blonde woman in a navy suit stood.

"Delia Redding, attorney from the law offices of Madison and Madison, for the plaintiff, Mr. Samuel Crossman." She spoke with a strong voice, her eyes locked in with the judge's.

Judge Whitten responded. "Attorney Redding, where is Madison and Madison located?"

"New York City, your honor." Slight murmurs echoed quietly through the courtroom until the judge lowered her reading glasses and glared at the gallery. It is widely known that judges and courts have disdain for outside counsel brought in for local proceedings, especially for lower-level matters.

The judge tilted her head toward the defendant's table and nodded.

Donovan rose from his seat and spoke directly to the judge. "Donovan Williams, on behalf of Ms. Emerald Woodley. I'm an attorney-at-law from right here in Falmouth." He took the first shot.

The judge looked down, shuffling some papers. "Attorney Williams. I'm not familiar with you in this courthouse. Have you been in front of me before?"

"No, your honor. My legal caseload is small, and I only work with select clients. I'm more on the consulting side and provide other services for clients and corporations. That being said, I'm perfectly capable of defending this motion on behalf of my client, Emerald Woodley."

"Thank you. And it is my understanding from the plaintiff's filing that you are also named as a defendant in this motion?"

"Yes, your honor."

"Care to explain? In two minutes or less."

Donovan concisely walked through the circumstances which brought him in front of the court. His client was fearful for her safety and well-being after a series of events that occurred in the week leading up to the execution of the agreement in question. He mentioned the reports from his client that she was being followed and harassed. He provided specific examples of her concerns and subsequent engagement of his services to provide protection for her and the property. He ended by saying that Emerald had reported directly to him, as her attorney, that she was afraid of harm from her husband, Samuel Crossman. The courtroom buzzed slightly.

"Your honor. That is hearsay." Redding was on her feet.

"Attorney Redding don't interrupt opposing counsel. You will have your turn to respond."

Redding persisted. "If I may, your honor..."

The judge folded her arms and leaned back in her chair. "You may."

"Your honor, this is a motion filed by the plaintiff to simply allow Samuel Crossman to return to his lawful residence. We are asking that the agreement assigning control of the marital property to Mr. Williams be vacated based on two key factors that are clear in case law. One, this agreement was entered into at a time when Ms. Woodley was under duress, and we contend coerced to enter into the agreement. And at a time when she was present and living at the property. She has since gone missing and is potentially deceased. As indicated in the filing, there is an attached police report that she jumped into Falmouth Harbor on Monday night and has not been rescued nor recovered. Two, Massachusetts law clearly outlines that an owner can't remove a tenant or their belongings from the home without first getting a summary process. This situation is tantamount to an illegal eviction. Lastly, these unfounded allegations of Ms. Woodley's fear of her husband come from a third party, even if it is a duly qualified attorney representing his client. This is not an order of protection proceeding and should, in our opinion, not be deemed relevant to your decision on our motion."

Judge Whitten nodded and looked at Donovan. "You may respond to her assertion."

"Attorney Redding missed more than one of the key words in MGL Chapter 239. Maybe the laws are different in New York. The Massachusetts laws on evictions speaks to the landlord and tenant relationship in cases where the tenant is paying the landlord for use of a domicile for lodging or other lawful purposes. This is not germane to the facts of this case nor to the lawfully executed agreement signed by Ms. Woodley and notarized by local attorney, Leonard Fiore. The bottom line is that the agreement assigns her attorney, me, to make decisions on her behalf if she is not available. Additionally, Mr. Crossman has a stable and more than suitable alternative residence in the local home of his father, William Crossman. We ask that the court stay the order for at least another week, given all circumstances, ceteris paribus."

The judge smirked at Donovan dropping legal phraseology in Latin. I knew from my time in court that it meant 'all things considered.' She looked over at the plaintiff's table.

"Your turn." Her voice projected sarcasm.

"Thank you, your honor. We simply ask the court to vacate the property assignment agreement and allow Mr. Samuel Crossman to reside in the marital home. This man was abducted and held against his will for over a week, only to return to find that his wife is missing and presumed dead. He has been through great trauma and is grieving the likely loss of his beloved wife. We believe that it is unnatural and unlawful for him to be prevented from living in their home, particularly without her being in the court to support the agreement and the position outlined by her attorney."

"Attorney Williams?" The judge looked over.

"We ask that the plaintiff's motion to vacate the lawfully executed property assignment be denied by the court, your honor."

Watching as the judge reviewed a small stack of documents, I made a mental note that Donovan did not give a compelling argument to void the order. In my mind, there was case law he had not evoked on behalf of his client. It surprised me that his case seemed insufficient, and he did not appear prepared for the shark from New York.

"Thank you to both attorneys for their concise and reasonable testimony on behalf of their clients. When I was assigned this case late yesterday, I was admittedly torn on the issue and can clearly see both sides of the argument. Both attorneys made compelling cases, and there is clearly gray area related to this matter. But I'm appointed by the great Commonwealth of Massachusetts to make tough decisions. Mr. Williams, your arguments have merit, however, since your client is not in this courtroom to—"

The judge stopped speaking as Donovan raised his arm.

"Mr. Williams, I really hope you are just stretching and not interrupting my decision."

"You are right, my client is not in this courtroom. May we approach your honor?"

The judge lowered her reading glasses to the bridge of her nose and her death stare rippled through the room. She waved the attorneys toward the bench. There was a heated conversation between the three in low, muffled tones. This persisted until the judge waved them back toward their respective tables. Redding looked angry, and Donovan walked back to his table, striding with purpose. He opened a laptop on the table and bent over it, slowly hitting keys while the judge continued to address the court.

"As I was saying, this is a complicated motion with many

different angles. I have made the decision, within my judicial discretion, to provide latitude to the defense based on his client being in absentia."

Redding waited until she finished her sentence, then spoke with an angry tone. "Objection, your honor."

"Objection noted. Proceed Mr. Williams."

"Thank you, your honor."

I watched as Donovan proceeded to the front of the courtroom and plugged the laptop into the monitor. His green phone icon was now mirrored on the screen, and he clicked on a contact labeled 172, clicking again on the FaceTime button. Within seconds of pressing send, his call was accepted. For five seconds the monitor displayed a blurred-out background, and then a figure moved onto the screen. Jaws dropped, and people in the courtroom gazed intently as the person spoke.

"Your honor, people in the courtroom, my name is Emerald Woodley, and I'm alive and in my home on Fay Road in Woods Hole. It is just after ten on Friday morning, May..."

The courtroom, which had been as quiet as a smalltown library on a late Friday night, suddenly sounded like an Irish bar in South Boston on St. Patrick's Day. The judge banged her gavel with authority and the echoes crackled through the court. The room slowly became silent again.

"I have been hiding in my home out of fear for my safety. My life is in danger, and I ask that the court grant me a temporary order of protection against Samuel Crossman, my husband, who tried to kill me and then pretended to be abducted."

The courtroom erupted again.

PART THREE
EMERALD

CHAPTER 7

DEAD MEN DO TELL TALES

As my bare feet hit the frigid water, shock waves of pain enveloped my body. I struggled to rise above the abyss, flailing my arms forward, reaching for something, anything. It was more painful than I had imagined. If I could have screamed, I would have, but my mouth was so filled with salty coldness that I was forced to swallow to breathe. This was not going to work, and I drifted back toward the rocks, catapulted by the cresting waves. I went under again and something grabbed me, pulling my stiff body forward and away from the rocks. Through eyes filled with forming ice, I saw him, and he pulled my frozen arms over the side of the slick synthetic rubber. A metal object was in his hands and a deafening explosion reverberated through the rocks, stifled by the blockage in my ears. The gun splashed into the water, and he quickly grabbed the back of my pants, hoisting my lifeless body into the dinghy.

The ride across the channel and into the harbor was quick, and in less than two minutes, the dinghy slammed into the wooden pier below a clam shack that was long closed for the night. I could see the flashing red and blue lights from the parking lot on the other side of the channel but knew, from their vantage point, they could not see us climbing the ladder and scurrying around the corner of the restaurant where the RV was waiting.

Because of the storm and the time of day, the area was vacant, and no other cars were parked in the small clam shack lot. We were back at the house, and I was in a warm shower in less than ten minutes. He warned me to resist the temptation to take a hot shower as it could send me into shock. He said we had thirty minutes until we needed to lock down. While I showered, Donovan filled the bureau drawers with bottles of water and bags of snacks that I had requested. He left the house after reminding me of his strict instructions and said he would be back at seven the next morning.

For the next three days, I was camped out in the guest suite in perpetual darkness. The blinds remained closed, and the bulbs had been removed from each of the lamps. My only light source was the new tablet that he had left in the room. My days were spent scrolling through the internet reading stories about my disappearance, binging the library of movies and shows that he had downloaded to the device. A weird selection of romantic comedies, the first ten seasons of Curb Your Enthusiasm, assorted documentaries, and real-time footage on the property courtesy of my security system. I spent an inordinate amount of time reading into Donovan's choices for me, trying to analyze what it meant. Putting that Harvard doctorate to work.

The tablet had the security application installed and would send a notification alert if anyone entered the house. He had warned me that the police would be there at some point on Tuesday, likely in the morning, and I watched like a voyeur as Chase, Donovan, and a female spoke in the driveway and then entered the RV. She looked like the officer that extinguished the fire on the night of the search warrant but was not in uniform. Donovan knew where the cameras were mounted, and he told me he would nod three times if the police were coming in to look around the house. I was instructed to hide underneath the bed when signaled. I watched him enter the house alone and he came up to check on me, letting me know that Chase was aware of the property authorization agreement. He did not think the police were coming in today but instructed me to be attentive.

On Wednesday morning, I heard some yelling out back and had to stop myself from looking out the bathroom window. I scrambled under the bed and logged onto the tablet, double-clicking the security system icon.

Selecting camera seven, which was above the rear slider, I watched as Donovan tied a masked man to one of the chairs around the fire pit. The camera feed was clear and, even before Chase and the female officer cut off the mask, I knew who it was without seeing his face. The return of Samuel was an eventuality that Donovan discussed with me, and he was proven correct.

Later that morning, Donovan signaled to me from the front camera that police were coming into the house. Hiding under the bed for an hour was not too difficult, it reminded me of childhood games. The difficult part was listening to Samuel yelling at Chase about only being allowed to grab some clothes and other belongings, and not being able to live in his home. His abusive tone and threats frightened me. I half expected them to come into the guest suite, and for Samuel to find me hiding under the bed, but they never came into the room. I finally breathed freely when hearing the front door slam.

On Thursday night, Donovan informed me that he was appearing in court the following morning, after being served papers earlier in the day. He presented an overview of his legal strategy and practiced his arguments, with me pretending to be the judge. He was transparent in telling me that there was a good chance that the plaintiff's motion would successfully vacate the property assignment. I thought he was joking when he told me his backup plan if the proceeding was not going the way he hoped, instructing me to be ready for a phone call to the tablet.

Feeling some freedom and safety on Friday morning after hearing the RV ramble out of the driveway, I had ventured out of the guest suite prison. The confinement of being in that room for more than three days had given me time to think about all that was happening in my life. The need to understand and put together the puzzle pieces of this chaos was messing with my fragile head. I desperately wanted clarity and needed closure.

My building emotions of anger, resentment, and confusion were further compounded when I went through some of Mary's belongings that had been stored in the basement. A dusty photo album I had not looked at in years was in the first box. I remember packing up the album around the time Samuel was moving in and was too rushed to flip through the pictures. The front cover of the album simply had the name of my mother. The book, more than four inches thick, was a chronological journey of her life. From the grainy, fuzzy baby pictures, through her childhood, and then early adulthood before she gave birth to me and passed away. The first fifteen years of her life dominated the thick pages of the album. After her school picture from her junior year in high school, there were less than five photos before the start of the blank pages. One of them was labeled her junior year homecoming dance and was a professionally taken photo of my mother and her date awkwardly posing for the camera under a gazebo with dramatic fall colors in the background. The photo was dated in October, the year before I was born.

Two things hit me, and hit me hard, while staring at that picture. First, my mother radiated beauty and my eyes welled up while looking at her smile. More importantly and shockingly, her date in the ill-fitting black tuxedo was someone who had recently come into my life. Puzzle pieces were coming together. I had taken the picture out of the plastic sleeve. The realization that the three men in my life, not including the Crossman's, had information and knew things they were not telling me was gnawing away at me, fueling my determination and resolve. I needed to take charge of this situation. No more fucking around. Ferguson, Chase, and Donovan. I would have it out with each of them, starting today. I'm getting the answers, one way or another.

THE FACETIME CALL ended abruptly shortly after the room had been spun into complete chaos. The judge had appeared flummoxed by the situation but did grant an order of protection that prevented Samuel from communicating with me and accessing the house. He was ordered to stay one hundred yards away. After her ruling, the feed from the courtroom was disconnected. As instructed by Donovan, I had Zoom-dressed for the possible virtual court appearance, wearing a white, button-down shirt and a gray, ribbed cardigan sweater. Not visible to the camera were my overpriced, black leggings and a pair of insanely expensive off-white, collaboration sneakers that I had worn exactly once. I had gone through a phase of socializing with kids at Harvard that had credit cards with no limits and had amassed a few items of luxury clothing that made me sick to look at, conflicting with my desire for simplicity and decency.

Today I needed to look different, and these props might help me achieve that goal. The shirt and sweater were quickly exchanged for a gray cashmere blend hoodie over a white shirt. When I bought the hoodie at the boutique on Newbury Street in Boston, the salesclerk informed me the color was 'shadow mélange.' I regret not walking out of the store empty handed. With the hoodie cinched tight around my head and with the help of oversized sunglasses, most of my face was hidden. A deep brown, hybrid crossbody bag adorned with the golden initials of the designer completed the ensemble that could best be described as bougie and bratty. I looked stupid and wanted to cry.

My first real dilemma of the day was transportation. While concocting this ill-advised plan, I came to the realization that my Jeep was not at the house. I seriously considered taking Samuel's BMW but thought that it would be a bad look given the court fiasco this morning. But I was tempted. *Do I really care about the fucking optics?*

Uber was a problem, as my iPhone, as far as I knew, was at the bottom of Falmouth Harbor, zipped in the pocket of my windbreaker. Regressing back twenty years, I used the tablet to find the number of the local taxi company and used the burner phone for the ride. Thinking on my feet, I set the taxi pickup for three houses down. That seemed smart and I could not be seen by the police car monitoring access to the house. Trudging through the woods to get to the meeting spot was a stroll down memory lane. I needed to avoid the police car that was parked at the end of the driveway, so I walked around the back of the house and through the trees, directly past the dilapidated shed and along the Morgan's property. I walked right by the tree that I crashed into on my birthday. Everything was confusing, but it all seemed connected. Exiting the neighbor's yard onto the street, I walked with my head down toward the pickup spot. The light blue minivan was seven minutes late, and I had to stand awkwardly on the sandy, dirt road, ready to hide behind trees if anyone drove down the desolate street. The overly friendly driver started the awkward conversation.

"Good day, my name is Bob, and I'll be your driver today. We don't pick up many people your age with all those rideshare applications out there. You might be my first passenger in a week that is under sixty."

"I don't have my phone with me. And I don't use Uber."

"Dispatch said your destination is Gardiner Road. We should be there at... ten of eleven if the drawbridge doesn't hold us up." He referred to the bridge on Water Street that lifts to allow sailboats and larger boats in and out of Woods Hole Harbor.

"Hopefully, we will not be held up." I pleaded. "I have an appointment right at eleven."

"This time of year, your chances are good. I could also avoid it by looping around on School Street. That's another option." I could see him looking back at me in his rearview mirror. "You here on vacation or something?"

"Just passing through."

"There has been a lot going on here over the past few weeks. There was this girl in town that they suspected had something to do with the disappearance of her husband. He had this big, fancy party for her, and she didn't show up, and then he goes missing. Then she dove into the harbor during a storm early this week, and a few days later, the husband reappears. Ethel, my wife, thinks this will be made into a *Lifetime* movie someday. Hey, are you with the media?"

"I'm not with the media." I'm the star of this movie, you dimwitted idiot.

Thankfully, the road was down across the inlet, and we breezed through the shops and restaurants before taking the right on Albatross Street which turns into Gardiner. I had Bob drop me off a few hundred feet past my intended destination and gave him thirty in cash to cover the fare and tip. He was in the middle of thanking me for my kindness when I abruptly shut the door and strolled down the sleepy road.

It would not be quiet for long.

AT FIVE MINUTES BEFORE ELEVEN, I was seated in the waiting room, next to a confused girl that looked to be in her early twenties. Like most people around her age, she was scrolling through her phone, and loud music was pulsing from her ear buds. She looked up at me with palpable anxiety, glaring at me from head to toe with her eyes widening when they landed on the crossbody bag. She then focused on my stupid sneakers. She nodded in approval and was still looking at them when she spoke, simultaneously removing her ear buds.

"My... I have an appointment now. Did he double book us or something? I really need to see him." Her voice and body were shaky.

"I don't have an appointment but need five minutes, just five minutes. Is that okay with you? What is your name?"

"Olivia. Five minutes, really?"

"Yes, Olivia. Just five minutes. Please." I said softly, using my best therapeutic voice.

"I don't know. I don't like my schedule interfered with and I have OCD and anxiety. You should wait until after I have my session."

I took off my sunglasses and flipped back the hoodie. "Do you know who I am, Olivia?" I sounded like a D-list celebrity trying to get a table at a crowded restaurant.

She took a hard look at me, and I saw the moment that she recognized who I was and hoped she would understand the urgency of my seeing the doctor.

"You are that crazy woman who jumped into the harbor this week. You are supposed to be dead." She started tilting her phone toward me and I immediately saw where this was going.

"Don't do it. No pictures, please. I'm alive and need five minutes of his time. Hey, what size are your feet?"

"Like a six or seven, depends."

Taking off the sneakers, I held them toward her. "These are sevens, I'll trade you for yours if you give me five minutes with him."

"Those are like five-hundred-dollar off-whites. These sandals are like five years old."

"Sounds like a fair deal. And when I go in there, turn your music back on for me, okay?"

We made the exchange, and the white plastic sandals squeezed my feet in abhorrent discomfort. The door opened before I could put the sunglasses back on, and Ferguson looked directly at me as shock filled his spectacled eyes.

"What... what are you doing here?" His tanned face paled. He did not seem surprised that I was alive, which made sense to me.

"We need to talk, and Olivia said it was okay if I took five minutes of her time."

I leapt out of my chair and moved furtively toward his office, looking back at Olivia. She placed the ear buds back in and smiled at me, then stretched out her feet and smiled at her new sneakers. Ferguson stood by the door, standing his ground and I drove a shoulder into him and shoved him back into the office, shutting the door behind me. He retreated behind his desk and grabbed the receiver to a landline.

"I'm going to call 911. You can't come in here without an appointment and assault me. I don't care if you are a patient."

"I did not assault you." Not yet anyway.

"You pushed me, and your body language is indicative of violence."

"Please, I just need five minutes. Please."

He slowly replaced the phone and motioned me toward the uncomfortable patient chair.

"You have three minutes. I don't keep patients waiting."

He came around the side of the desk, grabbing his pen and

notepad. He took his normal posture on the nice chair and stared at me.

"I want to know why you and my mother were in Florida at the same time. She ran away, and you were down there. She was pregnant with me when she left. I know that she went down there with you. That sabbatical nonsense. I don't believe that's a coincidence."

"You are out of line Ms. Woodley. I did not know that your mother was pregnant, I did not know that she went to Florida, and she certainly did not go there with me. You have two minutes. If this is not about me helping you in a clinical, therapeutic way, then you can leave now. I'm not going to entertain your wild and unfounded accusations." He pointed at the front door.

"Someone is trying to kill me. You know something. Help me." I feigned tears and balled up on the chair with my knees tight to my chest. "Please help me."

"Who is trying to kill you?"

"I don't know. But they are watching me. Waiting. Trying to take me to find the hidden treasure. And then they will kill me."

"You know... your mother used to say the same thing. She was convinced that people were following her, and she talked about the gold."

"Did she tell you where it is buried?" I asked, sobbing ever so slightly.

He paused and leaned back in his chair. "She talked about it during many of our sessions. She seemed to have some ideas. I tried to help her but—"

Leaping out of my chair with ninja-like coordination, I landed on top of the doctor. My left hand pushed into his weak chest, pinning him against the chair, and my right hand grabbed the thick, unopened pen from his fingers and pressed it hard against his neck.

"Tell me what I want to know." I demanded, speaking through my teeth, trying to muffle my voice. I could taste the violence in my mouth and smelled the fear that emanated from his limp body, shaken from the sudden act of aggression.

"I don't have anything to tell you. Let me go. Help!" He yelled the last part loudly and I wondered if Olivia's ear bud volume was high enough to mask the commotion in the office.

"Tell me. Tell me right now. Are you my father?"

He shook his head back and forth and was about to speak before being interrupted by a knock on the door, coming from the waiting area.

"Everything okay in there? I heard some noises." Olivia asked from the other side of the door.

"Yes. We'll be done in a minute." I answered as calmly as the endorphins would allow.

"Something is wrong, I'm calling 911. I don't want the doctor to hurt you."

Pushing the pen harder into Ferguson's carotid, I mouthed the question again. He continued to shake his head back and forth, eyes welling with water.

"If I find out that you are lying to me, I'll be back, and I'll fucking kill you."

I ran out the front door and down the walkway, taking a right turn onto the street, running as fast as the sandals would permit, suddenly regretting my decision to swap shoes with Olivia.

TIMING IN LIFE IS EVERYTHING, and I had traversed the quiet streets and made it to the Marine Biological Laboratory complex just as two Falmouth cruisers with lights and blaring sirens ripped down Millfield Street and skidded right onto Gardiner, headed toward the psychiatrist's office. The area was busy this late morning, with students and teachers milling around the buildings, and they seemed focused on whatever they were doing and not paying attention to me. The hoodie was back on, and somehow my sunglasses were not lost in the struggle and back covering my reddened face. I did not fully have this planned out but knew that I wanted to avoid transportation by police car.

Staying off the downtown roads, I powerwalked behind the largest building in the complex and made my own pathway along Eel Pond to circumvent being seen on the streets. I made it to the wooden pier behind Shucker's Raw Bar, finding a bench and watching people slurping oysters and enjoying an early lunch. The smell of fried seafood lingered in the air and my stomach grumbled. I wondered if I could go in there, order, and then enjoy lunch before the police found me and carted me away. I didn't want to take that chance as it would really make me angry if I was handcuffed and led away just as my food was arriving. As I debated on taking the risk, I could see the top of a cruiser slowly rolling down Water Street.

My attention was diverted by a man and a woman walking past me toward the row of slips behind the bench. The man was older and screamed freshly retired, dressed like he was going on an April cod fishing trip with a heavy jacket and thick pants. His bulky arms struggled to balance an oversized cooler that had a designer duffle bag sliding back and forth across the top. The woman looked much younger, wearing a boutique sundress, large sunhat, and sunglasses that reflected like mirrors. She sashayed down the dock with the elegance of a runway model, with a matching designer beach bag draped over her shoulders. She was not struggling like the man in front of her and walked with her head down while scrolling through a phone. As they approached, he said hello, commented on the peaceful morning, and proclaimed that it was a beautiful day for a boat ride. She smiled and complimented me on my fancy sweater and cross-body bag, speaking in an accent that sounded Portuguese. If only she had seen the off-whites that I was wearing an hour ago. After they passed, I watched them board a shiny, midsized cabin cruiser. The name of the boat, written in large green letters on the transom, was *Liquid Asset*, and I pegged him as a hedge fund manager or marginally successful venture capitalist. After they loaded the boat, I watched as the man tried to fire up the engines, but they refused to come to life. The woman was now seated in the portside seat, and just shook her head and started giving the man grief. The problem was obvious, and I took that as my sign and walked quickly over toward the boat.

"Hello again. Engine trouble this morning?"

"These engines don't like the cooler weather." He replied, nodding toward the twin Mercury 300 outboards on the boat. He introduced himself as John and told me that her name was Daniela.

"Mercs are like that, John. Temperamental." I replied.

"You know boats?" He gazed over at the woman with a look of validation.

"I do. Mind if I climb aboard and take a look?"

"Please. This is our first trip of the year. Dani and I just got the boat last summer. Thirty-footer. Still getting used to a boat this size. Twenty years ago, I had an eighteen."

The problem had a simple solution, one that plagued new boaters early in their marine experience or, in this case, a modern boat with improved safety features. The telltale sign was clear, the engine, which was on the verge of firing up, was not starting due to his failure to flip up the kill switch. Also called the engine cut off switch, it is connected to a lanyard that is supposed to be affixed to the captain's life jacket or other clothing as a safety feature. That way if, while navigating the boat, the driver hits a large wave and is thrown from the boat controls, the engine will stop and prevent a catastrophic accident. I decided to play this up and removed the cowlings from the top of the engines and adjusted each idle screw, telling him that this would help with the cooler weather. A stronger flow of the gas and oil combination would enter the carburetors and help the engine turn over. While surveying the engine, I noted that the oil reservoirs were low and asked him if he had a container of two stroke oil on board. He sheepishly shook his head.

"Well, you have enough for today if you're not going more than fifty or sixty miles. But I'd recommend that you always have at least a spare gallon on board."

"Fifty miles... we're not going anywhere if this boat doesn't start." Dani offered with a slight attitude. "We should have gone to the club today. It's a little chilly."

"It will be nice on the water, and it is going to be humid and near eighty this afternoon. I checked the forecast. Have some faith, Dani. She will start right up now that the idle is adjusted." John said to her, shaking his head.

Replacing the cowlings and making sure they were secure, I motioned for John to join me in the cockpit as I slyly flipped the kill switch to the correct position and affixed the lanyard to his heavy jacket. He looked down at the keys and I nodded. The boat fired right up, and he smiled from ear to ear and then leaned in toward me.

"Forgot about the kill switch. Thanks for covering for me." He whispered.

"You owe me. But the idle screws needed adjustments too, so you are all good." I said softly.

"What about the oil situation?" He asked, and I seized on the opportunity.

"I have an idea. Have you taken the boat to Falmouth Harbor before?"

John was thrilled with my idea and Dani's mood improved as the engines continued to idle and she popped opened a can of hard seltzer from the cooler. I had told him there was a marine store in Falmouth Harbor that sold the oil that he needed and would help him navigate there in exchange for a ride. I lied and said the harbor could be tricky. After releasing the boat from the wooden dock, John clumsily left the slip and almost hit a moored boat as he slowly navigated toward the Water Street drawbridge that we needed to go under to access the ocean. Timing was in my favor as I could see that the drawbridge was up and two sailboats in front of us were moving slowly through. As we approached the bridge, I saw the unmistakable dark uniform of a police officer standing to the right of the bridge looking down at the boats as they passed. Emerald the fugitive needed to think quickly.

"John, this boat is amazing. Okay if I check out the cabin below?"

"Be my guest." He replied with a grin.

Sliding the fiberglass door along the aluminum tracks, I stepped into the cabin and slowly closed the door. I watched out the portside window as we glided toward the bridge, holding my breath and almost choking when I heard the strong voice from high above.

"Good morning, Captain. Just the two of you on the boat?" *I'm dead.*

"Good morning officer." John said firmly, and then started singing an old song about just the two of them making it if they tried. His voice was off-key, and he mixed up the lyrics badly.

"Okay then, enjoy the calm seas." The voice from above bellowed.

~

I WATCHED out the small cabin window as John navigated past the steamships, and when he was nearing the marker that signified the open ocean, I opened the door and climbed back up on the deck. Dani was seated across from him in the cockpit area, and he was steering the boat with one hand and holding a beer can with the other. He gave me a curious look.

"Hello, stowaway. How do you like the cabin? What might you be running from?"

"It's a beautiful cabin." I took off my sunglasses and removed the hoodie. They both looked at me.

Dani was quick to recognize me. "Wait. You're that girl that they thought drowned in the harbor. You're all over the news and social." John was silent and more focused on navigation.

"Something like that. Listen, I'm sorry."

"Why did you hide? Everyone is looking for you." She asked with her thick accent.

"It's a long story. They know that I'm alive. There was a thing this morning. And then another thing." I debated on how much to say and noticed that John's beer was an IPA from a local brewing company that had splashed on the scene in recent years. It was one of my favorite beers.

"A thing? And another thing? Mysterious." John said, sipping the beer. I was jealous.

"I had a little altercation with a psychiatrist on Gardiner Street. It got ugly."

"Ferguson? He is an arrogant asshole." John grunted.

"That's the one. I got a little physical with him."

"Well, have a cerveza and sit back and relax." Dani smiled as she spoke. "Grab me another seltzer, hon. Cooler is in the back."

"I thought you would never ask. Thank you for helping me."

Seated in the back of the boat next to the engines, I enjoyed the quick cruise around the lighthouse and toward Falmouth Harbor. The ocean was glassy, and John had slipped out of his jacket and blasted yacht rock while awkwardly dancing. I wanted to be happy like John one day.

The beer had bright mango, peach, and passionfruit notes and the perfect amount of hops to accentuate the mouth feel. I had my eyes closed as the engines revved down and we slowly idled into the channel. I looked to my right and saw the red marker and the rock that I had jumped off a lifetime ago, or so it seemed. After another minute, the clam shack was on my left, and I watched people eating at the tables above where we scuttled the dinghy. John turned and pointed at his can, signaling that he wanted a fresh one. I knew that move from Harold. I drained the rest of my can and dug my hand into the ice-filled cooler to grab another round.

We docked at the inner end of the harbor, next to the pump-out station and below the raw bar that was bustling with activity on this early Friday afternoon. John had radioed the harbormaster and was granted permission to dock at this spot for a few hours. I sat on the floor of the boat with my back resting against the door to the cabin. My attempt to lay low. The raw bar had a live musician that was playing acoustic covers and his singing voice was comforting. John started singing along until Dani shot him a look and he stopped. It was clear that she was the boss. The second beer went down smoothly, and I commented on how much I enjoyed it. The grin on John's goofy face widened.

"Glad you like it. I brewed it myself." He said with a prideful smile while tapping Dani on the arm.

"What do you mean?" I asked.

"I started that craft brewery five years ago. I didn't technically brew that can, but it is my recipe and my company that makes it. That is why I named the boat *Liquid Asset*."

"Nice. I had no idea. How about getting me another one?" I handed him my empty can.

Over the next hour, I had two more of his beers and we made small talk and listened to the music from the raw bar. I felt some level of happiness, partly from the strong beer but mostly because of the kindness from John and Dani. As the afternoon progressed, more boats entered the harbor and there was a nice vibe happening in the midday sun. There was something to be said about the early spring optimism on days like this after long Cape Cod winters. I had forgotten about my mess of a life for a while, but it was coming back now. My happiness never hung around.

After finishing a soulful rendition of Prince's *Purple Rain*, the singer announced that he was going to take a quick break. John turned back on the satellite radio and began bumping some bass-heavy music on a station that Dani requested. She took off her sundress to expose her impressive physique that glowed from a quality spray tan. She danced rhythmically and provocatively in a micro bikini on the deck of the boat to the delight of John and the others lucky enough to be gathered at the end of the harbor on this beautiful afternoon. I wanted to stay on this boat for a long time but had things to do and needed to stop procrastinating. My next stop was a quarter mile away on foot. After a few impressive dances from Dani, John shut off the stereo in deference to the acoustic singer who had returned to the bar. This was met with a chorus of boos from the gathered crowd of men, and some women, who preferred to watch Dani. She addressed the crowd with her sultry voice.

"I'll be here all night and we will resume the dance party when the singer is done with his set. But only if you all go up there and give him a good tip. He's a great singer. Please go support him so we can hear more!"

That gesture of kindness was unexpected and made me feel good about humanity. As the group scrambled up the sidewalk to drop money in the tip jar, she explained that her brother was a musician from Brazil and supporting local artists was important to her. She then suggested that we go up to the restaurant. As she was explaining this to me, I heard John on the radio with the harbor-master to secure a transient slip for the night. He was not going to let the party end.

"I want some fresh fish and we also need to tip him. Join us?" She asked me.

"I'd like nothing better than to join you, but I have something to take care of and need to leave. Next time."

"What do you have to do? Please join us, I enjoy your company." She pleaded sweetly.

"It is time. I'm going to turn myself in. And besides, I'm lucky that no one has recognized me. Just a matter of time and I don't want to ruin your day."

DESPITE THEIR CONTINUED pleas to join them for an early dinner and the realization that I had not eaten real food in a long time, I stood my ground and started the trek to the police station. John had poured another one of his beers into a large, red plastic cup, telling me I should at least enjoy a road soda during the walk. Dani had written her number on the back of a receipt found inside the cabin and warned me that they would be too drunk to bail me out but if I got out of jail and needed a place to stay, I could sleep on the boat.

He told me the slip number. I was touched by their thoughtful gesture.

Sitting under an oak tree on a small patch of grass adjacent to the police station, I slowly drank the beer and watched the cars moving in and out of the parking lot. It seemed like it was change of shift based on the foot traffic going through the side door. Then, I saw the familiar walk of the person I wanted to speak with headed out the door toward a blue SUV. I yelled to him.

"Chase! Over here."

He looked over and shrugged his shoulders. I removed the hoodie and sunglasses. He shook his head and walked toward me.

"What are you doing?" He folded his arms. I couldn't tell if he was angry or concerned or confused.

"Drinking a cold beer and getting ready to turn myself in. Want a sip?" I bounced to my feet and held out the cup.

"I'm all set. Finish it and we go inside." Gulping down the beer like a pledge at a frat party, I burped and handed him the empty cup. *Classy.*

He walked me through the side door and dropped my empty cup into a trash can. I kept my head down as we walked through the station and within minutes, we were back in the stark interrogation room. He handed me a bottle of water and we sat across from each other and exchanged smiles. He spoke first.

"First, I'm glad you're alive. And we need to discuss that. But we should start with what happened today. And I need to read you your rights." He recited the warning off a card. "Do you want your lawyer or are you waiving that right?"

"How do you think he did today? Donovan. You were in the courtroom, right?"

"I was." He nodded. "Do you want a lawyer?"

"Scale of one to ten, what do you give him for his legal acumen based on court today?"

He shook his head. "I'm not in the mood. You want a lawyer or not?"

"You're no fun. I'm all set for now to speak with you without an attorney present. Unless you are planning to pin a murder on me. Then I'll request counsel."

"For the record, Ms. Woodley is waiving her right to counsel. You told me outside that you were turning yourself in, can you explain the reason for that statement?" He looked up at the camera.

"I'm turning myself in because there was a disagreement at my psychiatrist's office earlier today. Dr. Ferguson. I may have said some things during the heated discussion. If there is a fine for that or if I need to write a letter saying that I'm sorry, I'm happy to do so to clear this up."

"Are you intoxicated Ms. Woodley?"

"Yes. I'll pay that fine as well. Public intoxication, is that a felony?" I smiled obnoxiously and suddenly regretted not having dinner with my new friends. I was hungry and being on that boat was much more fun than being here.

"Dr. Ferguson reported that you shoved him in his office and also jammed a pen into his neck, threatening to kill him."

"For the record and for the camera, that is not my recollection of the events. We had a disagreement. I did not shove him or jam anything into his neck. I may have, under extreme emotional conditions, made a vague threat and I'm sorry about that. Deeply sorry."

"There was a witness."

"Who, Olivia? What did she say about this? And Chase, can you get me some food? I haven't eaten today. Actually, I haven't eaten real food in a while."

He shook his head and walked out of the room. Taking off and rolling up my finely knit hoodie, I used it as a pillow and rested my head on the table. Hopefully, he would bring back something good and not crackers from the vending machine. After fifteen minutes and a quick nap evidenced by a boozy drool stain on the cashmere, I heard the door open, and Chase walked in with a pizza box and some plates. *Nice.*

"Not sure what you like so I got a bunch of different slices."

"Thanks Chase. You're a good guy. Where have you been all my life?"

Grabbing an oversized slice that had chicken, olives, and banana peppers, I started eating and finished it like I was competing in a speed eating contest. I looked up and sensed a smirk of disgust on his face, noticing that he had taken exactly one bite of the cheese slice that he selected. *Boring man*.

"The camera is off, by the way."

"Nice try, Chase. I was born on a Thursday but not yesterday." I grabbed another slice, this one with pepperoni.

"Believe what you will. Good chance you will be summoned to appear in court for disorderly conduct. I don't think that they will charge you with assault given everything going on. Who knows, they might let it slide. Depends on how much Ferguson pushes the issue. I'm serious about the camera being off by the way."

"I don't really care anyway. This is the least of my problems. Thanks for the pizza."

"Tell me about Ferguson." He said softly. "I'm interested in him."

"He's friends with Samuel and his father. I found that out during my first appointment. I also found out that he treated my mother. When she was ten, and again when she was sixteen. Which is pretty messed up."

"He has been around for a while and there are few psychiatrists in the area. Why do you take issue with that?"

"He was treating her when she got pregnant with me. And then he took off to Florida around the time that she was down there. You don't like coincidences and neither do I."

"When was your mother in Florida?" He asked and tilted his head.

"Not exactly sure. Mary told me that she was a mess. Struggling mentally and using drugs. She took off to Florida, and returned when she was eight months pregnant. I was born in May, so she came back in April. I know she was here in October. My theory is that she was with Ferguson during his sabbatical."

Chase nodded and finally finished his first slice while I grabbed my third. It was time to confront him.

"I have another theory though." Drama exuded from my voice.

"Which is?"

"Hand me my bag." He had taken it from me when we entered the room and placed it on the empty chair next to him. He passed over the bag and I took out the picture, dramatically slapping it on the table in front of him. He tilted his head down for a brief second and then looked directly in my eyes.

"Nice picture. I have the same one tucked inside my yearbook. It was fun, and a beautiful October day at the farm."

"You didn't think that I needed to know about this?"

"There is nothing to know. We were friends. Six of us went as a group."

"She was pregnant with me by this time."

"That math works but that has nothing to do with me."

"Nothing to do with you. Are you... did you... are you my father?"

"I'm not. We never... I said it and I mean it. We were friends. Nothing more than that." He paused. "But I knew something was off that night."

"What do you mean?"

"Before the dance, we were down at the beach. Your mother, she... seemed different. I offered her a beer and she said that she couldn't drink. She offered to be our designated driver. After the dance, the six of us stayed at a house on the beach. The next morning, I heard her throwing up in the bathroom. We all went to a cafe for breakfast. Five of us hungover and scarfing down eggs and bacon. Your mother, she did not drink anything, and she threw up on the table. I took her home after that and I never saw her again."

"Never saw her again? Mary told me she was spiraling out of control. Drinking, maybe doing drugs. Hurting herself. She said that my mother ran off to Florida."

"I never saw her again. She didn't go back to school after that weekend. I'm not sure she was harming herself or drinking or using drugs. If she was, I never saw or heard anything about that. And I don't think that she went to Florida."

"Why do you say that?"

"She wrote me letters. Told me she was okay but taking a break from school and going through some things. That is how we communicated back in those days. Letters or landlines. She wrote me these letters every week or so, telling me that she was okay. There was never a return address, but I remember that the postmarks were local."

This information confused me. "What else did she say in the letters?"

"Nothing really. They were just letters. Honestly, I stopped opening them after about a month. The whole thing was weird. And no, I did not keep them. But she never went to Florida. And there is no conceivable way that I'm your father. Trust me on that."

CHASE OFFERED to give me a ride home from the station. He seemed genuinely sorry for telling me what he knew about my mother, and it left more questions in my head than answers. Walking out of the station, we were met by sweltering warmth. Odd that it was getting warmer and more humid as the afternoon turned into early evening. Normally it would cool down by now. As we pulled out of the station, I asked Chase if he would make a quick stop at a cell phone store. He looped around and pulled into a strip mall that had one of those independent wireless carrier retailers. I jumped out of the car and ran into the store. On the way in, I debated about changing my number but decided to hold off on that for at least a few days. The kid working there clearly knew who I was and was overly helpful in getting the device activated and all my apps and contacts loaded on the new phone. He asked for a selfie, and I politely declined. Back in the car with my new purchase, Chase asked if we could make a stop on the way to the house. I shrugged and closed my eyes. When I opened them, we were in the parking lot near the harbor where I last saw my Jeep. The parking lot was crowded at this hour with a mix of cars and people walking around. There was a line of people fishing from the walkway and casual onlookers watching the action. He shifted his SUV into park and looked over at me.

"I investigated the sailboat incident with your grandparents. And had another detective look into it as well."

"And?" I asked softly.

"Nothing helpful at this point. I requested a file with the photos and reports. I should get them tomorrow but talked to the guy in charge of the investigation. He said there was no evidence of anything off with the initial ruling of a faulty generator. Cards on the table, I don't think this goes anywhere. Hard to prove anything at this point. If there was tampering with the boat, at least a dozen people had access to it."

"So, Samuel gets away with it?"

"No evidence he did anything, but I'll still investigate. Between you and I, we are looking at him for the murder of the NYPD detective, Marcus. He was last seen with the Crossman's. You know that he is dead right?"

"I may have heard that." I wasn't sure about confirming Donovan shared this information with me during my confinement. He was matter of fact when he shared the news, telling me that Marcus would not be around anymore to bother me. I asked if that meant that he went back to New York or whatever, and Donovan proceeded to make a trigger finger and pointed to the back of his head. Chase looked over toward the harbor and directed his arm at the channel marker with the swiveling red light.

"I'd like to know what happened here on Monday night."

"Am I in trouble for that?" I asked. "I mean, is what I did illegal?

"Depends. But probably not."

"It's a long story, and I'm not sure that I want to get into it now. I'm tired and want to go home."

"Give me the quick version." He pleaded.

"Samuel went missing and I... was not sure what happened. Then people started harassing me... the father, the NYPD detective, your partner Simon, the media. Then Donovan suddenly appears around the same time that I find evidence that Samuel killed my grandparents. I learn about the gold... the secrets and lies. Ferguson had told me about my mother. This all happened within a week. I was overwhelmed and scared."

"Donovan, he has you sign the documents authorizing his access to the property and him becoming the executor of your estate. Later that night you—"

Before he could finish his sentence, the navigation screen between us lit up showing an incoming call from Jenelle Keith. He pressed the accept button.

"Jenelle, you on patrol tonight?"

"Chase, we have another dead body. Where are you?"

He looked over at me. "Falmouth Harbor. Sitting in the car, talking with Emerald. You're on speaker."

"That is... interesting." Her voice crackled.

"Why is that interesting?" He asked.

"Interesting because the body is near her house." Jenelle said with caution in her voice.

"Near her house? What do you mean? How near?" Chase replied.

"Top of her driveway, resting against the mailbox."

ONCE AGAIN, chaos reigned over the normally sleepy dirt road leading to *Indigobird*, and we were met with a cavalcade of police vehicles and a gathering crowd of onlookers surrounding the yellow crime scene tape that partially blocked the street. It was just after seven when Chase swiftly navigated through the gauntlet and parked just past the cobblestone section at the end of my driveway. The car was forced wide around the neatly manicured garden where the mailbox stood, and I strained my neck to see the body, but it was not visible because of police and other people blocking my view. As far as I knew, there was only one person at the house today and I realized that there was no communication between us since the courtroom theatrics. Chase halfheartedly told me to stay in the car, but defiant Emerald leapt out of the passenger seat and followed him up the road toward the peak of the driveway. We approached the yellow police tape guarded by officers standing with hands tucked in their belt buckles. As we reached these officers, Chase told one of them to keep me there, and the officer slid his bulky frame to prevent me from following Chase as he weaved through the crowd. The mailbox was less than ten feet away, but I still did not have a clear view of the body.

My mind cycled through the possibilities of who lay dead in my yard. Donovan first came to mind. I could see the RV silhouette through the trees and suspected he had returned to the house after court. The burner phone was in my crossbody bag, but I had turned it off after calling for the taxi. My new phone was also in the bag, but he did not know that I had just gotten a new one. It was my plan to distance myself from him, at least for today. And now, maybe that distance would be permanent. The next thought was Samuel. Had he returned to the house, in violation of the protection order, and then had an altercation with Donovan? That seemed logical and somewhat fitting. Samuel coming back and meeting his fate outside my house after everything that happened. That thought provided me with a level of eerie comfort. Whatever it took to get him out of my life. Or maybe it was just a random jogger who went into cardiac arrest, slumping to the mailbox as his life faded away. That would be too much of a coincidence and my mind dismissed that possibility.

The bulky officer turned his back for a moment as a two-toned blue police van approached the street. The blue lights were whirling but no sirens sounded. Medical Examiner. The officer moved some of the crowd away for the van to back up close to the mailbox while I slithered away toward the Morgan's house. Creeping through the dense trees near the shed, I circled back up the driveway. My timing was perfect. As I approached the top of the driveway, the crowd thinned, and disbelief filled my eyes as I saw the gray, scruffy beard, and the glasses with clear frames of the man neatly positioned against the mailbox atop a bed of star flowers. This had to be a cruel joke. The man I threatened to kill just eight hours ago was dead in my yard. This was not happening to me. Something touched my shoulder, and I swung around.

"Donovan, what the fuck?"

"Where have you been all day?" He asked, and I could not tell if he was oblivious or just asking the question.

"I've been around. Doing things. Did you do this?"

"No. Did you?"

"Of course not... no."

"I heard there was an incident at his office this morning." Donovan paused. "Chase called me. They were looking for you all day."

"I left the house before eleven this morning and haven't been back since. I went to his office and that was the last time I saw him."

"I hope you have a good alibi for this afternoon."

"That won't be a problem." I laughed out loud just as Chase and a uniformed state police officer came out of nowhere and stood in front of us. Chase spoke.

"Where can we talk?" He did not seem amused. I motioned toward the house.

Seated at the kitchen table, Chase and the state police officer, Hamlin, were across from us. Donovan had spoken to me in private before we entered the house, advising me to say nothing and not let the police in the house. He was acting weird, and his guidance was rejected. Hamlin spoke first.

"Appreciate your speaking with us Ms. Woodley and understand that your attorney is present. We would prefer to do this at Falmouth PD or our barracks, but I understand that you are unwilling to go at this point."

"That is correct."

Hamlin continued. "The information that we have so far is that you had an altercation with the deceased, earlier today in his office on Gardiner. And this evening, a neighbor walking her dog called 911 to report an unresponsive person on your property. Is that accurate?"

Donovan interjected. "My client does not describe the meeting with her medical provider as an altercation. Her version is that they had a verbal argument. And she has no knowledge of that call to 911. Also, the body was found close to the road, and we do not agree, at this point, to your statement that the body was found on her property. It is possible that the body was not on her property."

Hamlin ignored him and continued. "Can you tell us where you were today, Ms. Woodley?"

"I was home until shortly before eleven. I took a taxi to Gardiner and had a verbal argument with Ferguson, my psychiatrist. I left after ten minutes of being in his office, and he was alive and well. I walked to the harbor and was on a boat from that point on until around four when I walked to the police station. I was with Chase and then in his car before he drove me here after getting the call."

"You were on a boat from around eleven until four?" Hamlin asked.

"Yes. *Liquid Asset* is the name of the boat. The owner's name is John, and he was with a woman named Dani. They are staying in Falmouth harbor in the transient slips if you would like to confirm my story."

Chase nodded at Hamlin and then spoke.

"Donovan, where were you today?"

There was a pause. "I was in the courthouse until eleven. I returned here and spent the afternoon doing some work inside the RV. I tried to contact Emerald a few times, but she did not answer my calls."

"You were here all day?" Chase asked. "Anyone that can verify that?"

"No. I did not have contact with anyone other than when Chase called me around noon. I was in the RV most of the day. I went inside the house a few times."

"You did not hear any commotion? The body was found less than fifty yards from the RV. You heard nothing?" Hamlin pressed.

"I heard nothing out of the ordinary. It was a warm day, and I had the air conditioner on."

Chase nodded and pulled out his phone.

"Ferguson had a note in his hand." He opened and enlarged an image and held it so that Donovan and I could see the screen. At the top of the piece of paper it said, *Indigobird*. The bottom words of the note sent cold waves through my body. It was something that I heard many times in my life, mostly when Harold was telling stories about pirates and buried treasure.

Dead men tell no tales.

CHAPTER 8
DOUBLE CROSS

Soft sunlight swept through my window this morning, and the sweet melody of singing birds served as my alarm clock. I had slept with the bedroom windows open as the wave of heat and humidity continued to stall over Cape Cod. If this were July or August, it would be normal, but in the month of May, when your blood was still thin from the winter chill, this weather was uncomfortable and created havoc with my hair. Sleep came surprisingly easy given that my psychiatrist, who also treated my mother, was found dead at the top of my driveway. Although Donovan counseled me to deny the police request to search the house, I overruled his decision and allowed Chase and Hamlin to walk through the house and even showed them the security camera footage for the entire day. Donovan seemed displeased and that surprised me. I had sensed that he was hiding something.

Chase and the state police techs were impressed with the coverage and quality of the system. The exterior camera had a clear view of the driveway but did not extend all the way up the lengthy entryway to the property. It did, however, possibly confirm Donovan's alibi, as the cameras did not have him on any camera from late afternoon until the body was found. The tech noted that there were some blind spots, and Donovan could have eluded the camera coverage if he exited the RV from the rear and entered the opposite neighbor's yard. Donovan scoffed at that assertion. Chase was on the scene throughout the entire ordeal, leaving at midnight after the forensic techs completed their work where the body was found, and after the video review and walkthrough of the house. He told me there was no indication that Ferguson's death occurred at that location, and he was believed to be killed elsewhere with his body dumped there, in the continuing efforts to torment me. He also said that the cause of death would not be determined until toxicology is completed, but it was considered, at that point, a homicide. *Dead men tell no tales.*

Staring out the window at the calmness of the sea, I started thinking about how all these things in my life were connected. It was clear that the Crossman's were in my life because of the death of my grandparents and their hunt for the *Whydah* gold, and that Ferguson was in my life because of Samuel. And the man camped in my driveway would not be there if not for whatever happened the night of my party. I still don't have that answer and made a mental note to get it from Donovan today. The jigsaw puzzle in my mind was interrupted by a text notification on my new phone. Donovan asking me to brew coffee. *How did he know that I replaced the phone?*

Walking through the front door while juggling two overfilled mugs was challenging, but I was able to make it to the RV without spilling a drop. I used my elbow to bang on the door and he opened it with a smile.

"Great service. Thank you." He took one of the mugs and stepped back for me to enter.

"It's too hot, Donovan. Can we walk around back and sit by the water?"

"I want to stay up front, keep an eye on things."

"Can we at least go in the garage for shade? It is like ninety out here already. I have some beach chairs in there." It came out obnoxiously whiny.

He nodded and walked toward the garage, punching in the code to open the door on the left side where my Jeep used to be parked. He pulled down two chairs that were hanging on the wall and slid over a stack of boxes to hold our drinks. I noted that the empty boxes from the video equipment were still neatly stacked on the hand cart. Seemed like so long ago that this man entered my life.

"When can I get my Jeep back?"

"Probably any time you want. It's at the state police barracks in Bourne near the bridge. What are you going to do with the BMW?" He tilted his head toward Samuel's car.

"It's his car. Surprised he hasn't tried to pick it up or get it somehow. Can you help me get rid of it? Can I get it towed to a junkyard? I don't want it here anymore."

"I'll call him to arrange that today. I presume that you are going to divorce him. My guidance would be to play nice and not do anything to fuel the fire. Take the high road."

"Fuck him. He killed my grandparents. I know he did."

"Anything new on that from Chase?"

"It doesn't look good. It has been almost a year. Chase started to investigate and there is no obvious evidence of tampering, and even though Samuel had access to the boat... it is all circumstantial. No way to prove anything."

"Chase is a good detective. Maybe he will get them on the other murders."

"The other murders?" I asked.

"It's not coincidental that two of the people associated with the Crossman's were murdered this week. Marcus and now Ferguson. My guess is that they are responsible for those deaths."

"Chase knows this?"

"Yes."

"Well, it is still not good enough for me. They can't get away with murdering my grandparents."

Heat and humidity continued to build through the morning and by noon I was forced to turn on the central air conditioning system to cool down the house. Donovan and I had lunch under the large, blue umbrella that he had retrieved from the garage and set up on the patio. In addition to his protective and legal services, he was also handy around the house. Still wanting to lay low from the world, we had groceries delivered to the house this morning, and he had grilled burgers while I made a salad. We had forgotten to order bacon as part of the delivery, and that was a problem. I had an agenda for this lunch meeting, but he started the conversation before I could get my items out there. Chewing on the subpar, bacon-less burger, he broke the silence.

"I called the state police barracks, they are dropping off the Jeep at two this afternoon. Originally, they said to pick it up, but I explained the situation and they agreed to tow it here."

"Nice of them."

"Yeah. And I spoke to Samuel."

"How did that go?" I wasn't sure I wanted to know.

"Good. I arranged for him to meet me up on the road at two. I'm going to drive the car up to the street for him. Figure, if the staties are timely, at least they will be around if things go sideways. He was surprisingly pleasant and sends his regards."

I nodded. "How long do we have to hide out here and avoid going in public? I had fun being out yesterday and feel trapped here. I notice that there are no more media vans or cars lining the street anymore. What's the deal with that?"

"Town manager and police chief sought and were granted a temporary order to prevent parking or standing on the street citing safety complaints from your neighbors. It is a narrow road and there have been three minor accidents."

"Tell me what happened the night of the party. This conversation is long overdue. I want to know why I had fentanyl and naloxone in my system, and why I woke up in the back of my car. And how my dress was splattered in blood with a knife wrapped inside. You owe me that."

He looked down at his plate. "Not now, but soon. How about tonight? I have an idea. Pass the dressing."

I passed him the homemade raspberry vinaigrette that I whisked together while he was grilling. He slowly drizzled the red liquid over the kale and spinach salad and a smile emerged on his face. "How do you feel about going out on the water again? A late afternoon sail? We will have privacy, get out of the house, and be able to talk."

"Where did that come from? After everything, you want to go out on the water?"

"You have a better idea?"

No great idea came into my head, and I debated this for a minute. Other than my fugitive ride yesterday, the last time I was on a boat was with Samuel on the *Woodley*, the day that he proposed. Being back out on the water seemed like a terrible idea, but it also intrigued me. Something also clicked in my head from past conversations with Donovan.

"You have a boat?" I asked.

"Not right now, but I have access to a few. The guy from WHOI that I rent from has a sailboat and a large, offshore fishing boat. He is out of town for the month. I take care of the boats for him, fix things that need fixing. He charges me next to nothing for living in the in-law suite above his garage. I reciprocate by cooking for him at summer parties and maintaining the boats."

"You sail... and work on boats?"

"Yes. I have been around boats my whole life. My father was a lobsterman. I went to the maritime academy. My life has been all about boats."

"Where would we sail?" I asked, trying to piece together this information as goosebumps popped through on my arms.

"I'd have to check the marine forecast, look at the winds and the tide. I like to sail around Uncatena and then through Pasque, head toward Aquinnah and then tack back toward the harbor if we have the upwind."

He had named two islands that were east of town. These were familiar to me and a route that Harold liked to take around this time of year.

"Let me give it some thought." Something felt off.

"Obviously up to you." He wiped his sweaty brow. "We could just stay here and swelter in the heat."

"No. I want to do it. Only if you tell me what happened the night of the party."

"Deal. But I'll tell you on the boat. It is a longer conversation, and we don't have time now. They should be dropping off your Jeep soon, and I need to get the BMW out to the street."

"Okay. This sail. I'm not going to regret it?"

"Trust me. It will be an adventure."

PULSING THROUGH THE QUIET HARBOR, feelings of freedom and strength overcame my body as the late afternoon sun warmed my face. I wore off-white pants designed specifically for sailing, paired with a matching blue and white horizontally striped shirt. My hair was pulled back tight and, in a ponytail, and my eyes were protected from the glaring sun by oversized, polarized lenses. Donovan was also dressed in a nautical theme, wearing similar style pants and a lightweight windbreaker. His shoulder length hair danced in the sea breeze, and his smile continued to widen as his hands gripped the large, wooden steering wheel of the sailboat. An oversized backpack was secured by his feet, and I was mentally devising a plan to take control of this situation. He was oblivious to what was going to happen on this sail. At least that was my hope.

The winds favored the initial leg of the journey. Not too strong to be uncomfortable, but enough to power the main sail that I unfurled as we exited the harbor. Swinging the mast to the starboard side, we sailed peacefully through Woods Hole and banked left around Uncatena. I smiled and waved to the other boats that were enjoying this beautiful afternoon. Winds continued to be in our favor as we easily navigated through the Pasque Island channel and we were back in Vineyard Sound, as the sun glistened over the horizon and beamed on the colorful, clay cliffs of Aquinnah. Fond memories swirled in my head. Shortly after seven, we bypassed the entrance to the harbor in Woods Hole and continued along the coast, around the lighthouse, and went wide past the rocky area that had caused headaches for inexperienced mariners over the years. Donovan continued to navigate, and I knew where he was headed.

"Come up to the bow and drop the anchor." I yelled back at him. I had brought down the sail of the main mast and we were drifting about a half mile behind *Indigobird.*

As he bounced up toward the front of the boat, I retreated on the opposite side back to the large steering wheel. He turned his back to me and loosened the anchor from the windlass. Ducking down, I unzipped his backpack, and it was sitting right on top. I took it out, closed the pack, and stuffed the object underneath the maroon and green striped cushion that covered the bench at the back of the boat. Once the anchor took hold, the wind, tide, and current had positioned the boat perpendicular to the shore, and I looked over at the beautiful house that seemed like a stone's throw away. The lowering sun flickered in the horizon and the back lights of *Indigobird* emitted golden rays of light over the water. While admiring the view, small pelts of precipitation started to fall from above. *Nothing good in my life ever lasts.*

He looked up at the sky and spoke. "I didn't see rain in the forecast until later. Radar had a storm coming in before midnight though. Low pressure front stalled over the area." *The meteorologist is back.*

"Seems like a passing shower to me. How about we go down in the galley and have a drink?"

He nodded, looking down at the backpack. "Sure."

He grabbed his pack and ambled down the steps to the galley where we had stored our provisions for the trip. I reached under the cushion, and then followed his lead down the stairs. He spoke when I entered the spacious and well-appointed galley.

"My bag is a little lighter than it was earlier. You take something out?" He said casually as he turned toward me.

"As a matter of fact." I had the gun pointed directly at his head.

He nodded. "Can we have a drink, and can I tell you the story before you shoot me?"

Without showing any fear or concern, he turned his back to me and opened the whiskey bottle, splashing two healthy pours into plastic cups. He handed me one and took a seat at the far end of the portside bench. He took a sip and placed the cup on the table.

"Take a seat. I'll tell you what you want to know."

"Don't try anything or I'll shoot."

"Mutiny on the ship. You would have made a good pirate Emerald." He laughed sarcastically.

"Start talking." I ordered.

"Where to begin... about two years ago, Samuel was drifting around, working here and there. I knew of him... it is a small town, but we never crossed paths. One day, there was a problem with this boat, and Samuel was called by the owner to troubleshoot the issue. I happened to be on the boat working on something else, and we got to talking."

"Just happened to be on the boat?" I asked.

"Initially, I thought it was a coincidence, but soon realized that the meet was intentional. Samuel started hanging around, kept running into me at various places in town. We went fishing and had drinks on occasion. I keep to myself mostly, but he kept pressing me to hang out. It was... suspicious."

"You're friends with Samuel? Seriously?"

"I'll get to that. One night, after a long day of fishing and too many boat beers, we anchored across the sound in Lake Tashmoo. We were on Ferguson's boat. Samuel, Bill, the NYPD detective, another guy. They started talking about the legend of the *Whydah* gold. They seemed to know that I was friendly with Harold. Then it clicked. I was there because they thought I could get to Harold. Find out where he hid the gold."

"So, you've been part of this all along." I knew something was off.

"Let me continue. The next day, I went to Harold and told him what happened. Warned him that these assholes were trying to find the gold. Harold laughed and said they would never find it. He was getting up in years and it concerned me that he did not take this seriously." He paused to take a sip of the drink.

"Then what?"

"Harold asked me to play along. Double agent, he called me, and seemed to enjoy it. The whole thing was... stupid. But I liked Harold. At times, after he had a few drinks, we would take a ride in the Jeep. Shovels in the back seat. He had these maps, and I'd drive us down to a certain beach or a state forest, he would tell me where to dig. I obliged him. Again, he thought it was funny and I went along with him because he enjoyed it."

"You ever find anything?"

"No. There was nothing to find." He said emphatically.

"Then what happened?"

"I told the Crossman crew that Harold was full of it, and I had no more information and was no longer interested in searching for the gold. I had played along that I wanted my share of what they believed to be more than ten million in treasure. I stopped engaging with Samuel and everyone but stayed friendly with Harold. He really liked me. Told me I was like family to him and someday he would tell me everything. But I just chalked it up to his games which had grown tiresome. I was living in Hawaii that winter and spring. When I returned in July, I was shocked to hear that he and Mary passed away."

"You were not here when they died?"

"I was not. I was living in Ehukai, Hawaii, near the state beach. Beautiful place and I'll be back there some day very soon. It might have been a midlife crisis. Surfing during the day, tending bar at night. I had moved there in January and had a six-month rental. I went off the grid and had no contact with anyone. Then, I came back here for the summer and within a week of being back, Samuel banged on my door and said the crew was back together and had new information. Again, I played along, but did it for you."

"You did it for me? What the actual fuck does that mean?"

"Harold made me promise that I'd look after you after... he and Mary were gone. Samuel told me that he was spending time with you and getting closer to where the gold was hidden. I didn't know what to do. Do you know how many nights I spent lurking around your house, following you around town? I had game cameras set up in the trees in front of your house. I can't believe you never noticed me. You walk around in a fog... in a different world. I never wanted to approach you but hoped that you would notice me, and we would talk."

"Game cameras?" I asked.

"Remote, battery-operated cameras that hunters use to monitor activity on trails and in the woods. They are motion activated and you can watch footage from a phone or tablet."

"It is fucked up that you were spying on me, and I don't ever recall seeing you around town."

"You need to work on your situational awareness. But you are making progress." He nodded at the gun that had lowered to my lap while listening to his story. I quickly raised it back up again.

"Tell me about the party." The gun was heavy in my hand.

Donovan looked down at his watch and drank the rest of the whiskey. "Can I pour us another drink?"

Sliding my nearly empty cup toward him, I nodded, and he refilled the cups.

"A week before the party, I had drinks with the Crossman's. Samuel was talking to his father about you and said that you were spiraling... that you were taking prescription opioids. And drinking every night. I had offered to cook for the party, and I was aware that they were scheming something. But I had no idea."

"Go on."

"As you know, you never came down to the party. I saw Samuel going in and out of the house. It seemed... odd. They were panicked or something. The last time Samuel came out, I had just plated the chicken. The people at the party were eating and I snuck around the side of the house and entered through the front door. You were in your room, on the bed, barely breathing, respirations shallow. Your lips were blue. I gave you two doses of Narcan, and you started breathing more normally. I carried you to the bathroom and splashed water on your face. The cut over your eye started dripping blood on your dress, so I put some clean clothes on you."

"You carry Narcan needles... that does not make any sense."

"They're not shots. It's nasal and goes up your nose. Within an hour of the conversation where Samuel said you had an opioid problem, I got Narcan from a local rehab center and always carried it with me."

"Then what happened?"

"I had been in the house for about fifteen minutes, and I was concerned that someone was going to come in. I threw you over my shoulders and locked the bedroom door behind me while leaving. I carried you down the stairs and ducked into the garage because someone was in the bathroom across from the garage entryway. I heard voices on the outside on the driveway, so I put you in the back of the Jeep and covered you in a blanket."

"You expect me to believe all that?"

"You tell me. Did you wake up in the Jeep?" He took a sip of his drink and again looked at his watch.

"How can I believe you? All of these lies and secrets. Easy story for a smart guy like you to make up with a gun pointed at your head."

"Every word is true. Can I show you something in my pocket?"

"Slowly."

He reached in and pulled out a silver object that reminded me of a harmonica.

"What is that?"

"It is the clip for that gun in your hand. It's not loaded." He drained his cup.

I sipped from my cup while gradually tilting the gun and confirming that the cartridge slot was empty.

Silence flooded the room, and I looked out the opened galley window noticing that the sun had receded, and darkness had filled the night. The peaceful, calm water glistened with rays from the moon, and I heard splashes of fish surfacing for bait and the distant rumble of a small boat engine.

"Where do we go from here? It is almost eight and I'd prefer to navigate back before it gets too late and ahead of the weather." He said as he stood in the galley.

"First tell me about the bloody knife, and how that fits in—" My demand was interrupted by a loud thud and sudden rocking of the boat. His empty cup flew off the table as we continued to rock back and forth.

"Give me the gun!" He yelled.

"No fucking..." He lurched forward, grabbed the gun from my hand, and slammed in the clip.

"Stay here. Don't leave the galley."

Frozen to my seat, I watched him bounce up the steps to the deck of the boat, banging shut the wooden door behind him.

Muffled through the wooden door, I heard an eerily familiar voice say, 'what the fuck Donovan' and then suddenly the night was filled with a chorus of rapid gunfire. Seven, eight shots boomed through the air, echoing off the ocean water. Paralyzed by fear and cowering in the soft cushioned seat, I closed my eyes as the wooden door opened. I heard a voice.

"It is almost over. Close your eyes, you're not going to want to see this."

My hands covered my face but, through my partially spaced

fingers, I could see him digging deep into his backpack and extracting a shiny, metal object. I shut my eyes completely and may briefly have lost consciousness. Time stood still. Two more explosions ripped through the night and the corresponding sounds of splintering wood pierced my ears. It jolted me backward and I could taste the darkness.

~

STANDING on the deck of a smaller Coast Guard boat, I was fully alert now and my mind was processing the series of events that occurred less than an hour ago. In the distance, I could see Donovan and Chase on a different boat rafted to the sailboat. The boat where I stood was idling in the water, and two Coast Guard medics kept asking me if I needed medical attention. The cool rain was steadier, and we were sheltered under a hard top that was keeping us out of the elements.

"I want to go home. That is my house right over there." I pointed.

"It should not be long now Ms. Woodley. The detective is headed over to speak with you. Here he is now."

Chase boarded the boat, and we started moving, picking up speed as we left the flotilla and headed east towards Woods Hole. Donovan's figure got smaller and smaller as we pulled away.

"You okay?" Chase asked with requisite sympathy.

"Sure. How are you this evening?"

He looked at me sideways. "Another day. More dead bodies. Just want to get your version of events."

Summoning my inner Harold, I told him the tale of the mystical adventure, setting sail on the high seas with Captain Donovan, navigating through the choppy waters and treacherous channels, and anchoring in the calm waters before being approached by pirates. The ensuing battle that resulted in the deaths of the swashbuckling pirates by the strong and charming Captain, who saved the maiden and preserved the treasure."

"Nice tale. Sounds like a movie. Back in the real world, tell me what really happened, this time for the record."

"Ironically, my tale is close to reality. We were anchored behind the house, having a drink in the galley and the boat slammed into us. I stayed in there and Donovan grabbed his gun, and he went up the stairs to the deck. I heard yelling and then gunshots, ten or twelve of them. I had no idea what was going on. I stayed in the cabin until he came down to get me. He warned me to stay in there while he radioed for help, but I didn't listen. I followed him up on the deck and saw the black, rubber boat tied to the starboard of the sailboat. I looked down, and with the help of the moonlight, I saw Samuel and Bill Crossman. They were riddled with bullet holes and... dead. Donovan radioed for help, and the harbormaster and the other boats showed up, and here I am, talking with you."

"Did you hear what they were yelling?" He asked.

"Not really. I was scared and confused. It was a blur."

As we motored around the lighthouse and rounded the corner toward the Coast Guard station, one of the crew members warned us of increasing chop and rough seas for the next few minutes before we entered the safety of the harbor. He told us another violent storm was moving through the area. He barely finished speaking before the skies opened and rain battered the boat. Distant thunder rumbled in the air.

"Anything else?" Chase asked me.

"Not that I recall. Is this finally over?"

"That is a good question." He said as an ominous bolt of lightning flashed through the sky.

It was after midnight, and I sat on the window ledge in my room watching the flashes of lightning and listening to the crackling thunder over the sound. Donovan was not back at the house as far as I knew or at least he hadn't answered my knocks on the RV door.

Chase had dropped me at the house, and I knew that Donovan would not have gotten back before me. An hour into being mesmerized by the storm above the ocean, my phone vibrated. Falmouth Police Department. I answered it.

"Hey, it's Donovan. I'm at the police station on one of their phones. On the police line." *Translation – don't say anything stupid because they are listening.*

"I can see that."

"Alright. Just finished here and wanted to check in with you before coming back to the house. That... cool with you?"

"Yeah. That is fine."

"Great. We can talk then." He ended the call.

Fifteen minutes later, I was sitting at the kitchen table when I saw the lights beaming down the driveway. As the taillights drifted away, I went out the front door and saw that Donovan was standing outside the RV.

"Figured you would come by." Thunder crackled as he spoke. "In here?"

Sitting inside the RV, we stared at each other across the dinette table. I was not sure who was going to break the silence until he spoke.

"Ready to talk about this?"

"I am. What happened at the station?"

"They took my statement. I told them what happened."

"What did you tell them?"

"The truth. That you and I were having a drink in the cabin and a boat slammed against us. That I went above to see what happened and one of the two men had a gun and fired at me, and, in self-defense, I returned fire. Killing both men. Emerald, these men were after you. I was just protecting you. Clearly self-defense. But the department will investigate. I told them I'd cooperate and stick around to be available if they had any more questions."

I scoffed at him. "The police believe that they randomly found me on a sailboat, hidden below in the cabin?"

"Not sure how they found us, I mean Samuel knew the boat, and it was parked right behind your house. They've been following you."

"You did not tell them where we would be?" I thought about his frequent glances at his watch while we were in the galley and knew that he talked with Samuel during the day.

He ignored the question. "Don't tell me you feel bad about this."

"I'm not sure how I feel. So, the crew is gone, and I'm no longer in danger. Marcus, Ferguson, the Crossman's. You are the only pirate left. All four murdered this week."

"Technically, the Crossman's were not murdered..." His voice trailed off.

"You know what you did. You told them where we would be, set up a meeting time, killed them, and then... and then you shot up the sailboat with a different gun and threw it on the dead bodies."

"That will be difficult to prove. And I'd do it again if I had to. Without hesitation."

"So, you think this is over?" I asked with an attitude.

"Yes, it is over."

"Not for me." I said shaking my head.

"What do you mean?" He asked with a confused look on his face.

"This is over when I find the gold."

AFTER THE LATE-NIGHT conversation in the RV and not being able to get to sleep because of the storm outside my window, I struggled to get out of bed in the morning. When I finally got up, I saw that my bedside digital clock was a blank screen, and the room was dark. Looking at my watch, it was after ten. I brushed my teeth and walked downstairs in a fuzzy bathrobe. Donovan was sitting at the kitchen table with a white carafe next to a pair of *Indigobird* mugs.

"Good morning. You lost power in the middle of the night from the storm. I brewed coffee in the RV and thought you would want some." He pointed at the carafe.

I poured coffee into the mugs, handed him one, and took a seat across the table.

"How can you brew coffee without power?"

"The RV has a solar generator that stores electricity. I checked with your service provider and the estimated restore time is between six and eight tonight. If you need to charge your phone or tablet, let me know and I can take care of that for you."

I looked down at my phone to check the battery level and saw that there was a text from Chase asking me to come into the station at noon for follow-up questions. I flashed the screen toward Donovan.

"Chase wants me down at the station. More questions."

"I know. He called me this morning. They are playing this one by the book. Lot of national media coverage on this. The Chief is a little... anxious."

"What do I tell them? I mean... I already gave a statement."

"Tell them what happened, stick to your statement. You did not do anything wrong."

I just stared at him. "Should I bring legal counsel?"

Back in the uncomfortable seat in the interrogation room, I sat across from Chase and a man who identified himself as Chief Charell. It must have been a casual day at the station as Chase was wearing a blue FPD pullover and matching hat. The chief, who I had only seen in passing and was always in a power suit, had on a maroon sweater and dark dress pants. He did most of the talking and, after I provided a detailed version of events of the previous evening, he had follow-up questions that I answered to the best of my recollection. My story did not change. The meeting went on for over an hour before he thanked me for my time and excused himself. He left the room and Chase looked at me and then nodded his head at the camera. His signal to not say anything more. He stood and walked toward the door and motioned me to follow him. We ended up in a small conference room.

"No cameras or audio in here." He said softly.

"Okay. What's up?" Whispering back.

"I'm just trying to make sense of everything. There is something here that does not sit well with me. It is too neat. In the last year, there are six people killed under... weirdly connected circumstances. Your grandparents on the boat. Marcus Amato executed and dumped in the harbor. Ferguson killed and left at front of your house. Holding that note. Samuel and Bill Crossman... killed in... self-defense right behind your house." His changed inflection was noticeable when he said 'self-defense.'

"What do you want me to say?"

"You don't have to say anything. I have two unsolved murders on my desk and am still looking into what happened with Harold and Mary. I have this feeling that something is off in all of this..."

"It is comforting to me that you are looking into my grandparents even though the Crossman's are no longer around."

"My theory is that Samuel murdered them... he had access to the boat and had an agenda. Then Samuel, his father, Ferguson, and Amato are working together to find the gold. Something happens between them, and the Crossman's take out Amato and Ferguson. And then the Crossman's are dead. It all fits but something is missing. It seems too neat."

"I wish I could help you."

"Did Donovan tell you about Harold's tattoo?"

"Harold's what?" I laughed. "He didn't have a tattoo. At least I never saw one. And how would Donovan know about it even if he did have one?"

"The investigative reports from the sailboat incident came in. I showed him an autopsy photo last night when he was at the station. He was friends with Harold, and I wanted to know if he knew about it. We believe it was recent. I figured it was nothing but wanted to check."

"What was the tattoo? Don't tell me it was the fucking bird. And where was it?"

"It was on his right bicep. Just black letters that were hard to read on the autopsy photo." He looked down at his phone, which was vibrating on his desk. He picked it up and nodded his head.

"Can I see it? The photo?"

"I'll have to show you later. Chief has a press conference in five, and he just texted me that he wants me there. You parked in the back?"

"Yes."

He took off this hat and placed it on my head. "I'll take you out the side door. The media circus is back. Keep your head down."

THE RAIN HAD STOPPED while I was in the station, and sunlight peaked through the clouds as I headed back to the house. Chase spooked me with his theory of what had been going on, and the nerves in my body had returned. There was more to the story, I'm convinced of that and determined to understand. As the Jeep ripped into the driveway with purpose, I noticed that both garage doors were open. The RV was backed up to the side of the garage where Samuel's car was normally parked, and I pulled into my side of the garage. Donovan gave me a strange look as I stepped out of the car.

"Back already?" He asked.

"Seemed like I was there forever. Power is back?"

"Not yet." He shook his head.

"Then how did you open the garage doors?"

"I pulled that cord to release the tracks from the garage door opener and did it manually. Like I did this morning when you left. Remember?" He pointed at the hanging cord.

"I guess I was not paying attention."

"Situational awareness, Em. You need to work on that."

I shrugged. "What are you doing?" I noticed that the rear doors of the RV were open, and most of the cardboard boxes that he had trucked in for the security system were stacked in the back.

"Just getting rid of these boxes, cleaning up." He grabbed the last box from the garage floor and lugged it over to the RV where it weirdly thudded when it landed on another box. He placed the convertible hand truck on top of the boxes and slammed the rear doors shut.

The thudding sound of the empty boxes confused me. "Wait. Did you uninstall the cameras and the system?"

"No. Cameras and system are still there. Just cleaning up the boxes and the leftover equipment and packing materials. The system is down due to the power outage. Once the power is back, you will have to reset everything."

"Do I still need it? I mean, the pirates are all gone. Well, most of them."

"Funny. Yes. Keep the system and when the power is back on and you reset it, change the password. I don't need access to it anymore."

"Are you leaving?" I asked.

"That's up to you. We are done here. The bad guys are out of your life."

"Can I think about it... I mean, there are still things we need to talk about. I want to know about the knife. And Chase told me about the tattoo."

"The tattoo?"

"Harold's new tattoo?"

"Chase showed me a picture last night. It was... letters. It didn't make sense to me. I told him I knew nothing about Harold getting a tattoo. I'm planning to leave the house for a while. I have a meeting with the police later today and want to take a real shower at my apartment. I need to get my mail and stuff like that."

"Will you come back later? We need to finish the conversation about the night of the party."

"Yes. Or how about we meet somewhere?" He asked. "Kidd's will be quiet tonight. We can grab a booth in the back, and I'll finish the story. We can have dinner and a drink. You might not have power anyway."

"Seriously?" He is hiding something. I can feel it. Why is no one straight with me?

"We can finish our conversation over dinner."

"You really want to meet at Captain Kidd's? That seriously seems like a bad idea."

"Meet me there at seven."

"No promises." I said and walked backwards toward the house. I watched him jump in the RV and pull out of the driveway.

Right before seven, I was seated in the far corner booth behind the bar. The power had not been restored before leaving the house, and after a warm shower that was getting colder toward the end, I dressed in partial darkness, doing my best to alter my appearance. My hair was braided, and I wore a baseball hat and reading glasses. I threw on a faded New England Patriots sweatshirt and flipped the hood over my hat. The other day was the bougie and bratty look, today was the overzealous sportsgirl disguise. I could play this game all week. The server that took my drink order did not display any recognition of my unintentional celebrity status. I was slightly offended and pleased at the same time. The duality of my life.

After a few sips of a beer that was not hoppy enough, my new phone vibrated with a text from Donovan telling me that he was finishing with Chase's partner and would be running a little behind. While sipping on the beer, I gazed across the room at the mural on the wall that displayed a pirate standing on a tropical beach with chests brimming with gold. The eye-patched man with the large barrel belly and glowing red pants with his shiny, black boots resting on a bag of gold coins. My mind went back to Harold, and his endless stories of pirates and gold. These memories were interrupted by a man sliding into the booth across from me.

"Seat taken?" Chase asked, sounding like the bus scene from Forrest Gump.

"Chase... what are you doing here?"

"Meeting Donovan. We spoke earlier and I have something to tell him. He told me to meet him here. I did not expect to see you. I almost didn't recognize you."

He had a bottle of beer in his hand and took a large swallow.

"You alright?" He asked.

"Sure. Not bad. Donovan is running a few minutes late."

"Give you credit for being out in public. Curious that you chose here."

"No power at the house. And I want some warm food, and don't want to sit in the dark. Donovan picked the place, by the way."

"Still no power? Weird."

"The storm and darkness of my life never end. What do you have to tell Donovan? Related to the... whatever you are working on? Does it have to do with me?"

He paused. "It relates to you. But you and he should speak about it. It should come from him."

"That is ominous."

Chase shrugged. We ordered another round of beers and made awkward small talk about the weather, plans for the summer, and unimportant matters. He checked his watch and then looked at me.

"Almost forgot. I have something to show you." He opened his phone and showed me an image, using his fingers to enlarge it. On the screen was a bare arm with unspaced, capitalized letters.

"What is that?"

"Harold's tattoo. P-O-S-T-A-V-I-S." He spelled it out. "Mean anything to you?"

"Postavis? Maybe... it sounds like a character in the stories he used to tell me about the pirates. Maybe one of the maidens in the tales he told. Sounds vaguely familiar. Postavis?"

"I looked it up online and all that came up were local post offices.

When I first saw the tattoo, it had some vague familiarity, but I can't place it." He shrugged and sipped his beer.

"And you showed Donovan this last night?"

"Yes. But it was the actual photo which I could not find in my files today. I downloaded this to show you. Where is he anyway?"

"He said he was meeting with your partner and would be down after. Simon...that guy gives me the creeps."

"Simon? Call Donovan, call him now!" Confused, I pressed send to call him and got a strange, recorded message.

"What? The phone is no longer in service." I said, thoroughly confused.

Chase stood quickly and threw a fifty-dollar bill on the table. "We need to leave, now."

~

WE WERE in Chase's car, speeding down Fay Road headed toward *Indigobird*. I was not exactly sure what was happening, and his agitation level was unsettling. Rounding the corner near the house, I noted that the lights of the few houses on the street were on, and I was thankful that the power had been restored. Then, we pulled into the driveway of empty darkness.

"Why are my lights not on?" I asked.

"Not sure. I have a spotlight in the back."

We exited his Toyota, and he popped the hatch, pulling out the light to combat the darkness. He held a gun in his other hand.

"Do you know what is going on?" I asked.

"Something is off here and I'm not taking any chances."

With my shaky hands, I keyed into the dark house. We entered as he shined the light in patterns throughout the open foyer before speaking in a low tone.

"Take me to your fuse box."

We went down into the basement, trailing the beams of light that he shined from side to side. Chase handed me the light once we were at the metallic panel, and he opened it. Shaking his head, he flipped one of the switches. Taking back the spotlight, he walked toward the wall and flipped up the light for the basement. The power was back.

"What was that all about? Fuse tripped?" I asked.

"I don't think so. Someone turned off the main power switch."

"Who would do that?"

"Who was in the house when the power went down, not too many possibilities."

"What the fuck?" *Why would he shut off the power?*

We walked back up the stairs and turned on the lights. Chase walked through the first floor searching for something. I stood in the kitchen trying to process what was going on. Things were starting to add up in my head. He returned and looked at me.

"Assuming it was not you, why would Donovan kill the power?" Chase stared.

"I have no idea." I said, knowing that was not completely truthful. The security system. Chase changed the subject as my head grappled with trying to understand why Donovan would kill the power to subvert the cameras. Chase spoke.

"Simon. He is close to the Crossman's. The other night I saw them together. Samuel, Bill, Ferguson, and Simon. They were on Ferguson's boat. He was part of the crew. Chief put Simon on leave this week because of concerns about him."

"He is in on this? And Donovan went to meet him? Did you tell Donovan about Simon?"

"It never came up." Chase shrugged.

"I hope Donovan is okay. Simon, is he dangerous? Could he—"

"I'd be more concerned about Simon's safety. Where is that little yellow book of yours? Your diary from when you were a kid. I just remembered something."

"It is on top... no, behind the refrigerator. It fell that night."

We inched the refrigerator away from the wall and Chase was able to contort his small frame to reach behind the appliance and slide the small book across the kitchen floor. The diary ended up at my feet.

"What do you remember?" I asked, while bending down and opening the diary.

"Postavis. When I scanned the book when we first searched the house, you had that written on a few pages."

"You remember that now?"

"I do. But you spelled it differently, with an *e* instead of an *i*."

Opening the book, I flipped through the small pages of memories with the happy thoughts of Harold telling tales and singing pirate songs.

"Here is one entry. Maiden Postaves, with an *e*... she told the pirate where to hide the treasure and the pirate listened. That is what I wrote. I must have misspelled it."

"There must be more."

"Oh my god." I looked down at the words, written in my beautiful, obsessive-compulsive style. "He used to sing this to me. I remember it now."

Postaves wants to be a pirate, and sail around the sea,
And hide the buried treasure, so no one else can see.
If the captain can't tell the secret, no need to sound alarm,
The map for the buried treasure is written on his arm.
If the captain of the pirates happens to take a fall,
You can find the buried treasure, hidden in the wall!

"He sang this song to me at least once a week when I was a kid. Written on his arm... the tattoo. Postavis." I grabbed my phone, searching for a translation webpage. I found it. "I know where he hid it." I started crying.

Chase awkwardly tried to comfort me, but I was inconsolable.

We were standing in the living room as I tried to pull myself together. The memories and figuring out the secret were overwhelming. Chase looked at me and uncertainty filled his face. Through tears of pain and confusion, I pointed at the portrait above the fireplace.

"The gold is there... behind, behind the painting. In the song, the treasure is hidden in the wall, and the map is on the pirate's arm. Harold's tattoo."

Chase looked skeptical and rolled his eyes. "Come on Emerald. I mean, you know Harold did this to get people going. This has been going on for thirty years... maybe longer. If you want to take a sledgehammer to the wall, I can't stop you. It's your house."

"Post avis. It is Latin for *'behind the bird'*... it is there." Pointing at the large bird that was staring back at us.

Chase walked over to the wall and pounded to the left of the portrait and the thudding echoes seemed normal. He gave me the look of someone ready to prove they were right, and that I was wrong. His fists continued to move closer toward the painting and he thumped the wall with some aggression. Reaching the portrait, he flexed his hand, and using his knuckles, he lightly pounded on the indigobird on the painting. His hand oddly bounced back. He turned and shot me a look with a completely different facial expression, and then spoke.

"What the fuck?"

I quickly walked over to the other side of the massive portrait, and we simultaneously slid each side up in perfect synchronization, unhooking it from the mount. As we carefully lowered it to the floor in front of the fireplace, I saw that there was no wall behind the painting, just three rows of thick, shiplap shelves, running horizontally across where the painting had been. I pulled the iPhone from my pocket and used the small flashlight to cast illumination on the shelves. The sparkling reflections of dazzling light against the glittering and glowing golden treasure, hidden in the wall by my grandfather, is an image that will be tattooed indelibly in my brain.

I'll never forget it because the shelves were almost completely bare, the sparkling brightness was merely the reflection of my flashlight against the reinforced metal that secured the secret hiding spot that previously held the hidden treasure. In the center of the bottom shelf, I picked up the small shiny object – a single gold coin. The coin warmed my hand and pulsed energy through my body. It was in that very moment that I had a flashback to earlier this afternoon, and remembered the inconsistent thud of the empty security equipment box that Donovan had loaded into the back of the RV. I wanted to scream but could only smile. Amid this surreal revelation, Chase stepped close to me and whispered four words in my ear.

It was then that I screamed.

EPILOGUE

Early in the morning the following New Year's Day, I awoke in my hotel suite in downtown Boston thinking about breakfast and my meeting tomorrow with an academic advisor on the next steps in the dissertation process. *Life goes on.* The meeting had been set up many weeks ago and I had decided to come into the city a few days early to avoid sitting home alone for the new year. Instead, I celebrated alone in this room and fell asleep around nine. In my defense, I did spend the day walking throughout the city and found it enjoyable. I even watched part of the afternoon parade on Boylston Street and the early fireworks over the Commons. It wasn't until right before my eyes closed that I came to the realization that it also would have been my one-year wedding anniversary.

Coldness was in the room this morning and as I opened the curtains, the new year greeted me with grayness, a mix of rain, sleet, and large snowflakes splattering on the glass with a popping thud. I pulled the desk chair toward the window and used the limited natural light to read the room service menu. Eggs Benedict sounded like a good way to begin the new year.

About an hour later, there was a friendly knock on my door and a young woman pushed in a cart with the eggs, the French toast special, two orders of raisin toast, a plain croissant, carafe of coffee, and a bottle of sparkling water. There were two sets of white plates, coffee mugs, glass cups, and folded-up napkins with utensils which made me feel judged for my aggressive breakfast order for one. There was also a folded newspaper on the cart which struck me as odd. Do they still give out newspapers at hotels? I asked the woman about the paper, and she shrugged and told me it was by the door.

After the exceptional breakfast, I showered and dressed. My plan was to walk around the city this morning, saving the dissertation preparation work for the afternoon. As I cleaned up the dishes and prepared to roll the cart outside, the newspaper caught my eye and made me pause. I had expected it to be one of the Boston papers or a national one, but the odd font of the *Falmouth Enterprise* captured my attention. Why would someone leave my local paper outside of my room? My heart raced and my legs weakened as I unfolded the paper. Scanning above the fold, nothing caught my attention. Toward the bottom of the front page, one story jumped out at me - *Local Attorney Missing and Presumed Dead After Surfing Accident in Hawaii.*

The article was light on detail, and it read like an entry-level writer had picked up on a story from Oahu about a Christmas Day surfing accident and made the connection to the name of a missing Falmouth man. *Donovan Williams.* Witnesses reported the man paddled out into dangerous surf conditions including strong rip currents, high surf, and low visibility. Fifteen minutes later, the battered surfboard floated aimlessly toward the beach, but the man was never found despite an exhaustive search. The article noted that Donovan was a central figure in the chaos the previous spring in Woods Hole, and he had disappeared shortly after the shooting incident involving a local doctor and his son. I knew there was information not in the article, including the disappearance of Guy Simon who had not been seen since the incident. In conversations with Chase, he told me Donovan and Simon left together with the gold and likely had fled the country. I had a different opinion. Although we had different ideas on what happened, the gold angle was never discussed again and was not included in any of the police reports.

Shortly after nine in the morning, I picked up my phone to call Chase. As I scrolled to his contact information, the security system app pinged and I opened it, tilting the screen sideways. A dark figure, dressed in black and wearing a ski mask, was closing the rear sliding door and I switched cameras as the figure walked toward the alarm access panel. The app buzzed, indicating the alarm had been disengaged. The figure walked toward the kitchen, and I again switched cameras while following the person into the living room. The figure walked over to the *Indigobird* painting and, just as Chase and I had done just over seven months ago, unhooked it from the mount and slid something onto the hidden shelves before replacing the painting. On the way back to the rear sliding door, the hooded figure stopped for a second below the camera and made a peace sign.

Later that afternoon, I was in my living room, back in the oversized chair, envelope in my hand, and engaged in a staring contest with the bird. In this moment, I thought about Samuel and his many requests to remove the portrait and the times that I thought about ripping it down after he disappeared. I wondered what would have happened if I gave in, and we pulled down the painting together. The outside of the envelope had my name and a series of digits where the stamp would be placed. I opened the envelope and pulled out a piece of paper. Right before reading it, I thought about those four words Chase had whispered in my ear after we discovered the empty shelves. *Your DNA matches Donovan's.*

Emerald,

I was hoping to have this conversation in person and fully expected you would have tracked me down in Hawaii and we would talk in person. After you read this, please burn it. Not sure it is fully necessary, but I don't want to take any chances. By the time you read this, I will be on my way out of the country. I hope this information is helpful to you and provides some semblance of closure.

THAT NIGHT. *After I dealt with Samuel, I returned to the house to check on you. The knife was still in my pocket, and I put it in the bag in the laundry basket. I expected you to call the police in the morning and then I planned to come forward and tell the story once an investigation started. I had Samuel hidden and he was my leverage. I was monitoring the situation with the help of the game cameras hidden throughout your property. I watched you walking toward the shed with the package, which I assumed was the knife and dress. Then, I decided to use that to try and help you get out of this mess for good. Understand, it was a fluid situation, but I had your interests in mind throughout. Samuel and his father, they killed your grandparents, and they were going to kill you too. All for the gold.*

I WAS *skeptical about there really being any gold until I saw the picture of Harold's tattoo. He used to weave 'post avis' into conversations we had in the past, but it did not mean anything in context. Then I remembered when I scanned the living room with the device to check for surveillance equipment. Nothing was detected but the device gave off some weird signals when I scanned near the painting. Then, it clicked. That morning when you went to see Chase, I checked behind the painting.*

SIMON. *I called him when I left your house. I had him meet me at a rest stop in New Jersey. I told him the gold was in Arizona in a storage locker, even showed him a fake picture, and we started driving west. He was a loose end and would not give up, which kept you in danger. He is no longer a problem.*

• • •

THE GOLD. You have 12.1 million in the Central Bank of Cayman. It is in your name. What you do with it is up to you. As I said, I have no interest in blood money. The money was stolen from people and profits from slave trade. The banking information is on the front of the envelope. Keep those numbers and do what you want with the money. Knowing you, you will use it for a good purpose.

NOW THE HARD PART. When I returned from California, a few weeks after you were born, I learned my father engaged in a relationship with your mother and took advantage of her. She had been living in a suite above the garage at his house, hiding there while she was pregnant. I confronted him while we were on his lobster boat one morning. He fell off the boat and drowned shortly after. As shameful as it is for me to reconcile that my father did this to your mother, I hope you also understand your life was created due to this. Although he never told me directly, I suspect that Harold knew who your father was, and this was the reason that he got close to me. I will be in touch and trust we will meet again someday.

Your brother,

Donovan

ACKNOWLEDGMENTS

In no particular order, I would like to thank and acknowledge the following:

Ireland, Aidan, and Alana - for their love, support, and encouragement while I worked on this book. You all were immensely helpful in crafting the story. Your honest feedback, both positive and constructive, helped me bring the book to completion. I wouldn't be writing this acknowledgement if it weren't for you. Special thanks to my mother, Joan, who was instrumental in helping me understand the beauty of reading at an early age.

Thank you to the dozens of early readers who helped me through the process and provided insightful thoughts and recommendations. Many of these readers were sent one chapter at a time, and one of my favorite parts of this process was getting the middle of the night texts and emails from people asking for or demanding the next chapter. Your subtle encouragement kept me going.

Thank you to Kate Anslinger, a brilliant author and editor, for all of your assistance along the way. I would probably still be sending pdf chapters to people if it weren't for Kate.

Lastly and very important to me, thank you for reading the story. I truly hope you enjoyed your experience. My primary goal in this whole process was to write something people would like – I hope this goal was accomplished.

ABOUT THE AUTHOR

Michael Stuart is a behavioral healthcare professional with backgrounds in psychology and business. This is his debut novel in a series of stories set in Cape Cod, where he is a seasonal resident. He has dedicated his life in service to others and hopes this book brings entertainment to the readers. The story is dedicated to his amazing children; Ireland, Aidan, Alana, and Billy (Ireland's husband) who mean everything to him and are his inspiration in life.

Made in the USA
Middletown, DE
30 October 2023